EVIL EMBERS

VALE INVESTIGATION, BOOK TWO

CRISTELLE COMBY

ALSO BY CRISTELLE COMBY

The Neve & Egan Cases

RUSSIAN DOLLS

RUBY HEART

DANSE MACABRE

BLIND CHESS

Vale Investigation

HOSTILE TAKEOVER

EVIL EMBERS

AVENGING SPIRIT

Short Stories

Personal Favour (*Neve & Egan* prequel)

Redemption Road (*Vale Investigation* prequel)

The short stories are exclusively available on the author's website:

www.cristelle-comby.com/freebooks

Edition: 1

ISBN: 978-1792186714

Credits
Editor: Johnathon Haney
Cover artist: Miguel A. Ereza

PROLOGUE

SMOG MONSTERS

The door slammed shut as something grabbed at me. And by "grabbed", I mean "lifted me off the ground and rammed me into the nearest wall".

The structure bent under the impact while a nightmare that would have fit in an old-school John Carpenter movie screamed at me. With my gas mask on, I never heard it coming.

Dazed, I glanced up and faced sharp, yellow-tainted teeth. They formed a circular pit of canines, ready to swallow my head whole. I pulled a knife from my boot and slashed the creep at the center of its mass. The fiend's scream rose an octave as the cold steel struck home.

The creature dumped me back on the floor before dissipating into nothingness.

The attack sucked the air out of my lungs, and I spent the next few minutes coughing through the mask. I felt like kicking myself. I spent my first week here carving wards around the entire six-block area before going in for the first time. I should have known better than to cut one on this house's front door and move on. I forgot the back door. That mistake left that damned poltergeist way too much room to attack.

The monster *du jour* was a ghost, an escapee from the realm of death—the Underworld, Hell, or whatever else you call the place people go to once they're done with life. From what I knew, not everyone turns Casper in their afterlife. However, those who do become near-mindless creatures stuck in their own plane of existence. When they make it to our side of the border, they turn into full ectoplasmic savages.

The dead guy I stepped over near the open back doorway was proof enough of that. What was once an engineer working for the city now had his chest cavity cut down to the bone and his head severed from his body. Blood splatters all but drowned out the muted yellow of his shredded biohazard suit. Judging from the angle of what remained of his corpse, he was trying to flee the house when the poltergeist got him.

"Dammit," I muttered as I tightened the straps on my gas mask. Whoever this engineer was, I was pretty sure he didn't come in here alone, which meant I may have to explain what a six-foot PI in a surplus army jacket, a gas mask right out of the First World War and second-to-thirdhand leather gloves was doing in an area strictly reserved for city workers and engineers.

But that was the optimistic scenario. Something in my gut told me the rest of this guy's team was as dead as he was.

The house I was in hadn't been livable in a while. It was part of the many buildings that went up in flames when our former mayor, Jacinta Galatas, decided that opening a gate to hell downtown would help boost the economy. Even through the mask, the walls reeked of burned wood, urine and a few other foul chemicals I was glad I couldn't identify. The floor creaked like fracturing porcelain as I walked from the living room to the kitchen, and I was surprised my feet didn't go right through the weakened structure. But compared to what was waiting for me past the dead man, this was the ideal home.

A mix of late afternoon fog and toxic dust clouded the lenses of my mask as I walked out the back door. The mist was typical for Cold City in February, or "not-summer" as the locals call the three to four months a year when we get shitty weather.

The nasty chemical soup, on the other hand, was a newer addition. The strangled sunlight above me shone through the puffy cloudbanks of smog that swallowed the rest of the desolate landscape. Once upon a time, it was downtown Cold City. Now it was a glorified rubble pit whose entrance streets were sealed off by a police cordon. You could still make out shattered brick and glass fragments here and there, but otherwise, you could only see for inches.

The house I vacated opened on both sides of the cordon. It was sealed off, of course, but I'd long-since become a master in the fine art of lockpicking.

I pulled a compass from my pocket. The engraved golden artifact was an antique, the back and sides covered in complex symbols. I watched the needle dance and stop on a point that was definitely not true north.

Mad Mao, a Taoist sorcerer, assured me this compass was attuned to sniff ectoplasmic resonance—the nastier, the better. The last week proved the old Japanese man right. No matter how deep into the blast area they were, the compass always managed to point out the nearest Alterum Mundum escapee. I started off with twenty to put down. And if my boss told me the truth about this job, there was one left to dispatch.

Alterum Mundum is fancy Latin for "other world". It's a parallel realm that exists next to ours. There, you'll find all the afterlives known to mankind: Heaven, Hell, Valhalla, Elysium—you name it. For a couple of centuries now, Alterum Mundum has been the home of all the Gods you can think of and all the creatures and monsters you thought only folklore.

I took a second to carve out the proper Celtic Ogham onto the inside back door before shutting it and following the needle. It was pointing towards my left. My battered combat boots made a soft, muffled sound as various debris and gravel crunched under them on the uneven ground. I did my best to not think about the real possibility that some of the bumps I was stepping on might be bone. All this death and destruction in one place...I shivered to think how many of the formerly-living were going to turn into nasty supernatural manifestations themselves once they got enough dead time under their belts.

Between wisps of smog, I caught a fleeting glimpse of Cinema Leone. The old movie house stood tall and proud amidst the rest of its fallen brethren, a lonely survivor of a holocaust that took out nearly all its neighbors. I was relieved to see the needle was pointing away from it. The sight of that place conjured up way too many recent bad memories. But maybe I was short-selling it. There are bad memories; there are waking nightmares; there are things you'll never be able to get out of your brain for as long as you live—and there's what I saw coming out of the movie screen while surrounded by killer Vikings.

Something hissed through the smoky air, giving me the shivers even with the thick M65 field jacket on my back. I checked the compass; the needle stayed steady. The hiss came again a couple of seconds later, ahead of me. The acoustics of the place were so screwed up, it was impossible for me to tell how far ahead it was.

My discomfort gave way to irritation. Why was it always up to me to clean up the mess in this city, anyway? Was it my idea to blow up several blocks of downtown buildings so someone could open an interdimensional gate to hell? No. Was I the one who used a rare triple intersection of high-powered, geo-energy-feeding ley-lines to juice up my power and suck in necrotic energies from another world? Of course not. I was just plain old Bellamy Vale, the idiot goody-two-shoes PI who'd stopped the daemon's invasion, closed the gate to hell and saved the world. Hells, I almost died doing it too...Or, rather, I would have, if only my boss would let me.

Lady McDeath, as I liked to call her, wasn't my boss, strictly speaking. But she held enough shares of my soul to be a lot more than my client. She was...Damn, I wasn't sure what she was. A daemon? The Grim Reaper? The daughter of the God of Death who could kill me whenever it pleased her? Yeah, that last one sounded about right. All I knew for sure was that she was a cryptic *femme fatale*—emphasis on *fatale*.

A few years ago, we struck a bargain. I got a favor and the promise she would keep me alive so long as I worked for her.

That last part wasn't as involved as it sounds. The way it worked was she'd stop anything or anyone from killing me through the power of improbable coincidence. So long as I played the errand boy who takes care of the tasks she deems beneath her, the protection would hold. But, as she liked to remind me, she was going to kill me one day. Until then, nothing could end my life, no matter how hard they tried... and tried they did.

While the details in my books were sketchy, all of them agreed poltergeists have some bad juju in their makeup. The wards constrained them to stay within the area of the blast radius, but they would still suck the life out of any living soul they could get their claws on.

I swept the smog with my knife while I walked. Why not? I could always get lucky enough to snag this thing with a blind swipe, as I did with one of its brothers three days before. A paper cut would be enough; manifested poltergeists are so fragile when it comes to steel blades that they make a Ming vase look indestructible.

I achieved nothing for my trouble, and a sinking feeling that this thing had better prey prospects than me crept through my mind. I sighed as I struggled to keep my eyes open from the lack of sleep. I'd been playing Ghostbuster for a week now, cleaning up the residual spirits that managed to cross through the portal before I closed it down for good. They kept drifting about the rubble so much that tracking them was a long, grinding hunt. It took time for them to become tangible enough to interact within this reality, and while it meant they could kill humans, it also meant my blade had something to sink its teeth into. Today marked the first time I didn't get there soon enough. If only I had—

"Stop it, Vale," I muttered, shaking my head to clear out the smog in my brain. What was done was done. All I could do was try to save the rest of the team from their colleague's fate.

I made out another shape through the mists, a standing apartment building that managed to escape the explosions with shattered windows and some damage to the brickwork. I knew inside stood the remains of a lapis lazuli pyramid. That construct was one of the three relays Mayor Galatas used to harvest ley-line energy and power up her gate. My friend Zian blew it to dust with plastic explosives while I fought off Galatas and her minions within Cinema Leone.

I wasn't surprised to see the compass aimed straight at the building. The residual necrotic flux still floating about the demolished stones made it the ideal hideout for the ghost I was after. The hiss that emanated from the open front door confirmed my guess.

I pushed through the door and found all-consuming darkness. The hallway ahead was solid blackness despite the light streaming in behind me. The compass needle started spinning like a 1980s breakdancer, something it only did when I was within striking distance of my prey. I closed the door behind me with my foot while I put the compass back in my pocket. I pulled my angle-head flashlight out and clipped it to my belt.

The light never went past a couple of feet, a photo negative version of the fog outside. I strained to hear anything to make up for my lack of sight as I walked deeper into the hallway. I tried sniffing too, but the only thing making it past the mask's filter was a nasty stench that reminded me of burning garbage. Every step I took made a muffled sound on the wooden floor, whose echoes died within the radius of the light. I made it six steps when I heard what sounded like human screams under my feet.

"Oh, shit," I whispered, picking up my pace.

To the left was a door marked *Basement*. It was ajar. Not wanting to be attacked from behind again, I scratched a ward on the inside of the metal door before closing it behind me and running downstairs.

A pale glowstick greeted me on the stairwell, casting a sickly green light that matched the feeling in my stomach. More sticks dotted the staircase like breadcrumbs. Another engineer, or whoever I was after, left them to find their way back to the door. Handy, but it might have let the creature I was hunting know somebody was in its home.

I heard the screams again as I hit the bottom of the stairs. It sounded like two voices, a man and woman, muffled by their hazard masks. The man was screaming something, but I couldn't make it out. Didn't matter; the noise told me where they were. I took off down the corridor to my right.

I saw my first flash of yellow when the man's screams turned shrill. One of the engineers collided into me and smacked me with an impressive right hook to the head, which staggered me. Meanwhile, the hissing added some screaming of its own as the sickening crunch of smashing bone filled the air.

Dammit, I don't have time for this, I thought as I picked myself up. Pushing my attacker aside with a rough shove, I ran towards the slasher movie soundtrack with my knife out.

My light caught a glimpse of what looked like an oily black worm with four eyes and half-a-dozen wispy tentacles.

It was ripping apart the yellow packaging on the floor to get to the human inside.

With a war cry, I leaped at the creep, my arm pulled back for a slash, but the creature was faster than me. One thick tentacle brushed me aside, knocking me into the wall as though I were a ragdoll. I fell to my knees, the air knocked from my lungs. I kept a tight grip on my knife and readied myself for the next swing. The monster's mass stretched like taffy, most of its tentacles still focused on the man on the floor, who'd stopped screaming.

I reached for the creature again, but one sturdy tentacle wrapped around my knife hand, pinning it to the floor. In the dimness, I could see two of the beast's eyes set on me. They went comically round when something hit its head from behind.

The engineer that clocked me earlier was swinging a broken plank of wood, yelling incoherently at the creature. She distracted the ectoplasmic savage enough for all four of its eyes to focus on her.

Big mistake.

I flicked the knife up in the air and rolled to catch it with my free hand. With a *Psycho*-style stab, I jabbed the point right into the tentacle pinning me. The giant worm puffed out of existence with a scream.

The remaining engineer ran past me to get to her colleague. "Phil!" she said, kneeling next to the unmoving man. "Oh my God, Phil!"

I crouched by her side. From up close, it was obvious Phil wasn't coming back. His head was at an unnatural angle, and blood caked the inside of his mask. It took a few seconds for understanding to hit the woman, and when it did, it hit her hard. Her frame trembled, muted screams smothered by sobs.

I waited for her to calm down before asking, "What's your name?"

"Dana," she breathed through the mask. "Dana Mulgrew...Who the hell are you? What are you doing here?"

"I was hunting the monsters that got your partner here," I said, standing up. "I wish I'd gotten to this one in time."

"There's more of those...those things?" Dana asked in alarm as she leaped to her feet. She swayed a little, and I steadied her.

I shook my head and kept a hand at her elbow. "That was the last one. It should be...well, safe isn't the right word for this biohazard area. But they won't be coming back."

"There was another guy with us," Dana said with urgency in her voice. "Jacob. We were outside to check on Cinema Leone when—"

"Was he the only other guy on your team?" I asked.

"Yeah, it was the three of us," Dana said, desperate hope coloring her voice. "Did you—?"

"He didn't make it either," I whispered.

"But you said this thing was—"

"It was another one. Jacob was dead when I got there."

The sigh from her lips was tinged with sadness.

"We should get out of here," I said as I steered us towards the stairs. "I'll show you the house where Jacob is on the way."

I climbed up before her, my flashlight showing us the steps.

"Why not show me Jacob?" she asked.

"Because he's in roughly the same state Phil's in."

By the time we got to the front door, I had given her my name and my occupation as a private investigator. The cover story I fed her was that I was hired by a private client who knew about the creatures that infested the site and paid me to get rid of them. I wasn't straining the truth too much. The only falsehood was the part about me getting paid for the work.

Yeah, being Death Incarnate's errand boy didn't get you a dime in the pocket.

"How did you get in?" Dana asked as we walked away from the apartment building.

"There are a few loopholes through the debris the cops don't know about," I explained. "I've been using them to get in and out for the past week."

"A week? In those clothes...This gunk can't be safe for you," she said, pointing at my jacket.

"Sorry, my hazmat suit was in the wash today," I said dryly.

It surprised me when Dana laughed at my answer. It hadn't been that funny, and we both knew it. It didn't take long for her laugh to morph into tears. She leaned on me as she sobbed into her mask for a minute or two.

"Sorry," she said, shying away as she gulped, getting her breathing back under control.

It was hard to see through the mask, but she was young, maybe her mid-thirties, with a keen round face, tall and a little bit on the heavy side. I'm sure she was a sweet girl, and she didn't deserve any of the nightmares that would fall on her shoulders. Hells, I wished I could do more to help, but I was at a loss.

"It's shock," I assured her, giving her shoulder a friendly squeeze. "It's never easy to see death up close the first time."

"Does it ever get any easier?" she asked me.

I shook my head. "No. It doesn't."

"What do I tell people about how my team died?"

"Anything but the truth," I advised her, "or they'll lock you up with the crazies." I peered around to see if we were near the perimeter yet. "My suggestion is you wound up tangling with a lone survivor of the bombings who thought you all looked like an appetizing meal."

"And where was he when the blast hit?" Dana asked.

"Sewers," I answered without missing a beat. "The survivor must have stayed down there for longer than he should have. By the time he found a utility hole cover that wasn't blocked by debris, he was crazy from the isolation. And that was before the crap in the air drove him even more out of his mind."

"And where is he or his body now?" This question had a real edge in it.

"How should you know? Last you saw him, he was running away, back down in the sewers he popped out of earlier. You were a little too busy trying to figure out how you were going to survive to notice."

I could make out the house I was in earlier when Dana said, "You've had a lot of practice at lying."

"Occupational hazard," I replied, pointing at the building we were standing by. "That's the place where Jacob checked out."

Dana started walking towards it when I caught her shoulder again. "I meant what I said about the shape he's in."

"I'm not a child!" Dana argued back, shrugging my hand from her shoulder.

"No, you're a traumatized young woman who is going to have a lifetime of nightmares," I retorted. "Do you want to add to them?"

Dana took a breath but shook her head. "I owe it to him to see it."

"You owe it to him to remember him as an un-dismembered human being," I said back.

I could feel Dana wavering, but I didn't have anything else to add. The call was hers. She nodded. "So, where's the police cordon from here?"

I led her through the debris until we reached one of the gaps I'd found. It was an easy one that wouldn't require her to lift or push anything. I gave her enough directions to make it out on her own. I wish I could have accompanied her, but the passage opened onto a street too busy to exit out there with her. She had a story to stick to, and I had no place in it.

I took a long hike back across the ruins to another exit, left of the building where Jacob died. I wound up going through the broken septic tank of another house, which gave way to the root cellar of the house next door.

The latest mission for my boss of a dubious nature was over, but I felt no sense of accomplishment. Lady McDeath always threw me into the most messed-up situations imaginable with the bare minimum of information to guide me. Hells, it took me two weeks to figure out I was dealing with poltergeists on this one, then another week to educate myself enough on the subject, in order to have a chance at surviving them with my limbs attached.

"Ah, what did you expect, Vale?" I asked myself as I

opened the cellar door to climb outside. "When has one of her missions *ever* gone according to plan, huh?"

I could feel myself fading as I got out onto Wolfman Street. My adrenaline tank ran dry with the end of the job, as it usually did. I took the gas mask off and stuffed it in my pocket.

Dusk graced the city, and a soft wind chilled the air. I wish I could go home and sleep, but there was one more thing I had to do. I pulled out my smartphone and dialed my girlfriend.

"Sergeant Ramirez," a Spanish-accented voice said on the other end.

It brought a smile to my lips. Melanie Ramirez lived in the US for the better part of the last twenty years, but a thick Dominican accent still colored her every word.

"Mel, it's me," I said, walking away from the house.

"Oh, don't tell me you're calling up to cancel our date," she said, her tone rising in warning.

"I'm afraid it's more than that," I said. "Got a body to report close to the reconstruction site, an engineer from the looks of him."

"And what were *you* doing anywhere near that site?" she asked, her voice switching to her cop tone. "It's off-limits to civilians. And you are a civilian, Bell."

I sighed. A scolding was precisely the kind of conversation I did not want to have. But it was one of the hazards of being in a relationship with one of Cold City's best detective sergeants.

It was our third try at the whole boyfriend/girlfriend thing. We got back together shortly after downtown Cold City went ka-boom. Ramirez had no idea what went on that day, of course. No mortal should ever know, and I'm speaking as one who does. But she was a smart cookie on top of being a worthy homicide detective. I'm pretty sure she knew I was involved somehow and stopped it from being worse than it was. Maybe that was why she'd decided to give us another chance.

"Look, get Lieutenant Morgan and a CSI team over to... 329 Wolfman," I said, powering through my exhaustion enough to remember the address. "I'll be waiting in the front yard."

Ramirez blew an annoyed breath into the phone. "You said you wanted it to be different this time, Bell."

"I still do," I replied, stone truth behind my words. "But I am what I am, Mel, whether I'm involved with you or not."

"Alright, fine," she said. "But you better make this up to me later, *entiendes*?"

"Scout's honor," I said with a pirate grin on my face. "We'll get that date rescheduled for a better night, I promise."

We said our goodbyes, and I found a nearby porch to sit on. I was nodding off when I heard the sirens grow close.

As expected, Detective Lieutenant Morgan was at the front of his troops, making a beeline for me. He was tall, with dark short-cropped hair and bushy eyebrows. He towered above me as he asked in his usual gruff basso voice, "Alright, Vale, what did you do this time?"

"Found a dismembered corpse," I answered, jerking one of my gloved thumbs towards the house and what lay inside.

His face glowered at me. "Uh-huh, and did that knife in your hand do anything to put it there?"

Shit, I thought, looking down at my hand. *I know better than that.*

I threw the blade into the ground between us. "Take a closer look, Lieutenant. There's not a drop of blood on it and never has been."

Morgan pulled out some cuffs, prompting me to say, "I wouldn't recommend you touching me." I used my free hand to tap my clothes for emphasis. A dust cloud puffed from me to help me make my point.

Ramirez came up with the CSI team right behind her. Her cute button nose wrinkled at the sight and smell of me. Everything else about her was lovely too, from her shapely legs to her well-put-together face. She had long dark hair she pulled back in a ponytail. The t-shirt and blue jeans looked like they'd been thrown on in haste, making me wonder what kind of dress she would have worn if I'd kept my date.

I gave the CSI team directions to where Jacob was, skipping the part explaining how I got past the cordon.

Ramirez stayed behind with Morgan and me. That made the lieutenant's frown deepen. "You got something to tell me, sergeant, or do you like this punk's company that much?" he asked.

"Just got a call from one of the patrols at another junction of the cordon," she explained. "One of the city engineers got back with a story about how a maniac killed the rest of her team. One of them was apparently in this house."

"One of them?" Morgan asked. "There's another casualty?"

"Deeper in the zone," Ramirez said, giving me a look. "According to her, she ran into the guy who did it. Almost suffered the same fate as our vic."

"She got a good look at him? Please tell me she said it was a tall thirty-something guy with short brown hair."

Ramirez shook her head. "Happened too fast for her to get a good look."

"Fine. Could be anyone then," Morgan said, as he came at me to snap the cuffs on.

"Hey, remember what I said about—"

"I'll take a delousing shower later," he cut me off, pulling my knife out of the ground with gloved fingers. "Look at that, Sargent Ramirez, we've found ourselves an armed suspect."

1

SCENT OF A WOMAN

As I figured, Morgan kept me for most of the night, trying to break my cover story. While Dana's tale wasn't an exact match for mine, I gathered it was enough to corroborate what I told him about my fighting off our imaginary thug after I found poor Jacob. I covered for the lack of blood by saying I'd only managed to brain him with the butt of the hilt.

I know I could have sat this one out and avoided an evening on the grill, but I couldn't let Dana face this alone. One person telling a crazy story was just that. But two unrelated witnesses coming up with a similar tale? That went into the record.

It was a little after five in the morning when I was cut loose. Some of the officers even threw in a free delousing shower and complete disposal of my clothes. I wound up walking out of the station wearing some ugly hand-me-downs that I intended on dropping off at Goodwill as soon as possible.

I had a cab hailed for me and took it back to the Walgreen's parking lot where I'd left my car. As usual, no one got near the dark-gray Corvette Stingray that stood out like Megan Fox in the middle of your local Walmart. But then, considering the car was a *gift* from Lady McDeath, why should I have been surprised? I swear she made it thief repellant or something.

I pulled the plastic cover from the driver's seat and stored it in the trunk. It was put there to keep the chemicals out of the car, but that was already taken care of by my friends in blue. I got back home without too much trouble.

The sun was rising on the horizon, faint hues of red and pink over a dark blue ocean, when I stopped the car in the underground parking lot of my building. I took the lift up to the third floor without running into any of my neighbors.

I owned a small flat in a tall apartment building, close to the shoreline. Past the front door, a small kitchen opened onto a living room crammed with mismatched bookshelves, worn sofas and a TV on a tiny stand. A bedroom and a shower room completed the lot, just past the living room proper.

It wasn't much, but it was home, and it was mine. Honestly, I'd paid too much for that flat, but at least it came with a view. A tiny view. Oh, who was I kidding? Whatever was wrong with my life, a look at the ocean between the two neighboring buildings made it all worthwhile.

I went out on the deck and breathed in the early morning air. The sight of the sunrise on the horizon made me feel like this was going to be the start of a glorious day. Then I felt my aches and pains from my Ghostbusting and realized I'd cracked a rib. I went back inside and patched myself up with some bandages and popped down a few painkillers. I drowned them in milk and limped all the way to my bed.

So what if it was mid-February? The way I was feeling that morning, I planned to sleep until New Year came around again. Hells, as far as I was concerned, I earned it ten times over. I put an end to a string of gruesome killings, prevented the apocalypse our former mayor intended for us, and I'd stuck around long enough to clean up the mess she and her minions left behind. All that thinking took out the last bit of energy I had. I closed my eyes, found a way to lie down that didn't hurt too much, and let sleep throw its soothing blanket over me.

And then someone knocked at the door.

I groaned at the wrong timing but kept my eyes shut. There was no way in Tartarus that I was getting back up again so soon. Whoever it was could get lost.

The knocking came again.

It was more insistent this time. I could hear a sense of urgency to the motion. I forced one eye open and frowned. The sunlight streaming in from the window was too bright for it to be morning, and the angle it bounced off the floorboards was all wrong. I opened my second eye and glanced at the clock on the bedside table...Three in the afternoon.

"The hells?" I muttered, wondering where the day went while I shook my head to clear out the cobwebs.

The knock came a third time, and I got up, grumbling all the way to the door. I didn't bother to put clothes on or to tidy myself up before opening it. I was clad only in an old pair of sweatpants with a variety of cuts, bruises, and bandages on full display throughout my upper body. I hadn't shaved in a week, and I was sure my hair was a sweaty mess of brown locks and dried blood.

Who knows, I thought, *maybe the sight of me will convince my uninvited guest to let me get back to my coma.*

If the man in the hallway took notice of my state, he didn't let it show. He was tall and sickly thin under his rumpled three-piece suit. His pale skin provided some severe contrast with the purple bags under his brown eyes. He was somewhere between forty and forty-five. His angular face wasn't familiar, and my frown deepened.

He looked like a potential client, the I-want-to-know-who-my-wife-is-banging type, but they rarely showed up to my private address unannounced. I made a lot of enemies in my professional career, not all of them on this side of the border, so my business card only listed my cell number.

The suit he wore appeared brand-new, but I frowned more as I realized something didn't add up. I was no fashion expert, but the matching of colors between the vest and shirt was off, brownish-orange shirt covered by a purple jacket. Oh, and he wore a tie that matched his jacket...ugh. The light brown shoes were also at odds with the indigo blue pants. And there was the smell on the guy. It wasn't a garbage smell—I'd been around enough of that over the last month to know it at first whiff—but there was a smoky quality about it that stood out.

I filed the information away for later and looked at the man squarely in the eye. "What?" I croaked, my tongue feeling too thick and my mouth too dry.

"Bellamy Vale?" he asked, with an accent that wasn't from around here...Middle Eastern, maybe?

I jerked my thumb at the bell next to the door. It had my name on it.

The man peered down at it, perplexed, then pressed the round button. A shrill ringing shot out of the tiny plastic box above the door, and the sound sent sharp needles dancing through my brain. I winced in pain.

"Yeah—yeah, that's me." I rushed the words out, eager to make the noise stop. Damn, but my head was killing me. My odd gentleman caller took his finger off the button to look at me again.

"I need your help," he said, "to find my sister."

I needed help too, preferably in the form of another round of painkillers. But that was going to have to wait. I waved my potential new client inside.

As soon as I closed and locked the door behind me, I racked my brain to remember where I'd put my Sig Sauer and knife. I remembered the blade was in police lockup while the P226 was tucked away in the kitchen next to my dust-covered bottle of Bowmore. Granted, the guy didn't seem like a threat, but as I said, I have a lot of enemies.

The stranger sat down on my loveseat and waited for me to do the same on the couch. The funny thing was that his eyes never left me for a minute, which I considered a little spooky. But maybe it was nerves on his part. That smoky odor was still there; could it be his aftershave? It was familiar—sage or sandalwood.

"So," I began, "what can you tell me about your sister, Mister...?"

"Eli," the man answered. "Eli Smith, at your service, sir."

No way he'd given me his real name. But he would be far from the first client I had who wanted anonymity. I'd lost count of how many Jones and Smiths I talked to. The first name felt genuine, though.

"My sister's name is Sarit," Eli went on to say. "She came here on business a little over a month ago."

I felt a knot in my stomach. Even half-asleep, I knew that would have been right around the time Galatas leveled downtown Cold City. "Was she caught up in the—"

"Oh, no, no, no," Eli corrected me, holding up both of his hands for emphasis. "I am pleased to say she managed to escape unscathed from the wanton destruction that destroyed part of this city. Indeed, once she arrived, she took great pains to reassure me that she was hale and hearty."

"When was the last time you contacted her?" I asked, my brain changing gears.

"A few days past. However, my sister has gone missing, and I have no idea where she could be now."

I felt the slight tickle of exhaustion get the better of me. "Look...Mr. Smith. It's not that I'm not flattered by your thinking that I can find her. But there are any number of innocent reasons why she could be out of touch; she could be out partying, or her cell died or—"

"Why would she have a cell, and how could it die?"

"A cell phone," I said, pointing at my smartphone resting on the coffee table. "Like this one, see?"

"Ahh, of course," Eli said, but his eyes told me he still didn't know what I was talking about. How far out of town was he?

"Anyway," I said. "Why don't you go to the police for this one? I know a good detective there I can personally—"

Eli cut me off like a butchers' knife going through beef. "No! I need to find her now!"

His eyes flared, and his face grew frightened. I knew that look. A long time ago, it was the face I saw in the mirror every morning. Nothing hurts worse than losing family while you're drowning in unanswered questions. Whatever my would-be client might be hiding, there was nothing faked about his love and concern for his sister.

Eli took a breath and made himself relax. "I must apologize for my outburst, Mr. Vale. It is rather unseemly for me to be so insistent of a man whose time I am imposing upon."

"You're scared," I said, holding up a hand. "It's understandable."

Eli pulled out his wallet and started handing me some bills from it. Hundred-dollar bills. "Would this be sufficient payment for you to take this case?"

Money talks. The last paid job I had was the Townsend case about two months ago—a kidnapped young girl I safely returned home to her parents.

After a quick calculation of how many bills I could put this cash towards, I said, "Fine; you've bought yourself twenty-four hours of my time. After that, no promises."

Eli sighed in relief at my words, putting the wallet back in his pocket. "To God be the glory."

He had a higher opinion about the universe than I had. "Do you have a photo of Sarit?"

"Alas, no."

"Well, what about her last address? Phone number?"

I noticed a different kind of fear coming back into his eyes as he shook his head.

"C'mon, you said you were in contact with her until a few days ago. Why don't you have any of those things?"

"I...I am afraid I do not know the ways of this city well,"

he said, pulling at his tie. "It is so hard to...find anyone. The smells are constantly distracting."

I was still trying to parse out why he was saying what he was saying when he spotted a blank piece of paper on the coffee table between us. He pulled out a pencil and began sketching on it. Within the space of a few minutes, he had rendered a complete portrait of a young woman. He handed me the sketch. "This is what Sarit looks like."

Comparing this picture with my client's face, I didn't see the resemblance. The woman in the portrait only had the dark eyes in common. She had rounded cheekbones and lush lips.

"She's lovely," I said, eyes on the sketch. "How old is she?"

"Twenty-eight," Eli said. "She is my everything, Mr. Vale. I have spent days upon days attempting to catch her scent with nothing to show for my pains."

I glanced up from the sketch to him. "Nothing?"

A frustrated breath came out of Eli's mouth. "I am explaining this badly...Again, I apologize. I did have one place I was able to track her scent back to."

"Which was...?"

"An old abandoned place of storage on the docks. But it was empty."

Eli started getting that panicky look in his eyes again when I asked him where. I sighed and put the money he had handed me away. "Let me ask it like this...Could you show me the way?"

"Absolutely," Eli said, brightening up. "If you have an automobile, the trip will be much faster."

"It usually is," I said, rising from my seat. "If you can give me a few minutes to get dressed, we'll head that way."

I went back to the bedroom to put on a fresh shirt and a pair of jeans. We were off ten minutes later, the Stingray easily sliding into the mid-afternoon traffic.

Whatever strangeness was going on with my new client, his sense of direction was impeccable. Within about twenty minutes, we pulled the car up to a deserted part of the docks off Thames Street. The abandoned building he motioned to was far from the only one. A lot of commercial shipwrights and warehouses went down for the count during the Great Recession. The vast empty buildings left behind marked the corpses of those defunct businesses. I drove past the warehouse we'd be looking over, aiming the car for an office building a block up.

"Mr. Vale," Eli said, confused. "I told you that—"

"We're still going there," I explained as I turned the corner. "But a car like this draws attention." It wasn't the truth, but something about the man's attitude made me want to keep some cards close to my chest. I didn't have enough fingers to count on the number of times where leaving my car at least a block away from my destination saved my bacon. It became a habit, same as the one I had of leaving my keys in the ignition for a quick getaway.

I parked the car on the curb next to the offices, and we made a quick hike over to the warehouse. Looking at the big metal building from the outside, it felt empty in every sense of the word: of space, of life, of purpose. When was the last time anyone bothered to glance its way?

The answer to that question presented itself in the form of black liquid on the gravel. I walked over to it and got down on my haunches. I put my fingers through the stuff to smell it. Looking over my shoulder, Eli sniffed as well. "Petroleum?"

"Car oil," I agreed, wiping off the oil on a nearby patch of grass. "Somebody with a leaky oil pan has been here recently."

The door was locked, but that was hardly a problem. I pulled my picks from my jacket and had it open in under two minutes. Eli didn't even blink at my little B&E routine, but what's a little break-in compared to finding a beloved family member?

The vast space echoed back our footsteps as we peered around inside, dirty windows filtering the dimming light of the setting sun. I went down into a crouch again and rubbed my hands along the floor.

"No dust," I said, getting back up. "Someone's been here recently."

"Now that we are inside, is there any way I can be useful?" Eli asked, energized by the prospect of some headway.

"Look around," I said. "See anything unusual, point it out to me."

While Eli started flitting here and there, searching the place in a random pattern, I did a grid search to make sure I was getting everything. Whatever this place had to give would still be there when we found it.

I saw some brown spots on the otherwise grey floor in the corner. A quick inspection showed them to be cigarette butts, unfiltered Camels by the smell of them. Underneath the pile was a small stick pin, the kind used in fashion design circles.

"Mr. Vale," Eli said, holding up some strips of cloth. "I found these at the far end of the warehouse."

I gave them an intense look over. The material was dirty from the grime but still elegant in quality. The bright, vivid colors made me think of designer dresses, custom lingerie, and other fashionista accessories.

"This feels like the site of a sweatshop operation," I declared. "An out-of-the-way place like this next to the water would be perfect for it."

That's when I realized my nose was picking up something ever since I walked through the door. "Do you smell that? Smells like something burning in here."

"Like burned what?" my client asked.

"I dunno," I admitted. "Maybe burning wires or—"

"Coal?" Eli said, which sounded a little too much like a presupposed answer.

"I wouldn't know. Never was around much burning coal. Sure stinks, though."

I watched Eli breathing in the air like an overachieving bloodhound. What was it with this guy and smells? But I put that aside. Trust me or not, a client with an olfactory preoccupation was far from the weirdest thing I'd seen in my line of work.

After we swept the building as thoroughly as we could, we stepped outside. A glance at my smartphone confirmed I had enough bars to make a call. Three rings later, a familiar voice answered, "Sergeant Ramirez."

"Mel, I think I might have something for you," I said.

"*Madre de Dios*, I would think a *cabrón* like you would know better than to dig more into that corpse you helped us find," she huffed, the Spanish accent sharpening the edges of her disdain.

"The *cabrón* does, *mi corazóne*. I am on another case right now," I explained. "What can you tell me about the warehouse at—" I looked up at the numbers over the door "—458 Thames Street? Was it ever used for a sweatshop operation that got caught up in a raid? Or a spot you wanted to keep an eye on?"

"I'm homicide, Bell. Why would I know about any of that?"

"C'mon, Mel. Surely it's something you can check."

Ramirez sighed into the phone. "Fine, sure, of course. I mean, it's not like I haven't got a slew of missing person reports on my plate."

"Since when?" I asked as I leaned against the wall. "Thought you were homicide."

"Since I got in this morning," she explained. "Missing persons is swamped. It's all leftover business from the Galatas Incident. Clearing them should be a relative slam dunk if we can determine they died in the bombing. But there are so damn many of them." I could hear the steady stream of rapid keystrokes tapping away in the background. "I don't know who I pissed off," she continued, "but I wish I were secretly awesome at something better than inviting the boss's wrath. Guess that's the price I pay for dating your scheming ass."

"Hey, how is this one my fault again?"

Ramirez chose to ignore that jab by telling me, "Found it. We've got it flagged as a potential location for a sweatshop op but that's it. No search warrant or even a request for one... What did you find on-site?"

I gave her the rundown of the evidence Eli and I found,

including the fact it was now vacant. More keystrokes took down the info.

"Done, consider the file up to date," she said. "Can I say it's a pleasure to get a crime this low-key out of you for once?"

"Sure can," I said, feeling the grin come back on my face. "Anyway, I can make up for last night a little later?"

Ramirez hummed into the phone. "Well...I've got to print out and organize all these case files, which should take up the rest of the day. After, if I've got the time, I need to hunt down a witness for a missing cab driver. Tell you what...why don't I text you later, and we'll see about getting a bite to eat?"

"Sounds nice," I said. "Hope your afternoon isn't too terrible."

I could hear the smile in her voice on the other end. "Truthfully, *mi corazón*, you've been the best part of my day so far. Good luck with your case."

After we hung up, Eli peered at me in curiosity.

"Girlfriend," I explained, pushing myself off the wall.

"You care for this woman?" Eli asked, gauging me as though I were some strange alien artifact.

"Yeah," I said as a dumpster caught my eye. "A lot."

Eli followed my gaze and said, "What is so interesting about that receptacle?"

"Well, take it from a professional. You can find out a lot more about a person by looking through their trash than you ever could their possessions," I said, walking towards the dumpster. "Maybe the previous occupants left us something useful."

My nose was screaming bloody murder at me for the

smells inside that dumpster. It was only a quarter full, which made the search more manageable than it could have been.

I found a few more duplicates of what we saw inside: stick pins, cloth samples and a whole forest of Camel cigarette butts. But there were also some new things buried under the throwaway food wrappers and banana peels. One of them was a pile of partially-ruined sketches for designer dresses. They looked like they could have been at home somewhere a bit tonier than a Walmart. The overall quality on them was astounding, all elegant straps, discreet seams, and ruffled sleeves. What was something this detailed and professional doing here?

The next thing I pried off the bottom was a man's button-up shirt. It was of similar quality to the dresses, but tar stained its fabric to the point of sheer ruin. A quick sniff of the material revealed it had a couple of distinctive scents upon it: the unknown burning smell I'd tagged inside and the Camels. I flipped through the samples in the dumpster, only to find there was no match.

"Can I see those fabric samples again?" I asked Eli, who was standing outside. He handed them to me. None of them matched the shirt, either. It looks like the material was meant strictly for the dresses.

A faint glint of light caught something underneath the shirt, a small green stone that resembled an emerald. It was likely dyed glass supposed to have gone with one of the dresses but, fake or not, it belonged here as much as the sketches did.

"Have you had any success, Mr. Vale?" Eli called out to me as I pocketed the stone, samples and sketches.

"Maybe," I said, standing back up. "All this stuff confirms the sweatshop guess I had about this place."

I climbed back out, almost falling on my ass on the other side as my cracked rib flared up. Eli caught me with surprisingly strong hands before I hit the ground.

"Thanks," I said with appreciation as he pulled me to my feet.

"Think nothing of it," Eli assured me. "Does any of this point to where my sister could be?"

I pulled off my plastic gloves and threw them in the dumpster. "As tired as I am getting of saying this, I dunno. Did Sarit ever work in the fashion industry?"

"No, why would she?" Eli said, puzzled.

"Well, what kind of work did she do?"

His puzzlement turned to alarm in the space of a second. "Many different things but...nothing specific."

"She went through a lot of jobs then?"

"Yes, many, many jobs. I can no longer recall what she said she was doing currently."

God, he was such a lousy liar. But that was his business for the time being. Mine was helping him. "Listen...I need to follow up on these leads we've found." Sniffing myself and wincing, I added, "And I need yet another change of clothes and a shower. Can I drive you back to where you're staying?"

Eli glanced at me with more than a bit of suspicion.

"Look, you know where I live," I said, holding up my hand. "Even if I wanted to rip you off, you know where to find me. By my count, you've still got" —One glance at my watch— "twenty-one hours left of my time."

Eli didn't look thrilled with my wanting to put him aside, but he said, "Very well...I shall leave you to it, then."

He started walking away.

"Wait! I said I could give you a ride," I called after him.

"That will be unnecessary," Eli assured me.

"Don't you at least want my phone number?"

He didn't answer and kept walking until he turned in the opposite direction of where the Stingray was parked.

I hauled the plastic back out of the trunk and put it on the driver's seat. Given the highly questionable substances all over my clothes, the last thing I wanted to do was smear them on the Stingray's posh interior. I wasted no time pulling the stinking clothes off my body once I got back to the apartment.

As I showered, I racked my brains over who I could talk to about the designs and fabrics I found at the warehouse. I needed somebody who had an inside track on the fashion world and who could point out things I'd miss. My best friend was more into geek t-shirts, and my number one street-level informant had a fetish for denim and flannel straight out of the eighties. I could have called Ramirez again, but I had already pushed my luck twice within the space of a day. The third time might not be the charm.

I all but groaned as I shut off the shower. That only left one person, and I'd been doing my best to keep her on the sidelines since the Galatas Incident, seeing as she'd found out way more about Alterum Mundum than she should have. But given how well she made a plaid skirt and cowboy boots look on her, maybe, just maybe, Kennedy would know something about what I found.

I put my soiled clothes in the washer before I rang her. Two rings later, a sweet Texas drawl answered, "Hello?"

"Hey, Kennedy, it's Vale," I said, trying to sound casual.

"Howdy, what case you working on now?" she asked without missing a beat.

"Who says I'm working a case?"

A full-throated laugh came through the line at that question. "You don't call for weeks, and then out of the blue—on a Saturday night, no less—you happen to get lonely enough to want to ring me up? What part of that smells right to you, Mr. Private Detective?"

I winced. My inability to bullshit Kennedy was as annoying as I remembered it being. "Fine, I'm working on a new case, and I thought you might be able to help."

"Ohh, like our last case?" Kennedy all but cooed, her reporter's hunger for a story shining through her voice.

"Nothing that flashy," I admitted, before laying out the particulars of the case of the missing Sarit.

"You know, it's kind of funny you should mention the sweatshop thing," Kennedy said. "I've been covering the first-ever Cold City Fashion Show this week."

"I didn't know we rated a fashion show."

"Surprised me too when the boss handed me the assignment," Kennedy said. "But your old client and newly minted mayor, Ian Townsend, pulled some strings to make it happen. I gotta say, it's a mighty good way to get a positive spotlight back on this town."

She had a point. Given the notoriety of Cold City in the wake of the explosions, we needed something to bring back the customers and tourists this city was dependent upon to survive.

"Is there any way I could meet you there and show some of the stuff I found to the people you're interviewing?" I asked. "I got a feeling your press pass could help make this nice and discreet."

"Level with me, Vale," Kennedy said. "You sure there's nothing else to this case? Nothing spooky?"

"None at all," I said. "Based on the evidence I have so far, I'm not convinced this isn't anything more than a little rich girl wanting to get away from her big brother's thumb."

There was a long pause on the line. "Okay, then. You can carry my bag the minute you get up to the Springfield Center. But the second you find something interesting that could land me a story, you *are* going to keep me in the loop, right?"

I wasn't in a position to argue. The fact Kennedy knew about the supernatural aspects of my job meant she had me over a barrel. Just the same, I hoped this little meet-and-greet I arranged was going to be as far from that end of my business as possible. Kennedy proved herself to be resourceful in a scrap, but my almost-boss made it clear she'd be in danger if she started sniffing into our business again.

2

WHERE THERE'S SMOKE

K ennedy's interview with designer Fritz Murnau was conducted in an empty conference room in the Springfield Center the next afternoon. It was a ritzy glass building on the oceanfront. You could hear the ongoing fashion show through the wall, but it was dull enough to have a conversation. To make sure they had quality sound, I helped Kennedy's cameraman set up in the farthest end of the room from the wall noise.

My hand to God (or whoever was in charge), I did my best to stay interested in the Q&A. From what I put together at the beginning, Murnau was a leading fashion designer in his field, a rising star with the potential to be the next Tommy Hilfiger. He grew up in the old East Berlin before the German Reunification gave him access to university and his lifelong dream to be a designer. All interesting, compelling stuff, even to a guy like me. But then the interview got into what went into putting together the collection he was showing off, and I felt my eyes and ears glaze over.

Everybody, Kennedy included, stopped paying attention to me the moment the camera started rolling, so I decided to pull up an older interview with Kennedy on my phone for distraction. I went to the back, plugged in my earbuds and sat down in the nearest straight-back chair to focus on what was onscreen.

It was Kennedy's last interview under her old news agency, the *Headliner*. A couple of months before, her bosses stuck her on the midnight shift, chasing down whatever random crime or story broke in the wee hours. Somehow, she found out I was investigating a string of alleged wolf attacks she was reporting on for her news outlet. Smelling an opportunity, she gave me a choice: help her break the story or she'd tell Detective Morgan about the depth of my involvement in it. I was in no position to say anything but yes.

After she went live with the story—minus a few details that needed to stay under wraps—she had no shortage of offers from the *Headliner*'s rivals. The interview I was looking at, with the freshly-elected Mayor Ian Townsend, was part of the *Headliner*'s efforts to get her to stay. Given that I knew for a fact she'd already made up her mind to leave for *Full Access News* at that point, I'd say the joke was on them.

"Thank you for agreeing to speak with us, Mr. Mayor," the onscreen Kennedy said, her usual Texas drawl restrained for the camera. Both she and her subject were seated in one of the *Headliner*'s interview rooms.

"Please, make it 'Mr. Townsend', Ms. Kennedy," Townsend said with a practiced smile. "I have a few days left before my new official title applies."

Kennedy smiled back at him. It was genuine, and my mind flashed back to the day monsters attacked both of them in the office of Townsend's maritime shipping company. She saved his life, and then I rescued both of them.

"It's no secret, in the wake of the bombings, that Cold City has a good many pressing issues," she said. "As mayor, how do you plan on handling them?"

"Well, as I see it, we best handle this situation the same way I did when my company met hard times after the Lehman Brothers financial meltdown: identify all the existing problems, see how many of them are related, prioritize the most urgent ones, and get those urgent cases dealt with before moving on to other matters. I can tell you and your viewers that my transition team is in the process of doing the first two items on that list."

"Do you feel intimidated by all this?"

"I know other people in my position would say they feel scared. But I don't. If my professional career has taught me anything, it's that fear alone never solves problems. When there's too much of it, you're not solving anything."

"So you are confident you can meet the challenges before you?"

Townsend looked over to the right for a minute, doing his best to figure out the correct way to answer that question. "I would say I am as concerned about what is going on in our city as the next private citizen. What we have in front of us will only get better if we deal with it. I will do everything I can, based on the information available, to fix these things. But I would ask that everyone else also do their part. We are in this together."

"Your election was unprecedented due to the extraordinary circumstances, how did—"

Someone tapped me on the shoulder, making me glance up—Kennedy. After pausing the video, I popped out my earbuds.

She peeked over my phone. "Looking at my greatest hits?"

"Killing time," I admitted. "Interview's over?"

"As of a minute ago," she confirmed. "I went ahead and told Mr. Murnau you had questions about some sketches you found."

"And that's all you told him?"

"Was I supposed to add anything else, hoss?"

I smiled at the nickname I hadn't heard in a while and put the phone in my pocket. Kennedy went to help her cameraman pack away the equipment.

Fritz Murnau was a big man with a surprisingly thin frame. He wore a standard three-piece suit that reflected better color coordination than Eli's. His placid face and eyes radiated urbane charm and manners as he shook my hand, but the calluses on his hands told me he had done a lot of hard work to get where he was in life.

"How might I be of assistance, *Herr* Vale?" he asked.

"I found these sketches in the trash not so long ago," I said, pulling the folded sketches out of my pocket. "They look like professional quality to me, but I'm no expert. So I wanted to get the opinion of an actual expert."

"Flattery will get you everywhere with me, young man," Murnau said with a muted smile. His brown eyes went wide as he unfolded the papers. He shuffled through them one by one, then repeated the process. "*Mein Gott,*" he breathed. "And you say you found these in the trash?"

"A dumpster, no less," I confirmed. "I'm guessing, from the way you're reacting, that was the last place they needed to be."

"*Ja genau!*" Murnau confirmed. "The designs on these dresses are inspired. I have every confidence, with the right material, they would become a major hit. *Wunderschön!*"

His expression changed as he glanced down at one of the drawings. "Now that I think on this, I believe I know who did this."

"Who?" I asked, doing my best not to let eagerness overwhelm me.

"Hellfire," Murnau said, after a moment's pause. "Local company. They were a last-minute addition to the show. Under normal circumstances, newcomers aren't considered, but..."

"There hasn't been anything normal happening in Cold City for a while."

Murnau suppressed a giggle.

"Still, I figure these Hellfire people would have to be good at their job to get their foot in the door."

"Unique design certainly is an indication of quality," Murnau said, turning the drawing around to me. "Take this particular dress. Note the placement of the gemstones. The shapes they make are very ethnic and far from the usual."

"What made you say these designs likely come from Hellfire?"

"Because, *Herr* Vale, I happened to see a dress very similar to this one on their clothing rack backstage."

I nodded and pulled out my Sarit sketch. "One more

thing...I was wondering if you have seen this woman around the show this week."

We exchanged sketches. Murnau's eyes lit up again, and he tilted his head slightly to the right. "I regret to say the answer is no. Who is she?"

"Someone I'm helping a friend find." I took the sketch back and handed him one of my cards. "If you happen to see her, would you mind giving me a call at this number?"

"Most assuredly," Murnau said, taking the card and putting it in his pocket.

By this point, Kennedy had sent the cameraman back to the van with the equipment. She was waiting for me by the door. "So...get anything juicy?"

"Local fashion company called Hellfire," I told her. "Heard anything about it?"

"Just the local part," Kennedy said. "They connected to this missing person of yours?"

"Might be," I said as we walked. "It's a place to start."

We asked around the center for any Hellfire representatives on-site, but none were present. We did, on the other hand, have a bit more luck in getting directions to their dressing rooms. They rented space situated towards the back of the Springfield Center, close to the stage.

The show itself was in full swing while we were doing our poking around. That meant a steady stream of models in various states of dress and undress walking through the corridors. Looking at all that heavenly flesh made me sorry I was on the clock.

Kennedy eventually gave me an elbow to the rib. "Sure you got your mind on business, hoss?"

I rubbed my ribcage. "Hey, no harm in looking."

"Wonder if your ex would have bought that line," Kennedy said as we got in front of the Hellfire dressing rooms.

"She isn't my ex anymore. But you're right; she didn't buy it when I tried," I said, peering down both ends of the corridor. We were alone. I pulled out my lockpicks and started jimmying the flimsy lock. Kennedy kept on the look-out, but things stayed all clear. Took me less than a minute to pop the lock.

"We searching for anything specific?" Kennedy asked once I closed the door behind us.

Spotting the clothes rack, I said, "I'll start with the dresses if you look around."

I pulled out the dress sketches again and laid them all out on a nearby table. A few minutes of flicking back and forth confirmed at least three of the designs had real-life counterparts on the racks. Even the gems were in the same spots.

"Oof, this place smells like the Taco Bell back home before it went smoke-free," Kennedy said while she waved a hand in front of the closet.

"Springfield's supposed to be a smoke-free building anyway, right?" I noted while I picked up the sketches to put back in my pocket.

"Tell that to the ashtray," Kennedy replied, pointing down to the amber, square basin in question. It was tucked away in a back corner of the closet, out of sight. That poor thing's maximum cigarette butt occupancy was exceeded by at least twenty. It made a small mole-hill that would fall over into the floor at the slightest puff of air. The butts were all unfiltered Camels like at the warehouse, except some of these had lipstick on them.

Kennedy kept looking around while I was giving the ashtray a once-over. Without taking her eyes off the model's stations, she asked, "Find any of those at the warehouse?"

"The same brand," I said. "This sort of thing's usual with models?"

"Put it like this. You're already stressing out about being stared at by a bunch of strangers and wearing clothes you couldn't afford if you worked for the next century. You're wondering if you're too fat and you're terrified about eating anything because it'll show. There's no coke to help you chill out, so you invest in a pack of smokes to get your nerves under control. Let the maintenance guys deal with the mess after."

"Sounds like the voice of experience talking there?"

"Did a little bit of modeling when I was in college," Kennedy admitted. "But I found out real quick there are better ways a girl can get by in this world."

The way she said it, it sounded like she was trying a little too hard to appear casual about the whole thing. There was a story there, but I didn't press the issue. We weren't close enough for me to pry into her life. Still, I filed that nugget of information away as I went back to the dresses.

I found what I was looking for on the third try. "The gemstones on this one match the green rock I found in the trash. If I had to make a guess, I'd say Hellfire set up at the warehouse on a strictly temporary basis to get ready for the show."

"Sure," Kennedy said, finishing up her search to join me. "Murnau did say they were a last-minute addition. Didn't have any time to get ready, so they rented out space, all nice and legal. Those designs you found were sketches that had a thing or two wrong with 'em."

I sighed and rubbed my face. "I dunno. I mean, every bit of this is checking out as legit so far. Nothing connects back to our missing girl."

"But...?"

I dropped my hand and shook my head. "Let's say my PI senses are still twitching. Any chance we could get with this fashion show's manager?"

"Yeah, I was supposed to do a follow-up interview with him anyway. Let's go back to the van and grab the gear one more time."

The cameraman was annoyed he had to go back to work again, but neither of us cared. The manager, one Roger Curry, was holed up in an office on the second floor. Nondescript in appearance, he was in his late forties with lightly tanned skin, a widow's peak, gray eyes, and an average frame. He wore a simple blue button-up shirt over slightly darker blue slacks. If he were a superhero, I'd have called him Blandman.

The windows in the office looked out onto the main floor, where we could see the fashion show in full swing. As tempting as it was to keep my eyes trained on those sweet young things down below, I made myself pay attention to Kennedy's interview this time around.

After a few questions that were unasked in her initial interview, she said, "So let's talk about Hellfire. I understand they are a local fashion company, correct?"

"Very much so," Curry confirmed, his hands clasped behind in parade rest. "Indeed, they are new players in this business; so new, in fact, they should not have been included in a show this high-profile. But His Honor, Mayor Townsend, made the sensible argument that if this show were meant to focus the world's attention on Cold City, a local company would only make sense."

A weird sort of rapture spread across this grey man's face as he added, "Of course, these things become less of a hardship when the designers are of Hellfire's caliber. Such an intricate blend of both old and new ideas...the talent at their beck and call is nothing short of extraordinary."

By the time he quit talking, he had the kind of loving devotion I associate with cults. Okay, Hellfire was good. Even a fashion illiterate like me could see that. But why was this annoying little man treating it like the Second Coming of Christ?

Kennedy wrapped up the interview officially a few minutes later. The cameraman glanced at her warily. "You sure you're done with me for the night?"

"Yeah, Ralph," Kennedy said. "Go ahead and wait by the van. I'll make sure Vale here gets the equipment back."

Ralph gave her a "you better mean it" look before walking out of the office. I was loading up the equipment when I popped a question of my own. "Mind if I ask something?"

Back to his default neutral way of interacting with the world, Curry shrugged. "Depends on the topic."

"Well, I was wondering...Who's in charge at Hellfire?"

"That would be Mr. Khalim Jones," Curry said. "Would I be correct in saying, Ms. Kennedy, that you would like to interview him as well?"

"It's an interesting enough angle. I'd like to pitch it to my bosses," Kennedy admitted. "Do you happen to have their business address?"

"Of course," Curry said. "I'll need to consult my listings here."

Once Curry found what he was looking for in a black book on his desk, he took out a notepad and pen from his pants pocket to write down the information.

"Does Mr. Jones smoke, by chance?" I asked.

"To put it mildly," Curry answered with a wry smile, his eyes fixed on writing out the address. "That man smokes a carton a day, I swear. We've had to turn a blind eye to his smoking in the dressing rooms with his models. But maybe that's the secret to his genius."

Tearing off the sheet, he handed the information to Kennedy. She gave him a smile she must have perfected during her modeling days. "I appreciate you taking the time, Mr. Curry."

The manager gave her a smile with a lot less wattage. "The pleasure, I assure you, was all mine."

With the equipment all packed up again, I lugged it towards the exit, Kennedy right behind me. She slipped the paper into my jacket pocket.

"So...got everything you need from me tonight?" Kennedy asked.

"Well...I can think of one more thing," I admitted.

Kennedy rolled her eyes. "Always something extra with you."

The last favor I got out of Kennedy wasn't too big. I wanted to use her press pass to get backstage one more time for a canvass. Officially, Kennedy was back there asking the models if they'd want to answer questions for her piece. Unofficially, I was showing them Eli's sketch of Sarit.

I got the same answer back each time: nobody had ever seen her. Still, I wouldn't call the time a total waste. Half-a-dozen models who didn't bat an eye at how little they were wearing, with the occasional nipple thrown in? Nights like this made me love my job.

3

WALKING WOUNDED

Out in the parking lot, Ralph the cameraman leaned against the hood of the news van with crossed arms and a closed-off expression.

"Love to tag along on whatever you're planning next," Kennedy said. "But I gotta get back."

"Is it past Ralphie's bedtime?" I quipped.

Kennedy snorted out a laugh. "Got a lot of footage to sort through. If I want my piece to air on time, gonna have to get on that tonight."

I was a little relieved by that.

"Don't look so broke up about it, Vale," Kennedy teased.

Her ability to read me was exasperating. "How do you stay so tuned into my thoughts?"

"Where I'm standing, you got a lousy poker face," Kennedy said with a playful poke in the ribs. "Seriously, though, you *are* gonna tell me if this turns out to be more than what it looks like, right?"

The words didn't come easy, but they did come. "I promise. It's not like I got a lot of people I can trust with business from—" I glanced at Ralph to confirm he was out of earshot. "Well, from over-the-border."

She stuck her pointer in my face. "I'm holding you to that."

We said our goodbyes, and Kennedy walked towards the van. Ralph uncrossed his arms and asked, "So, who's the new boyfriend?"

"Oh, shut up and drive," she snapped back.

———

The address for the Hellfire offices was in Heinz Point. Before the Galatas Incident, they were an out-of-the-way collection of office buildings in the northern part of the city, and had trouble keeping tenants. With the leveling of downtown turning many companies homeless, the owners of Heinz Point had to start a waiting list for the new applicants. With any luck, the businesses would stay when the reconstruction finished. Personally, I called it a coin toss.

It was getting close to ten by this point, and a fog bank was settling over the city, courtesy of moisture from the bay. The shape of Cold City was like a natural amphitheater, sandwiched between the ocean and a large mountain chain. With the lack of wind from the coast, the fog was likely to stay all night.

As I drove north from the Springfield Center, I got the feeling someone was following me. Believe it or not, there's nothing supernatural about that. When I was in the Navy, one of my sea daddies drilled into me the concept of pattern recognition. The more you're aware, the less of a chance you'll get caught flat-footed. I wasn't always able to pinpoint what was off, but I learned to trust that feeling enough to act on it.

I pulled the Stingray into an all-night diner a few blocks south of Hellfire's address. It straddled the border between Heinz Point and Sweeney with what I thought was a lot of traffic for a Sunday night. I stayed there for a few minutes, pretending to fiddle with my smartphone while I watched cars go by on the main road. Nothing stood out.

After ten minutes, I got out and walked towards Heinz Point proper. There were a few people out on the sidewalks at that time of night, but it was a thin crowd. The further north I went, the smaller the crowd got.

I started feeling eyes on me about two blocks up. I was hoping it was just one guy...and that it was the kind of guy I could win a fight against without losing all my teeth.

I turned off Maltese Street and into a familiar alley. The rusted-out dumpster was where it usually was, tall enough for me to hide behind in a crouch. I wished I had my knife with me. My gun might have been nice too, but too much noise would have put me back in Morgan's crosshairs. I was going to have to wing it.

Another set of footsteps came into the alley. They slowed down as they got closer. I heard labored breathing on top of the steps, like the guy was running a mile to get me. In a voice so low it barely echoed off the walls, he muttered, "Where is he?"

That's all I needed to hear. The moment the intruder got past the dumpster, I gave him a hip tackle that should have sent him into the opposite wall. But somehow, he managed to flip me around in mid-air, and I was the one that hit the wall with a thud. I was still shaking my head clear when I saw a fist aimed right at my nose. I jerked my head to the side, making the attacker's hand slam into the brick with a meaty slap. My right fist jabbed into his belly and side, working his body like a jackhammer.

I bucked my hips and used my left hand to help flip him over. But once again, he kept the flip going, and I wound up on the bottom before I could blink. This time, the fist struck, and my head went blank a couple of times as the blows hit home. I wrapped my hands around his arm as the third punch landed and applied pressure to the elbow. The strangled cry from my attacker's mouth sounded familiar.

"Smith?" I asked in confusion, relaxing the pressure.

"Mr. Vale," the shadowy figure replied, confirming my guess.

I released his arm, and we both got back on our feet, a bit unsteadily. Something about his gait told me he was a lot less steady than I was right then.

"I...I must apologize," he said. "I was quite certain you were a robber of some sort."

"A robber that doesn't use a gun or a knife?" I asked. "In this city?"

He sighed. "Yes...upon reflection, that theory does seem rather foolish."

I took the time to check myself over for any severe damage. Aside from new aches and pains, nothing was pressing. "What were you doing following me in the first place?"

"I was most interested to see if you had managed any progress on the leads we found."

"So, instead of waiting at my place for me to come back, you stalk me across town to make sure I'm on the job?" I admit I was more than a little offended. Sure, I can be a bit devious when it comes to getting the money I need, but I'm enough of a professional to stick with a job until I either figure out that it's not worth pursuing or I get paid.

It made me want to punch my client all over again.

Eli sagged at my words. "I have no excuse nor would I expect you to accept any on my behalf. I can only cry your pardon and ask your forgiveness."

The wording was as hokey as old-school pulp dialogue, but damn if the sincerity behind his words didn't touch me. "Alright, apology accepted. But if I'm going to keep working for you, I need to know that you trust me to do the work, okay?"

"Yes," he said, with an ever-quickening nod of his head. "I did hire you for a reason, after all."

"So where did you learn to fight like that?" I asked, while my hand massaged my cracked rib.

"It was a very long time ago. I am quite surprised I remember how to do so."

I thought about the constant flips he'd employed. "Was that aikido you were using?"

Eli leaned against the dumpster. "No, it is a far more ancient fighting style from the Arabian Peninsula. I doubt you would recognize the name."

Even after a throwdown that took a lot out of him, he still was tight-lipped about anything related to his past. "Does Sarit know these techniques too?"

"Indeed. If anything, of the two of us, my sister was always the more proficient."

So how did she wind up getting kidnapped, assuming you're right? I thought to myself. *Considering this style accounted for things like knives and guns, she'd be much tougher to bring down than her brother, based on this little demonstration.*

My client started leaning against the dumpster a bit more.

"Hey, I didn't hit you that hard, did I?"

"No, Mr. Vale. I assure you I am quite fine."

"Bullshit," I declared as I went over to him. "Take it from a professional...injured knows injured."

Eli sighed again and lifted up his shirt. Even in the dim light, the angry red of the gash in his side stood out on his pale-white skin. I put my hand on it to assess the damage. I would have expected a wound like this to be gushing a fountain of blood, but there was barely a trickle—and that was only when my fingers put pressure on the injury.

"When did this happen?" I asked, concerned.

The show over, he pushed my hand aside and pulled his shirt down. "It is not important. Yes, it hurts, but as you can attest, it is hardly as dire as it seems at first glance."

"Damn it, man. How am I supposed to help you if you won't level with me?"

The confusion returned to his expression. "What do you mean...level?"

"Every time I ask you a question about your past, you avoid a straight answer. Even your name is fake, isn't it...Mr. Smith?" I sighed. "Look, I don't ask these things for kicks. The more I know, the easier my job is."

Eli stopped leaning against the dumpster and stepped into the light. He hadn't looked great the first time I saw him, but time hadn't done him any favors since. His already-pale flesh tone was getting into "walking corpse" territory. His dark eyes, while still animated, were downright shallow and sunken. I fancied I could see more of his cheekbones than I should have.

"Please believe me when I say this, Mr. Vale," Eli said. "It is for your protection I have kept certain pieces of information secret. Should there be an urgent need to share these things, I will gladly do so."

"I'm holding you to that," I said, pointing the same sort of finger Kennedy had pointed at me, "*Eli.*"

"Now that this unpleasantness is settled for the time being, what have you found out about my sister?"

4

DANCING SHADOWS AND FIRELIGHT

The address for Hellfire put Eli and me in front of the Clarke Building. It was an anomaly in Cold City, a building older than ten years that avoided an extreme makeover courtesy of the wrecking ball. The one constant industry in this town was the tearing down and building up of new commercial properties in the hopes they would catch on enough to stay a decade. But there were a select few places that managed to sidestep the real estate not-so-merry-go-round. Some, like Cinema Leone, managed to be declared National Monuments. I couldn't guess why this neo-art deco monstrosity was still standing.

Past the soaring blank-faced statues at the halfway point up the structure, you'll find a building betrayed by its 1980s design origins. There were no security cameras in sight and plenty of places for both of us to hide in the shadows from the lone night watchman making a patrol around the area.

Regan was probably still in office when they changed the lock on the back entrance. I wouldn't be able to pop it as quick as I had the dressing rooms back at the Springfield Center, but it wouldn't take much longer.

I put that thought on hold and turned to my client. "What I'm about to do is highly illegal. I'd personally advise—"

"I know, and you would be wise to say so," Eli said, cutting off the request. "Nevertheless, permit me to stay with you."

Well, since he asked so nicely...

The lock turned out to be a little tighter than I imagined. I could hear the steps of the watchman coming back when I popped it open. The hinges were oiled enough for us to slip into the building with little fuss.

A quick scan of the directory gave us Hellfire's location, 318 on the third floor. I shut off the flashlight, and we located the door to the stairs, right next to the directory. We slipped inside and waited several minutes to make sure no one was patrolling. As quietly as the hard rubber and marble steps would allow, we went up to the third floor.

The slow pace we used to go up those stairs gave me time to think. I found myself impressed with how apt Eli was at sneaking around in the dark. Sure, he was wobbly from our fight, but that didn't impede his ability to be twice as quiet as I was. I was no slouch in that department, mind you, so that made me wonder the kind of training he had. Not to mention his mysterious wound. What else was he not telling me?

A beam of light shined under the door of the third floor. Eli and I stood on either side of the door and waited for it to pass. There must be a second guard patrolling the various levels.

I counted down from sixty and hazarded a peek out the

door. A soft set of footsteps walked around the corner, taking the light with it. I gestured for Eli to come through the door, and I quietly shut it behind him.

As luck would have it, 318 was two doors down from the stairs. I tapped Eli on the shoulder and pointed towards my eyes. Then I gestured to either end of the hallway. Getting it, he nodded and kept watch as I picked the lock.

Maybe because it wasn't as exposed to the elements as the back door was, it took a little longer for me to get through this lock. I tapped Eli on the shoulder as I put away the picks and, after one last glance to make sure the guard was still out of sight, we went in.

The room on the other side was set up like a doctor's office. There was a small lobby with a front desk and little equipment. It stood before a flimsy partition to give the impression of another room behind it. The back room was a cramped layout of three desks with 1990s vintage computers and a couple of filing cabinets. A quick sniff of the air confirmed my initial impression. The lack of Camels in the air meant Mr. Jones rarely ever came into this office.

I pointed Eli towards one of the filing cabinets, and I took the other one. I winced a little as the top drawer opened with a squeak. But another quick countdown later, nobody came through the door to investigate. I rifled through the files.

All I got for my trouble were invoices, electric bills and more designs like the ones I found in the dumpster. The address on Thames was marked on some of the invoices and statements, but there were no records of a new warehouse location. Ditto any information of any kind on a Sarit.

I glanced over at my client, and he shook his head. I had

a pass at his records myself and came up with more of the same. As I shut the bottom drawer of the cabinet, I whispered, "Dead end."

"Shall we go?" Eli whispered back.

"We'd better."

We'd arrived at the front desk when four shadowy figures appeared before us. They were blocky, indistinct forms, roughly shaped like men, standing between us and the door. I had just enough time to process all this when the nearest one screamed.

Even now, I can't describe the sound. All I can remember was the chill that ripped through me, making every one of my recent injuries hurt worse. Then the nearest one struck me in the gut with a vicious punch. I went down to my knees while Eli caught the blow of his attacker and tossed him to the floor. The creature hit the ground without so much as a sound, and Eli's hand passed through it as though the fiends were made of smoke.

I tried sweeping the front leg of my attacker, hitting nothing but air. Too bad his leg hit my face, busting up my nose for my trouble.

I wasn't surprised when the flashlight beam on the other side of the office door grew close in a hurry. We were making enough noise to get Helen Keller's attention. The guard opened up the jimmied door in a hurry, and his flashlight beam shined through the bodies of our attackers.

"What the—?" was all he had time to say before one of the smoky creatures grabbed him by the throat and smashed him against the wall outside.

I glanced over at Eli while I fended off my attacker's blows. He was holding his own against the other two killer shadows by flipping them around as he had me. But they were landing punches on him that he was in no shape to take. A few more minutes of this, and both he and the watchman were going to be dead.

Goddammit, I managed to avoid doing this all last week, I thought as I focused my concentration on my heart. Aside from the "not dying until it's my time" clause, Lady McDeath gave me some tools to do my jobs for her. None of them came with any label or instructions, mind you, but at least they were there. The one I was about to tap was amongst the nastiest.

I channeled the living power of my heart from my chest into my right hand while I blocked the shadow's blows. Once it felt right, I grabbed the punching hand of my foe and slammed its upper body against the wall. Next, I rammed my charged fist straight into my attacker's chest. It caught on some icky material, and the energy in my hand flared enough to make the entire entity dissipate.

I gasped for breath as the backlash hit me. The unwanted intrusion was why I used a knife to go after the ghosts downtown. My "vacuum fist", as I called it, was great for dispersing incorporeal creatures or anything composed of ectoplasm, but every time it landed, it took in the essence of whatever being I punched. In short, while it allowed me to connect to such entities and disperse them, it also guaranteed me about six hours of flu-like symptoms as my body processed out the nasty energies I was never meant to take in.

Hells, I was pretty sure that type of backlash would be fatal to any other human. A lot of Lady McDeath's boons worked the same way. It was hard to put it into words, but it always felt as though I was tapping into resources not meant for someone of my kind. There was little doubt in my mind that without the no-dying clause, I'd never have survived the tryouts.

I went after the attacker between Eli and me. The thing looked stunned by what happened to its mate. I didn't wait for it to connect the dots and hit it with a similar fist to the head. A cut-off version of the cry that started the fight came from whatever the thing used for vocal cords before it fell apart.

Eli's remaining foe noticed how I stumbled back from the force of my attack and aimed a punch at me. I was too dazed to fend it off. The world was spinning, and every beat of my heart hurt. It felt as though it was now pumping battery acid through my veins.

My opponent came at me fast, but Eli was faster, and he intercepted the blow. He gave the creature an over-the-shoulder toss onto the desk.

I fought through the increasing numbness in my body to muster up another vacuum fist. My nerves were on fire, and it hurt to even breathe, let alone stand and walk. I saw red, and my heart contracted and burned with pain. I let out a strangled cry as I threw my charged hand into the monster's shoulder, taking him out.

That left the watchman, still being strangled by the remaining shade. I shivered with cold, though heavy droplets of sweat ran down my brow. Try as I might, I was too weak to summon up another attack. Maybe I could beat the unwanted guest to death with my fists? That is, if I could get my feet moving in the right direction and raise my arms.

Eli aimed a kick at the fiend's back, and it staggered

under the impact. Pressing his advantage, he yanked it under its arms and pulled it away from the guard. The nightmarish creature thrashed and struggled, making yet more cries that aggravated my wounds, but Eli held on.

The poor guard fell into a fetal position, watching all this in disbelief. Couldn't say I blamed him...This thing was a nightmare beyond all reason.

Eli was still wrestling with the creature when I got my feet moving again. I was ten feet away from them, but it felt like ten miles.

The creature screamed again as it got one arm free. Its hand flew up to Eli's throat, constricting painfully. Eli's eyes flashed brighter, and he plunged his hand into the otherworldly devil. A burst of firelight sprung from its chest, and the shade fell apart in a spray of burning ash that floated down to the ground. A smell, reminiscent of dragon's blood incense, filled the room. It made me cough a little and brought tears to my eyes.

When my vision cleared, I saw Eli kneeling on the floor, his hand in a pile of ash. Whatever he'd done, it took a toll on him. He was swaying, and he looked inches away from passing out. The guard was still whining about what he saw, but he seemed alright. Whatever story he came up with later, it would involve the two of us, but I didn't have time to worry about it now.

Eli and I got out of the building as fast as our spent bodies allowed.

5

LIGHT OF DAY

I threw up in the alley where I ran into Eli earlier. My client had to lean against the nearest wall as I fell to my knees. I have drunk myself stupid more than once, a few years ago, but whatever spiritual essence I sucked up from those things made my worst binges feel like a pleasure cruise. Three dry heaves later, I was able to get back on my feet.

Eli's breath was growing more ragged. I grabbed his arm again. "We need to get you help."

He put his other hand on my chest while his eyes flared with the same intensity I'd seen in the fight. "No hospitals... It would be the first place the Azif would look."

"That's what those shadow things are called, Azif?"

That little outburst had robbed Eli of his lung power; all he could do was nod in response. The name meant nothing to me.

I left him there as I took a peek down both ends of Maltese Street...All clear. The foot traffic was nonexistent now. Too many people had work in the morning to be wandering around this close to midnight.

I did my best imitation of a barely functional drunk as I staggered alongside Eli back to the diner's parking lot. The nasty stuff in my system made that imitation a lot easier. I plopped my client down in the passenger seat and strapped him in with the seatbelt. An interminable minute later, I managed the same trick with the driver's seat.

Eli started whispering Arabic, something that sounded like an invocation.

"What'd you say?" I asked, reaching for the key.

Eli's head did a lazy turn in my direction. "I asked the Most High that we be protected and spared whatever cruel fate we may deserve."

I could get behind that prayer. I started up the engine and drove through the cold night.

Despite Eli's fears, going to the hospital never entered my mind. Years of dealing with things from over-the-border taught me there was no Geneva Convention that made such places neutral ground to Alternum Mundum's nastiest. I resorted to the one place where I knew we could go to ground and find time to recuperate.

Oddly enough, once I got going, it was easier to drive to my apartment building than it was to walk back to the diner. *Something else to mull over when I feel better,* I thought as I pulled into the parking lot.

I coughed up a solid black clot from my throat as I shut the car door. The slimy stuff floated in the air for a few seconds before dissipating into oblivion. I felt a small boost of energy after the coughing stopped. I used it to get Eli out of the car and to my front door.

I fumbled with my keys a little to find the one that got us inside. After dumping Eli on the couch, I wasted no time locking the door behind us. The wards I placed around my home would keep any immaterial baddies like these Azif from coming in, but for all I knew, they might have some physical backup looking for us too.

"Alright," I said, turning Eli over to face me. "Let's get a look at those wounds."

"There...there is only the one I...showed you," Eli protested, trying to keep my hand from his shirt.

"I say again...bullshit."

A quick lift of his shirt proved my hypothesis. In addition to the normal bruising from the Azif's punches, I noticed some fresh claw marks had joined the gash I'd seen earlier. If I had to guess, I'd say the Azif phased through the shirt to inflict the new wounds. Despite the freshness, those cuts weren't bleeding at all. Like the old one, there were barely trickles of clotted blood when I pressed my fingers to the wound. I was no doctor, but even I knew this wasn't right.

My patience for guessing games was over. Eli made it clear he was not going to answer my questions, but that didn't mean there wasn't another way for me to get to the truth.

I frowned in anticipation: this was going to make me feel worse than I already did, but my obtuse client left me little choice. I turned to one of my more regular tools from Lady McDeath's gifts. Slowing my breathing, I pushed past the pain and turned my attention to my senses. I focused on them until everything sharpened around me.

I could hear the slight buzz of a fly outside the window,

smell the stale blood coming out of Eli's wounds and hear my heartbeat like it was a bass drum. I watched specks of dust caught in mid-air under the lamplight's glow; they were dancing to their own rhythm. I heard a car drive along the street at the foot of the building. For a moment, it made me lose track of the steady rhythm of my heartbeat. There were two people inside, and the radio was blaring Bonnie Tyler's *Total Eclipse of the Heart*. The car passed, and the disturbance faded. Silence fell again on the apartment, and my attention returned to the bass drum of my heart and its steady thump, thump, thump. And then it hit me.

"I'll be damned," I muttered, as my eyes latched onto Eli's carotid artery, searching for something that wasn't there. No throbbing. It was the same for all the other veins and arteries on his exposed skin, no movement at all. No thumping sounds coming from his ribcage either. As I focused on him, the smell of sandalwood intensified in my nostrils, his skin exuding it like a strong aftershave.

I managed to latch onto that last detail when my "sixth sense" shut off with a headache-inducing jolt. I reached the end of my rope and reeled from the abrupt return to reality. I grabbed the armrest to prevent myself from toppling backward. My client gave me a curious look, and his expression gave way to alarm as he figured out what I must have seen.

It took the world a minute or ten to stop spinning enough for me to form a coherent sentence. The sixth sense was a useful tool for a detective like me, but it came at a massive cost. Whatever it was, it wasn't something a mere human like me should have access to. Then again, tapping into resources that weren't mine to use was all part of the gig with Lady McDeath.

"You're...dead, aren't you?" I asked through my pain. "I mean the body you're inhabiting. You're in a bloody stiff."

"Yes," Eli confirmed with a nod. "Though...it is hardly stiffer...than...any other...vessel would have been."

Shit. I reeled back from him on impulse. What kind of creature did I let in my flat? Was any of what he told me true? Did Sarit even exist?

I glanced down at the man-creature sprawled on my sofa. I didn't see a threat. And the more I thought about it, the more confident I was Sarit existed and that she was in danger.

"What in all the hells are you?" I asked. "And you better start telling me the truth. Otherwise, I'll walk. I swear it."

There was a long pause, before Eli replied, "Jinni."

Old Arabic mythology, my mind supplied, *Spirit creatures from the other side.* "You need a vessel to interact with people in our world, right?"

"Yes, we're only smoke...But this vessel, I fear...its usefulness may be—" Eli winced in pain before he could finish the thought.

It was enough to clear the supernatural fog from my head for a minute. "What do you need?"

"Seal off...the holes. I can...can get better once they..."

"Strip," I said, getting to my feet. "I want to be sure I get them all."

Eli may have given me a half-nod as I staggered towards the bedroom.

Most of the time, I could recover from common injuries with enough rest, thanks to Lady McDeath. Bruises that would take someone else weeks only took me days. Papercuts would get sealed up fast enough not even to need a Band-Aid. But whatever boost my immune system got when I sealed the deal with *her*, the job still required that I kept a very well-stocked first-aid kit under my bed.

I came back into the room with a handful of Ace bandages, a box of Band-Aids, a family-sized bottle of hydrogen peroxide and a tube of Neosporin. My injured client tossed his pants to the side, which landed right on top of the shirt and shoes he'd dumped there.

As I expected, he had a few more cuts on his legs and upper arms. I used up most of the Band-Aids sealing those off. For the gash, I used an Ace bandage treated with Neosporin to help with the sealing effect I was trying to achieve. I didn't know if hydrogen peroxide would help or hurt the process. Hells, the guy was a freaking jinni anyway, and I had not the foggiest what could help or hurt him. I poured some on all the open wounds I found.

I sensed time passing as I did this, but damned if I could tell you how long it took. Noticing Eli was shivering by the time I finished, I grabbed a blanket I hung on the back of the couch and pulled it over him. The shivers stopped in a few seconds.

Eli sighed and said, "Thank you, Mr. Vale. That...that will do nicely."

I took a minute to put all the supplies on the coffee table before dumping my weak ass on the loveseat. I could feel the Azifs' essence cloud my thoughts again.

"You know, Eli," I said, my voice a low rumble. "You could have saved us a lot of time and trouble if you'd told me the truth."

Eli's voice was a reedy whisper. "I can only...apologize.

My kind is bound...by strict rules we...we do not break lightly."

I closed my eyes. "How many did you break when you asked for my help?"

Eli's voice sharpened a little. "You...are different, Mr. Vale. I knew...the first time I saw you. Your scent...has a certain...taint about it. It...it smells of my world."

I smirked. "So you didn't look me up in the phonebook."

There was a long pause and then, "What is...a phonebook?"

I opened my eyes and craned my head to peer at my guest. His breath was steady again under the cover. "How long has it been since you were on this side of the border?"

"Far, far too long. This world...so strange...so different from...Baghdad of old. Every corner...poses a new ques— questions. Every turn, a new mystery. I thought scent alone could guide me. How...foolish I was. Those days...gone...like the practice of...hiding in open holes."

I frowned. "What's up with the whole scent thing anyway?"

The only answer I got was quiet, even snoring. Eli's exhaustion caught up with him. *Hells with it, I can ask him about it tomorrow.* I leaned my head back and closed my eyes again. Sleep wasn't too far behind.

———

I felt the first needles of daylight stab me through my eyelids. I winced from the light and pulled my stiff neck back into an upright position. The first thing I saw when I opened my eyes was the state of my clothes.

Overnight, they grew seriously slimy. A foul-smelling gel was now smeared all over me, from my underwear to my jacket. That could only mean the Azif were ghosts. Anything with ectoplasmic-based physiology always leaves this kind of mess in its wake. While it never stuck to furniture, the floor, the ceiling, the walls or even my skin, clothes always caught the stuff with the thoroughness of an air filter.

Eli was still out cold, so I did my best to be quiet as I got up. I could hear the faint squish of the slime with each step. And don't get me started on how it felt on my body.

I grabbed a garbage bag from the kitchen and went into the bedroom to do a little stripping of my own. Everything except my shoes went into the bag, which I sealed up tight. A quick run through the washer would send the stuff back to the dimension it came from, but it could wait until after I got a shower.

One clean change of clothes in my hands later, I took that shower, taking extra time to make sure I'd gotten every last bit of the goo off me. I dried off, put on fresh clothes and went back to the living room.

Eli was awake, looking a bit more animated than last night as he sat up. Just the same, I put a palm on his forehead and instinctively pulled it back at the clammy feel of his skin.

"I fear that is an inadequate way to check my well-being, Mr. Vale," my client said. "As you noted last night, this body is quite dead."

I once again sat down on the loveseat. "Who was he?" I asked, motioning vaguely at the body he inhabited.

"A victim of what you would call...'a mugging', I believe?" At my nod, he continued. "His attacker left him with the memento on my stomach that you spotted last night.

He was in the process of claiming his ill-gotten gains when I opened this body's eyes again."

"And made him drop his loot in the process."

Eli's smile leaned towards the predatory. "It was a bit more involved than that. I overpowered him, made him give me all the money he stole that night and swear by the Most High to reform his ways."

"Wouldn't that have violated some of those rules you mentioned?"

Eli held up a pointer. "On the contrary, one of our rules states we must see justice done whenever it is within our power to enact it."

"So how does justice tie in with the search for your sister...Is she your sister, by the way?"

Eli seemed hurt by my implication. "While I have been circumspect in my answers, good sir, have I directly lied to you?"

"Unless Sarit did have all those jobs you were talking about before, then yes."

Eli bowed his head, nodded.

I put my hands on my hips. "Alright, cards on the table. I want the full story. Now."

"Long ago, your kind called us the jinn," Eli said. "Our natural form is far from corporal; it is what you humans would call 'smoke'. We can communicate somewhat in that form, but it is constrained. Thus, if we are to interact with you, we need vessels."

I put my hands down. "What kind of vessels?"

"While we could possess anyone, our code is clear. Only those bodies whose souls have fled are to be used for such a purpose. Sarit—and yes, she is indeed my sister—took over the vessel of a young woman whose brain had burst less than a day before our arrival."

"Where do you come from?"

"None of your languages could get you close to its proper pronunciation. Suffice to say it is home, and I miss it very dearly." He threw off the blanket and picked up his pants.

While he put them on, I asked, "So why are you both here?"

"We are...were...chasing a criminal from my world, one of the worst," he explained, grabbing the shirt next. "He is an ifrit, a class of infernal jinn and an insult to the Most High and my people. He waged an eons-long war against us that snuffed out many lives that otherwise would still burn with the fire of life."

"So you weren't able to do something about him?"

"On the contrary, we were on the cusp of executing him at the Mountain of Judgment when a great portal formed over our heads. It was a cloud of swirling energies; bright blue...We had never seen anything like that before."

I groaned at the description—no fair guessing what had caused that portal to form in the first place. From what I saw at Cinema Leone, Galatas' door opened onto the Under-world...Could it have crossed through Eli's world in doing so?

"You know of what I speak?" Eli asked, putting it together while pulling on his shoes.

"Let's say I had a front-row seat to it opening on this side of the great divide," I said, wanting to keep the conversation on track. "I'm guessing your ifrit took that opportunity to escape."

"Killing my father in the process," Eli confirmed. "Many

others died along with him when the Azif moved in on us to cover his retreat."

"So what are these Azif?"

"In elder times, demons of shadow who prowled the lonely stretches of the desert to waylay vulnerable travelers. Praise be to King Suleiman ben Daud the Wise that their chilling cries are no more in this world."

"Until last night," I pointed out. "Are they the reason why Sarit's now the ifrit's prisoner, despite the fact she's a better fighter than you?"

My client blinked in surprise. "I said nothing about—"

"Process of elimination," I explained, walking back into the kitchen. "You wouldn't have shown me that sketch unless she was still in that body she took over. She's not going to stop until this ifrit is caught and sent back to your world. And she'd be right by your side this very minute if she could. So...she's the ifrit's prisoner."

I opened the drawer underneath the old Bowmore bottle. The Sig went straight into my pocket.

"It is reassuring to know I have chosen wisely in this matter at least," Eli said, and I could hear the smile in his voice. "I was not so careful during my first encounter with our enemy."

I smiled back as I came into the living room. "How about we keep talking about this over breakfast? I don't know if you get hungry but—"

"My inner fire does need stoking like any other," Eli admitted. "But what about discretion?"

I gave him a "are you kidding me?" look. "I may not have the code you guys have, but do you think I'd talk about this anywhere?"

Eli shrugged with one shoulder. "Fair point, Mr. Vale...Shall we?"

"Only if you agree to call me 'Bell' like everybody else," I said, grabbing my keys from the coffee table.

Eli frowned. "Very well...But only if you explain why you insist on being called the namesake of a relic from my time."

I did my best to suppress a sigh. It was going to take a lot of work to civilize this out-of-towner.

———

I didn't blame Eli for gawking at the sight of the Tombs as it came into view. The sight of a 1950s style diner, all done up in chrome and neon, squatting between a couple of high-rises, came off like a cross between Norman Rockwell and Salvador Dali. I noted that the parking lot was a little on the full side this morning.

Funny thing about the Tombs' parking lot, no matter how full it ever got, I never had a problem finding a parking slot somewhere I could fit the Stingray. I wasn't sure if that was Tommy's doing, another custom feature Lady MacDeath installed in the car, or a good old-fashioned coincidence that had nothing to do with either. All I knew was that's how it always worked out.

Today was no exception. A slot around the left side of the diner was waiting for us to park.

My client's nose worked overtime as I killed the engine on the car. "Odd...this place almost smells like my home."

"Yeah, about that smelling thing," I said, remembering

the question I tried to ask last night at last. "Why do you do that so often?"

Eli shrugged as he unhooked his seatbelt. "Just as your people tend to utilize sight as their primary sense, mine rely on our sense of smell. Every jinni in existence has a distinctive odor. We can recognize each other by our scent."

"Is that why you smell like a cross between sage and sandalwood?"

My client shrugged. "I suppose."

"And that burning coal smell at the warehouse...that was the ifrit?"

"Yes."

My stomach rumbled with an audible growl. "Let's take this conversation inside."

To Eli's uneasy expression, I added, "It'll be fine. We'll have to talk a little less straightforward than we did at the apartment, that's all."

We both got out and walked in.

As I expected, the breakfast rush was in full swing. There wasn't that much in the way of class distinctions amongst the customers. Stockbrokers sat alongside construction workers at the bar. In the booths, secretaries on their way to the office sat behind working girls from the world's oldest profession on their way home. The only real division was a smoking and non-smoking section, one of the last buildings in the city to have that classic setup. Every other restaurant went completely smoke-free years ago.

My regular booth—which was deserted, like it always is when I come by—was in the non-smoking section in the corner. Nothing against the nicotine addicts, but not all my clients wanted to inhale a mini smog cloud while telling me their problems. If this was the spot I was going to meet them rather than at home, I wanted them to be as comfortable as possible.

A cute girl, whose height and smooth off-white complexion made her look like she was twelve, came up to the table. She looked frazzled from working the morning crowd, and the perfect Cherokee that came out of her mouth upon greeting us confirmed it.

I smiled and said, "I'll start with some OJ, Tiffany. Eli...?"

Eli gave me a confused glance before turning to Tiffany and saying, "Coffee for me, please."

Thankfully, Tiffany reverted to English after writing the drinks down. "Okay, I'll be right back to take your order."

After she went to the back, Eli asked, "What was that language she—?"

"Cherokee, one of the few surviving native languages on this continent," I explained. "The owner insists on teaching it to his staff for talking to each other when they're getting the food ready. But I'm pretty sure Tiffany's family came straight from the rez for her to always use it when she's stressed."

"Rez?" Eli asked while giving the menu a severe look.

"Short for reservation...Nice word for what's essentially a concentration camp dedicated to the proposition of finishing off what Manifest Destiny started, isn't it? I mean, it'd be downright unchristian to wipe all the native tribes off the face of this earth with straight-up genocide. So let's stick them on poor plots of land and let poverty, alcoholism, and despair do that job instead."

My client put down his menu and stroked his chin. "You

play at being otherwise...but under your cynical façade lurks a man who is as dedicated to the proposition of justice as any of my kind."

The words touched me, but I didn't want him to see it. "You know, if you want to ask me out on a date, you could say it out loud."

Eli's face went back to being confused as Tiffany returned with the drinks. "Sorry about before, guys. It's been that kind of morning."

I shrugged. "I gathered."

"So what would you like to eat?"

I opted for a ham omelet and oatmeal. Eli asked for simple biscuits with butter. Tiffany nodded and took off for the kitchen.

"You don't eat meat?" I asked after she was out of earshot.

"I do not partake of pork," Eli corrected me. "I can tell my body has done so in the past. But I would like to do things differently going forward."

I nodded. Dietary restrictions were the least odd thing about the jinn code I'd put together so far. "So let's talk about that thing you mentioned before. The last time you ran into the guy who took your sister, how'd it go down?"

Eli gave our surroundings a nervous glance while sipping his coffee. I was taking a pull of my orange juice when he said, "You have to understand that when Sarit and I arrived, we were...separated for a time."

"Why?"

"You remember my speaking before of our need for...vehicles?"

"Sure."

"Well, as it happened, she found hers next to the city morgue, whereas I found mine at the local hospital."

Sounds like another good reason why he didn't want to go to one of those last night, I thought. "Those places can be a pretty good distance from each other."

"Indeed...though that was not what delayed me. There was the matter of my exit being a bit more...complicated than my sister's was. After all, the longtime patient of a doctor is likely to be more closely watched than the deceased resident of a mortuary."

I didn't like the sound of that. "Wouldn't this violate—"

Eli held up his free hand, anticipating the question. "Remember...the stipulation is that any vehicles are to be unoccupied. While the people who watched over this partic-ular one believed otherwise, the one I appropriated was deserted long before I arrived. It merely sat...idle, waiting for something to happen to it."

Decoding my client's flowery speech, it sounded like he'd taken over someone in a terminal coma. The brain activity would have been as flat as Morgan's sense of humor, but some grieving relative was maintaining the body in the hopes they'd beat the odds and come back to them. Not sure that was much better than the other nasty possibility I'd initially thought of.

"Okay, so you get out of there," I said. "Where was Sarit in the middle of all this?"

Eli shook his head with a long, steady exhale. "Despite my protests to wait for me, she was already tracking our mutual quarry. My sister has many virtues, but patience has never numbered amongst them."

"So, when you caught up...?"

"It was at the top of a very tall building, such as what flanks this place. I overestimated my strength in being able to handle our foe. I was certain that because my vessel was in a more...working condition than Sarit's own, I would have an advantage. That nearly proved to be a fatal mistake."

I could imagine. Sure, Eli had managed to snag a living body, which might have had a few more perks over the corpse he was sporting now. But it was a body that was deprived of exercise and critical nutrients for months, maybe years. Pee-Wee Herman could have kicked his ass in that kind of state.

"Sarit, to her eternal credit, had overcome the enemy's underlings," Eli continued between sips of his coffee. "The same underlings, I should add, we fought last night...but she was no match for our foe after such a gauntlet. Though I was much more rested, well...I have already hinted at my short-comings. My enemy made me fall both very long and very hard to the ground."

My eyes widened as I parsed out the meaning behind that statement. "You mean...?" I mimed a long fall with my hand.

Eli nodded. "I do."

The cops would rule that fatal topple from the top of the building a suicide to keep the caseload light, but I felt sorry for whoever that body was related to.

"So," I said, putting the nearly-drained cup back down. "Do I know the rest from there?"

"After...acquiring a new vehicle, I made some efforts on my own," Eli admitted. "They only got me as far as the ware-house we looked over. No surprise, truly; he now knew someone was searching for him. That was when I decided to contact you."

"The smartest choice you made since you hit town," a voice with more bass than Tiffany's said.

Tommy, in all his copper-skinned glory and chef's outfit, put down our orders with one of his trademark toothy grins. Eli's nose started sniffing the fresh biscuits like a 1980s corporate executive mainlining coke. I decided to dig into my omelet while he was doing that.

"These are positively heavenly," my client said with rapture. "My most sincere compliments to the creator of these fine examples of bread."

"Well, you happen to be talking to that creator you mentioned," Tommy said with a little laugh and an outstretched hand. "Name's Tommy...I own this place."

"An absolute pleasure, sir," Eli said, shaking the hand with enthusiasm.

The man who kept me fed gave him an off-hand wave. "Ahh, just make it 'Tommy.' Owner of a greasy spoon like this has got no business being all formal about things."

Tommy showing up when he did was no coincidence. While I'd never put together what exactly my favorite restaurant owner was, he knew enough about Alternum Mundum to be my best street-level source for across-the-border info. The way he was looking at Eli, I bet he knew what my client was better than I did.

"So how you'd hear about this reprobate I keep from starving on a regular basis?" Tommy asked, giving my shoulder an affectionate rub. I stuck my tongue out at him before going back to my omelet.

Eli froze, a biscuit halfway to his mouth, a worried

expression crossing his face. My mouth was full, so I gave him a "go on" gesture, to indicate it was safe for him to reply.

"I happened to find out about him when I first arrived in town," Eli said with a visible effort to weigh his words. "At the time, he was involved in what I can assume was some rather pressing business. But something about him stayed with me, as the matter I came here to resolve became more...complex."

I glanced up. I guess it wasn't a surprise that Eli saw me after I shut down the portal. Remembering that fatal day made me put down my knife and fork. I pulled out my smartphone instead.

"Well, I've got one question I want to ask you about all this," Tommy said, leaning over Eli as he gave him a sober, serious look. "Are you paying my boy for his time and trouble?"

While I put the phone away, I said to Eli, "Excuse Tommy's lack of self-control there. I've got this regular client who makes me work for free—"

"Does she ever," Tommy said with a roll of his eyes. "And you keep letting her do that to you, Bell. I mean, what the hell?"

I held up a hand while the other one put my oatmeal on my cleared plate. "Bottom line is the chef's always happy when I've got a paying client to work for."

"Especially when your tab is run up a little high."

I glowered at Tommy, who gave me a toothy grin and a shrug back. "What? I'm running a business here, not a soup kitchen. The only reason I let you get away with not paying upfront is that you've always been good about paying me back eventually."

Eli did his best to hold back a bemused smile of his own. "It would seem you are both quite fortunate to have such a reliable friend in the other."

"Well, that's an idea my stomach and his balance books can agree on," I said, picking up a spoon to dip into the oatmeal.

As Eli dug into his biscuits at last, Tommy winked at me with an appreciative smile. "So, in the interest of keeping that cash flowing in the right direction, anything I can do to help out with this case?"

I swallowed before answering. "Matter of fact, yeah, there is. A fashion outfit calling itself Hellfire recently started up here in Cold City...Think you could do some sniffing around their operations?"

Tommy's face got serious again. "Got a place I can start looking?"

I mentioned the warehouse on Thames and the office building at Heinz Point.

"Might want to get your gamer boy on the Heinz Point angle," Tommy suggested. "If you can stay out of sight of his papa, that is. I'll see what I can run down on the other thing."

The breakfast crowd thinned out while we talked. Tommy took one careful look around before whispering, "I don't suppose you've got enough cash left to put a dent on—"

I palmed him one of the hundreds. "Use this one to pay for our meal here and the rest on the tab."

Smiling, Tommy went back towards the kitchen while Eli asked in a whisper, "Is he always like that?"

"More or less," I answered in the same whisper. "As soon as we get done here, we're going to go see that 'gamer boy' he was talking about." I texted my hacker friend and arranged a meeting.

"Does this 'papa' Tommy mentioned have a grudge against you?" Eli asked.

"Not exactly. He doesn't like me being around his son... Thinks I'm a bad influence."

It seemed like a smart idea not to mention Zian's father was Hermes—the Messenger of the Gods, as he was known in Ancient Greece. The old man was the king of information, and it was a safe bet he knew I was up to something. Hells, it was a safe bet he knew more about the situation than even *I* did.

I could only pray his reaction to this new situation would be on par with how he took the last one...hopefully.

6

TRUST ISSUES

Two hours later, we walked up to what felt like yet another deserted warehouse on the docks. Up until a few months back, that was what it was, but then Zian needed someplace other than his usual spot at the club he worked at and that his father owned, the Indigo, to help me out with some data gathering. That's when he set up this off-site office.

The front door was repaired to the same dilapidated condition it was in before a giant scorpion bashed through it. I swear, even the rust spots on it were the same. I did a quick glance up at the mini-cam Zian set above the doorframe, and I heard a buzz. That was my signal to open the door.

As Eli gave the door a curious glance, I said, "Think of the buzz as the equivalent of 'open sesame'."

Sir Richard Burton must have gotten much of his translation of the *One Thousand and One Nights* right because Eli got the reference straight away. I heard the door shut behind us and click the lock in place.

Once upon a business, this place was a shipwright operation, which accounted for the cavernous space we walked through to get to the back office. I fancied I could still smell a whiff of burned giant scorpion coming from the concrete, even though there wasn't so much as a scorch mark. Natural lighting filtered in the dirty windows up top, but the office in the back was lit by fluorescent lights. I could make out a familiar figure as he paced about the office.

Eli pointed in the office's direction. "That is who we are to meet?"

I nodded. "If you spotted me when I think you did, you might recognize my friend as one of the people who was with me at the time."

We didn't say anything else and walked across the vast concrete prairie to the office.

The office door buzzed to let us in, and Zian turned around to greet us. Even though I knew he was on the edge of thirty, I was always struck by how much of a teen Zian still appeared to be. A lot of that impression came from his fashion choices. Today, he was sporting a *Space Invaders* t-shirt and black-dyed jeans. Those distinctly offset the hand-crafted dress shoes on his feet, the dark vest that looked like it should have been part of a three-piece suit and a red tie around his neck. It wasn't as off-putting as Eli's choice of wardrobe, but it was out there. Add in Zian's usual smirk, bleached-blond hair and round blue eyes, and the impression was complete.

Zian was a big contrast to the office, a dumpy 1970s relic with wood paneling, an oak desk and dusty, battered filing cabinets. The laptop on the counter and some of the tech along the walls for the wi-fi looked as out of place as Zian did.

"Well, Bell," he said with his usual rapid-fire, British-accented delivery. "I'm guessing whatever you've got going must be very interesting indeed." He glanced at Eli. "And I'd be correct in saying this gentleman here is the reason I'll be looking things over?"

I couldn't quite read the expression on Eli's face. To keep things from getting awkward, I decided formal introductions might smooth things over.

"Z, this is my client, Mr. Eli Smith. Eli, Zian, the best computer expert in the entire city, maybe the world."

Eli gave Zian an enthusiastic handshake that went on a little too long and ended awkwardly.

Over the next few minutes, we sketched out details of what we knew about Sarit, the ifrit and the possible Hellfire connection to this case.

"Okay," Zian said. "I could start by hacking into CCTV feeds to look over footage from the night the portal opened, check to see if any cold or open cases might match up to what we know and extrapolate some more facts from there."

To Eli's puzzled expression, I explained, "He's saying he'll use his machines to go dig up some more information for us."

"Ah," Eli said, grateful to be given the dumbed-down explanation. "And will this take some time?"

"It might," Zian admitted with a shrug. "But it should only take me a few minutes to get something that could give us a place to start looking."

"In which case, I noticed some rather unusual smells

coming into this area. With your permission and by your leave, I would like to take the opportunity to guess at them."

"We could tell you how they got there, you know," I said.

"Since the ifrit has successfully masked his scent, it would behoove me to work on improving my sense of smell on the slim chance he has not concealed his spoor beyond my ability to detect him."

Zian tilted his head to the side. "That makes sense. Knock yourself out."

Before Eli's face had time to register his confusion, I said, "In other words, go right ahead."

Eli smiled broadly as the door buzzed open again. He walked out, and the door lock clicked as he shut it behind him.

"I take it it's been a few centuries since he made it to our part of the universe?" Zian asked while his hands did their usual warp-speed tap dance across the keyboard.

"He won't say how many, but yeah," I admitted, watching the rapid succession of windows opening and closing on the laptop's screen. "I've been acting as a translator since I got him to trust me last night."

"And do you trust him in return?"

There was something behind the question that made a "yes" answer sound like a terrible idea. "What is it?"

Zian kept his eyes glued to the screen, but his words couldn't have been more pointed than if he'd been staring directly into my eyes. "One thing Father drilled into my head at an early age was to never, ever trust a jinni if your life depended on it...and it usually would. Even the general public knows that much, if I'm reading between the lines of their little fictions about 'genies' the right way."

"Eli wasn't eager to tell me what he was when we first met, but he didn't have any more reason to trust me than I did him. Why should I still be wary?"

Zian's fingers abruptly came to a standstill, though the windows kept flashing across the laptop's screen. He glanced out the office window to see Eli doing his best impersonation of a bloodhound. While I'd need Zian to confirm it, I was almost sure he was standing right on the spot where that scorpion and its human buddies burned.

"All jinni have a fairly deep bag of tricks to draw from," he said in the most serious tone I'd ever heard him take. "Black magic, poltergeists, witchcraft, mediums, some illusions and magicians' spells...Their powers can explain a lot."

"Well, I already knew about the body possession thing since—"

"It's more than humans they can possess, Bell. They can also take over things like rocks and trees or that pencil right next to my arm. And don't get me started on how they can traverse huge distances in a matter of seconds in their regular form."

Eli moved onto the front of the warehouse, his nose sniffing around the restored door we'd walked through. I shook my head, both at what Eli was doing and what Zian was saying. "So what about the stories of jinni granting humans whatever they ask for? Do we chalk that one up to wishful thinking inspired by a few balls of hashish?"

Zian gave his still-busy screen a quick peek before looking at me. "No, there's some truth to those stories. But all that power comes at a cost. No jinni likes being made to serve humans any more than your average human slave would. So any jinni stuck in that situation will use every trick in the book to turn the tables."

"Which is where the 'wishes not working out as planned' scenario comes in, right?"

"Pfft...Tip of the iceberg. They also can make predictions that have so many lies laced in amongst the truths that acting on them will do more harm than good. Then there's the bad dreams and hallucinations they can cause to completely warp the perspective of the human who thinks he's still in charge of the relationship. Give it enough time, and it's usually the magician who is made to serve the jinni instead of the other way around."

"Well, the only thing Eli's given me so far is cash, so I'd say I can still be saved."

"Yeah, not all of them are evil, but they're natural-born tricksters." Zian let out a frustrated breath as he turned his full attention back to the screen. "You can joke all you want, Bell, but there's a reason why my father has not bothered to make contact with their courts for close to a thousand years now. Stay on your toes, okay?"

"Isn't that usually my line?"

Before Zian could give me more grief, one of the windows stopped cold on some digital paperwork. Having been the subject of a few of these, I recognized it as a BOLO.

"Well, look at this," he said. "If I'm reading the details-light description right, your new client is wanted for assault on a security guard at Heinz Point."

"I was there too," I countered. "We saved the guy's life... Some gratitude, huh?"

Zian scrolled the window a little and saw the second BOLO right behind it. "Yeah...Apparently, there's one out for someone vaguely resembling you on this one too. Any chance this guard could identify either of—"

"The way that Azif wound up giving him that fit of cosmic horror? Doubtful. I'm surprised he had enough of a memory left to remember us."

Another window popped up, complete with a photo of a pale woman who vaguely resembled Eli's sketch of Sarit. "Here's a report of a corpse that decided to check out of their freezer in the morgue."

I showed him Eli's sketch. "That's her, that's Sarit."

"Alright, alright, I believe you, Bell," Zian said, pulling up another window. "Let's see if the rest of Eli's little story checks out."

The new morgue report he pulled up had an unfamiliar photo of a deceased male on it. The ME noted massive weakness in the arm and leg muscles from a lack of activity, as well as nutritional deficiencies, both brought on by eight months of being in a coma. Somehow this corpse walked a total of six city blocks and up several flights of stairs before falling to his death from forty stories up.

"That's the way Eli described it to me," I said, pointing at the window.

"No way the cops didn't investigate this." Zian ran his fingers across some more keys.

A polite knock rang out from the office door.

"Be with you in a minute!"

While Zian buzzed Eli in, I made a face when I saw Detective Lieutenant Morgan was the man assigned to look over our dead man's demise. There was enough physical evidence at the scene to rule it a homicide. Sarit's vessel left prints, of course, leaving Morgan to make some not-exactly-professional notes on how the hell a corpse can walk out of the morgue and straight into a fight. But there was a third set of prints left by the human the ifrit was using that had no matches in the system.

I barely noticed Eli coming back to my side as I took all this in. "I take it you found out some more unwelcome news?"

"You could say that," I admitted with a tight expression on my face. "Your first vessel's death is being investigated as a murder by a cop who I would like to avoid."

"What is a...cop?"

"Sort of like a city guardsman," Zian explained, drawing more from his experience with D&D than his dad's stories to cross the cultural gap. "Cops are the people who keep everyone from breaking the local laws."

"And you have had unpleasant dealings with this partic-ular...cop...before?"

"More than a few," I said. "Which is why we are going to have to be very, very careful going forward. If Morgan gets the slightest scent of me on this case, he'll have me thrown in jail faster than you can say 'probable cause'."

While we talked, Zian reviewed the CCTV footage from the night of the portal opening. All the cameras within the blast area were completely knocked out of commission, along with the power grid. But judging from the shot of Bloch Street I was now looking at, the cameras around the disaster zone remained functional.

A taxi came into view from further down the street. At first, it was being driven like any regular driver would. Then a nasty black smudge came over the windshield, and the car started acting like a junkie was at the wheel, weaving from the left to the right erratically.

"Back that up," I said, pointing at the screen. Zian wound it back to the start of the shot.

"I'll slow it down so we can get a better look," Zian said, putting the video at half-speed.

No question about it, the black thing on the taxi looked an awful lot like a smoke cloud. Going by the camera's timer counter, it was only in sight for roughly 1.2 seconds before disappearing entirely.

"That has to be the ifrit," Eli said. "It would make sense for him to take over such a person. He knew we would pursue him if possible, so the faster he could flee the area, the better."

"Plus, he took a taxi driver," Zian added. "That'd give him a little shade to be behind the wheel of a car for a bit. Still, if he's as unfamiliar with how to drive as I'm thinking, he wasn't in the taxi for long."

"Long enough to make a clean getaway," I said.

But not completely clean. Unless I missed my guess, I'd managed to stumble onto another active CCPD case that could land me in some serious trouble—Ramirez's missing cab driver.

7

ONCE BURNED…

Even with everything Zian said, I still asked him to bring Eli up to speed on this century and city. I argued that the more he was familiar with his environment, the less of a chance he'd stick out at precisely the wrong time. I knew Zian well enough to know he wasn't happy about being the designated babysitter, but he agreed with my logic, and so did Eli. Plus, Zian conceded it'd make the tedious task of waiting for his computers to come up with more interesting bits of information pass a little easier.

Just the same, Zian said he needed to go "check the server connection", which also happened to be on my way out the door. After extracting a promise from Eli not to touch anything, he walked me to the door.

Once we were a couple of feet from the office, Zian said in a low tone, "Don't think I didn't notice who landed the cab driver case...unless there's two Sgt. Melanie Ramirezes in the CCPD."

"Yeah, she mentioned having to talk to a witness about

it," I admitted. "Could be the witness was our cab driver's last fare before he got bodyjacked by our ifrit."

"Well, her latest reports didn't mention any witness testimony, so you might have a chance to get that from her today."

"We can hope...Like I hope you can keep Eli occupied while I'm checking that angle out."

"Speaking of which, why are you leaving your client out of the loop? Could it be you're taking my advice?"

I gave him a crooked grin. "It's not *just* that." But my face grew serious again as I said, "I'm...I don't want Mel to get any deeper into over-the-border business than she has to. We both know how dangerous it is. Having Eli around while he's still puzzling out what a Starbucks is would only make keeping her in the dark that much harder."

Zian hummed. "I don't know...Maybe she's tough enough to handle it. You know, like Candice was."

I shook my head. "With Kennedy, it was a case of 'we either tell her or go ahead and book her a room in the psych ward'. Mel's not deep in yet, and I'd like to keep it that way."

By then, we were at the door. Zian examined the wiring to the camera outside. I guessed it was part of his act of "checking the server connection".

"Look, Bell," he said as he ran his hands down the wires. "Maybe it's because I grew up around all this that I'm even going to say this, but you might want to reconsider either telling Ramirez or being in a relationship with her. The longer you two are involved, the more likely she's going to get wise."

I gave him a little laugh. "Excuse me, do my ears deceive

me? Is my little hacker friend, who has yet to score a girl-friend of his own, trying to give *me* dating tips?"

"Think about it, okay?" Zian said with a bit of a huff in his voice. "I'm not telling you anything my father didn't already tell me when I got to be a certain age."

His finger hit the door buzzer to let me out, which I was only too eager to do. "I'll see you later."

"Yes, you will," Hermes' hacker son promised.

———

The funny thing is, on the long walk back to my car, I did think about what Zian told me. Ramirez and I were cycling on and off in our relationship for a while now. The pattern was so predictable you could set your watch by it. We'd get together, our work would take us separate enough ways to make it suitable for a while, I'd get a case a bit more involved than my usual ones, Ramirez would get offended by what I was doing for it instead of for her, she would smell the lies, and we'd break up. Repeat as necessary.

So, on the surface, it would make some sense to let Ramirez into the reality of my world and what I dealt with on a regular basis. Hells, I was so creative in my lying some-times, it was getting hard to keep track. I sighed. If only it were that simple.

Lady McDeath still wasn't over Kennedy finding out about the basics of Alternum Mundum. She made it clear my journalist friend better not get too nosy on the subject; her life would be in danger. I could not get Ramirez into that situation as well.

Worse, the way I figured it, Lady McDeath may not be

the only aggrieved party. She was part of an outfit called the Conclave, a sort of supernatural border enforcement group that passed on its dirty work to people like me. The more ordinary people know about the supernatural end of things, the harder their job gets. While they allow for accidents happening, deliberate spreading of across-the-border knowledge is frowned upon. And I also had to factor in that Lady McDeath was accountable to Hades, the king of the Underworld.

Okay, so why don't I break it off with Ramirez? I thought as I saw my car, parked on the right side of the gas station. *You know, aside from the obvious reasons?*

Of course, I knew the answer to that one too. Ignorance was never protection from over-the-border nastiness, let alone bliss. I wouldn't put it past a particularly sadistic perp to do something awful to Ramirez to send me a message. So making sure she stayed safe from those things was a lot easier if I stayed in contact. Not that she was any damsel in distress; I had her back in a shoot-out not so long ago where she took the lead. But still...

I shook my head. I could go round and round with this for the rest of the day. Frankly, I had better things to do... Like call up Ramirez and see if I could figure out how to tease that witness statement out of her.

I waited until I got into the driver's seat before calling Ramirez. She picked up on the second ring.

"Sgt. Ramirez."

"It's me, Mel. Catch you at a bad time?"

"Kind of, yeah. I'm at the hospital to talk to the witness I told you about."

I let an instant pass before replying, making sure to wipe

all traces of eagerness from my voice. "Oh. How come you couldn't do it before now?"

She sighed. "Had to clear it with her doctors and mother first. From what I know, she has emotional as well as physical damage from taking a cab with our missing guy."

Given what I was learning about jinn and ifrit, it sounded like the poor kid got off lucky. "I'm guessing all this police work means no chance for dinner tonight?"

"And you know how I hate that, *mi corazóne,*" Ramirez said. "But work is work, and if I want to pay my bills—"

"Hey, I am the last person you have to explain that one to," I said, holding up a hand, though there was no way she could see it. "Never mind, I got an idea...Why don't I sit in on your interview with the witness?"

I heard a warning tone in my lovely sergeant's voice. "Bell..."

"C'mon, it's not like we haven't done this before," I pointed out. "Maybe I can spot an angle on what she's saying that could help with the case, also..." I paused and hated myself a little for what I said next, "...I miss you."

I could practically hear the gears turning in her head on the other end of the line. The last time we did something similar, she got a lot of useful information, but I also managed to get a client who paid in advance. To this day, she was still convinced that last part wasn't the happy coincidence it was. Just the same, one thing she's never accused me of was being bad at my job.

"Okay," she said. "I'll be by the front desk until you get here. But the usual rules apply: I'm in charge, do nothing to upset the witness, and any information you get out of it goes straight to me."

"I can live with that," I said, starting up my car. "Which hospital are you at?"

———

Despite the full parking lot, it was a quiet day on the inside of St. Jacqueline's. The hospital corridors had a smattering of staff and visitors, but most were deserted as Ramirez and I walked through them. I tapped her on the shoulder when I spotted room 371 on the left. A temporary name tag told us who was inside: Peggy Lawrence.

The first thing I noticed about Ramirez's witness was her haunted green eyes; it was a look I knew all too well. The first time you see something from over-the-border is always the hardest. The eyes were a good match for her pale, bruised face, which had the shape of an oval about it. A few strands of brown hair poked out from underneath the bandage around her head. It was hard to tell what kind of build she had underneath the covers and hospital gown, but her arms were reasonably thin, so I could imagine the rest of her wasn't much bulkier. She bit her lip at the sight of us, hard enough that I was surprised it didn't draw blood.

"Ms. Lawrence, I'm Sargent Ramirez," my girlfriend said, holding up her badge. "This is Mr. Bellamy Vale, a private investigator."

"What's he doing here?" Peggy asked, her tone a couple of steps from hostile.

Ramirez faltered for an answer, so I stepped in. "I was hired by the family of the cab driver to search for him. Sgt. Ramirez agreed to let me sit in on this interview, in the interest of saving everyone time and aggravation."

Peggy remained unsure.

"If he makes you uncomfortable in any way, Peggy, I can always have him leave," Ramirez added, giving me a pointed stare to reinforce how much she liked that idea.

"No, no, that's not it," Peggy said. "It's just ah...well...I'm sorry. I'm not sure I can talk about it yet. It was...real bad."

I leaned forward and put on my most understanding face as I lowered my tone, making it gentler, more comforting. "Anything you can tell us about it, even if it's a small detail, would be a big help."

A little smile crossed Peggy's face for the reassurance. It fell again when she realized what I was asking her to do. "I...I wish my mom was here. I mean, I told her it was alright if I talked to you alone. I wanted to help, as she did after the explosions downtown. But...but..."

"How did your mom help after the explosions?" Ramirez asked as she hit record on her smartphone's recorder app. She knew this part of the story, but she figured it might be enough to get Peggy talking.

"She's the relief coordinator for the local Red Cross," Peggy explained. "Usually, the disasters she's working on are way out of town. Global warming, you know? Sea storms are getting worse every year, and a lot of local communities keep getting devastated by it. But this..."

I thought I saw Peggy's hand shake a little before she went on. "I was three years old when 9/11 happened. I heard people talk about it after, and this was...this was a lot like those stories. My mom was in as much shock as everybody else, but an hour later, she's going out there to go look for survivors."

"What about the smog?" I asked. "Wasn't she worried about that?"

"Only all the time," Peggy assured me, warming up to the story. "She got scared when I said I wanted to help her out. But we took all the precautions, the reasonable precautions. I still think mom would have grabbed a couple of hazmat suits from the OSHA guys if she thought she could have gotten away with it." She giggled a little; it felt forced.

Peggy licked her lips, her eyes darting between the two of us. "Anyway...the night it happened...it would be the only night that Mom's car was in the shop. We had to get a cab ride over to the site, so of course we grabbed one back. I was kind of glad at the time, you know? We'd been going all day, and I wasn't sure either one of us was up to driving home. Mom fell asleep on the way."

Peggy stopped, peering down at her blanket-covered legs. Now we'd reached the part of the story where talking about things was going to be difficult.

"Take as much time as you need," Ramirez said, leaning over to give Peggy's hand a sisterly squeeze.

The touch was enough to get Peggy talking again. "It started off as this...light show, you know? When I was a kid, we went to this place in Georgia and saw a laser light show. It was like that but...different. You couldn't make out much in the rearview mirror other than the flashes."

Ramirez tapped her chin. "How did the cab driver react to it?"

"He was scared like I was. I mean, it was...we had no idea what was causing it. Was it another explosion? Something worse? We didn't know, none of us. I tried waking my mom, but she was fast asleep."

Peggy took a shallow breath. "That's when it happened. There was..." Her jaw clenched up as the tears spilled out of her eyes. "You're going to think I'm crazy for telling you this part. All my doctors think I am."

"Remember what I said about any little detail being a help," I reassured her. "Whatever you saw could be important."

The tears were still coming, but Peggy was choking back her sobs enough to speak. "It...it started off as this black cloud. It was big...big enough to blot out the light show for a minute. Next thing I know, it's right in front of us, looking at us through the windshield."

"Looking at you?" Ramirez asked, puzzled.

"There were these eyes," Peggy explained. "Big red eyes, right there in the cloud, staring at us. I thought I saw something else a little deeper, a big red ball. But...there wasn't time. It—it went through the car, right through the vents. It swarmed right over the top of the driver. He tried screaming, and it went into his mouth! I screamed and woke mom up. She screamed too, tried opening the doors. They were stuck! I-I-I..."

It was too much. She cried her eyes out over the memory. Ramirez glanced at me and shook her head. She needn't have bothered. The only way Peggy was going to be able to finish this story was if she took a break.

It took a while, but the tears ran their course. Peggy sniffed as I handed her some tissues. "Sorry...sorry..."

"Don't be," Ramirez said. "Whatever happened that night, it was a traumatic experience for you. I'm impressed you got this far into your story before you had to stop."

Peggy blew her nose, and I replaced her used tissue with

a fresh one. Once she was done using it to wipe away the tears, she took a breath and let it back out slowly. "Okay, I'm better." She paused, looking self-conscious for an instant. "I know how this sounds. I wouldn't believe myself either, but... I swear to you, that's what I saw."

Ramirez gave her a patient smile. "It's fine. Tell us what happened next, the way you remember it."

"Well, the cabbie, he...he clenched and shook for a second. There was this awful smell that came in with the cloud."

"How would you describe it? The smell," I asked, playing a hunch.

"What?" Peggy scrunched up her face in thought. "It was sort of like...burned wires or coal, you know? Not exactly like it, but..."

Ramirez gave me an annoyed glance before asking Peggy, "What did the driver do after he clenched up?"

"He...he looked back at us and...laughed. There was something different about his voice. It was...deeper, a little louder. And...I swear I'm not making this up but...I thought I saw some of that smoke come out of his mouth a little bit."

"Was the car still going down the road while he was doing this?" I asked, trying to picture the scene in my head.

"Yeah and I remember thinking how...how it was a good thing there wasn't anybody in front of us. But then...he drove off the road and right onto the sidewalk. There weren't many people around, but he kept swerving to hit them, laughing the whole time...Laughing." Peggy shuddered at the memory before adding, "Eventually... he—he tried to chase down someone who managed to jump out of the way. It's not like— like he's been careful, but this time...he winds up hitting something that flips the car over. Next thing, I know...I'm here."

Ramirez clicked off her smartphone's recorder. "Thank you for sharing all that with us, Peggy."

"Seriously," Peggy asked. "You don't think I'm crazy, do you? I know I hit my head, but..."

I put a reassuring hand on her shoulder. "Trust me, the very fact you're unsure about that question tells me you're the furthest thing from it."

She grabbed my hand and gave it a hard squeeze. My detective sergeant girlfriend slipped me another annoyed look as she handed Peggy her card. "If you can think of anything else, Peggy, please don't hesitate to call."

Peggy assured her that wouldn't be a problem and we left.

———

Ramirez waited until we got into the parking lot before giving me the tongue-lashing I expected.

"This wasn't about spending more time with me," she snapped. "This was about pumping me for information on a case you're working."

"No, I..." Something in her expression stopped the lies somewhere in my throat. "Honestly, Mel, I wasn't sure if this was connected."

"Oh, but you know it is now, don't you? I saw how you reacted to what that poor girl said."

"I wasn't that obvious, was I?"

Ramirez's frown deepened, and her Latino accent flared. "This is me you are talking to, remember? When have you ever been able to keep these kinds of secrets from me?"

I fought a smile, knowing there was the small matter of me keeping her in the dark over this hidden world parallel to ours being out there, in spite of the fact she survived a direct run-in with it alongside me. But it didn't seem like the right time to bring that up. "I meant it when I said I wasn't sure before now. And yes, now I am sure. But did I step outside your rules in any other way? It's not like I was going to ask you about active police business."

Ramirez took in a deep breath, always a sign she was trying to calm down. I kept my mouth shut, lest something stupid came out of it.

"Alright, Bell, I'll admit this is a fairly minor breach compared to some of your previous offenses. But I still have to know...what was that cloud she saw? Was it some toxic gas, or something?"

"Not sure yet," I said, which was the truth. "When I have a better idea, I'll fill you in. Fair?"

Ramirez got in my face. "You'd better. Busting you for interfering with a police investigation is a great way to make my boss's day. Try to keep that in mind."

Unexpectedly, she slipped something into my hand. I glanced down to see it was my knife, now safely out of Morgan's custody. By the time I looked up, she was walking towards her car. She didn't need to mention we wouldn't be getting together again for the rest of the day.

8

BEST LAID PLANS

I t felt reassuring to have my knife back in my boot as I walked towards Zian's office. Sure, it was a little thing, but as anyone in my business can tell you, it's the little things that count. Besides, it distracted me from wondering if my little play at the hospital was sending Ramirez and me towards yet another breakup.

Zian gave me a calculating look as he buzzed me in. Eli was much too wrapped up with looking over a tablet playing back some reality TV show to acknowledge my appearance.

"So...did your date with the sergeant go great or shitty?" Zian asked as the door closed behind me.

"Kind of in-between," I admitted while Eli put the tablet next to my hacker buddy's laptop. "Got some useful information that could help."

The video footage ran without pause as Eli stared at me. Zian must have found it annoying because he reached over to pause it.

"Forgive me," Eli said. "I was unsure about how to make it stop."

"Tap the video screen to stop and start it," Zian explained. "Couldn't be simpler."

"Yes, I will remember. So what have you learned, Mr. Va —Bell?"

I smirked a little. Guess my client couldn't help being polite.

I filled them on the witness's testimony about the possessed cabdriver. Eli nodded as I finished. "That was most certainly the ifrit. Such unholy possessions are very much their stock in trade."

"Any chance he'd still be using that body?" I asked.

"You mean, assuming his carelessness did not result in him being forced to abandon that vessel from causing it an excess of injury?"

"Well, when you put it like that..."

"Again, forgive me," Eli said with a sigh. "I fear as this vessel continues to decay, it is becoming harder and harder to both think and act in the manner I would wish."

"Well, technically, you *are* an old man, so..." Zian said.

Eli and I cracked up at the joke. I noticed Eli's laughter had golden tones to it, almost like a trumpet. I also thought I saw one or two wisps of cloud come out of his mouth. How different was his kind from the ifrit?

"To more fully answer your question, Bell," he said as the laughter died down, "the vessel of the driver was a mere convenience. Yes, it was the vessel I encountered on the roof, but to better cover his trail, he would have to abandon it. And knowing him, he would have no qualms about choosing someone of a higher status."

I sighed. "So it's another dead end."

"At least until the CCPD finds the body," Zian said. "So...we've got the last known location of our perp, what he might have looked like and a possible connection to all this through the fashion company Hellfire. Sound like everything?"

"Well, there's also those Azif we ran into at Hellfire's listed company HQ," I added. "Somehow, I doubt they were there to take in the sights."

"I did some online snooping around," Zian said, summoning us to the monitors. "A lot of Hellfire's company records are strictly offline, so my info has got serious limits."

That made sense from a security standpoint. Sure, piles of paperwork were slower and more tedious to deal with, but the most sophisticated computer system on the planet can't open a file cabinet.

"Still, because they are a company operating in this century, I got a few hits on them," Zian went on, opening up some windows. "Mostly, it's been tax records and LLC filings."

"This isn't another shell corporation, is it?" I asked, remembering how the late, unlamented Mayor Galatas used one of those to help carry out her dirty work.

"Uh-uh, this has been operating as a regular small business up until recently."

Eli raised his eyebrows. "How recently was this change you are hinting at, young master?"

Zian did his best to squelch a flattered smile, but didn't quite get there. "A few weeks ago. They were marketing their designs to the locals without any success, for something like five years. Then, out of the blue, they've got stuff the local boutiques can't get enough of. That was enough to get Hell-fire's designs put in Cold City's Fashion Week."

"Like someone else took over the business...or something else." Zian nodded, and I asked him, "Any chance you can pull up the current location of their head honcho, Khalim Jones, on the CCTV feed?"

"But we have no idea what Mr. Jones looks like," Eli protested. "The Hellfire office certainly had no such—"

Zian made a short "tadaa" sound, and the picture of a man popped up on the screen at the press of a button. I raised a questioning eyebrow. "If anyone asks, I did not hack into the DMV files," Zian said with a bemused smile and half-hearted shake of his head. "He'd have to show his face in public sometime." Zian pulled up a new window while working the keys. "I've got the license plate number and make of his car. All I need is one shot of him on camera, and I can tell you where he is as long as he's in the city limits."

"How long will this take?" Eli asked, sliding up a spare office chair.

"A minute, two hours, a couple of days...There's no way to tell," Zian said. "It depends on his schedul—" A bip coming from his computer interrupted him.

"What is it?" I asked, leaning in closer.

"We got him," Zian said, smiling widely. "Check this out."

The video in the window showed the exterior of another warehouse. The lack of landmarks made it impossible for me to figure out where it was. A vintage Maserati in pristine condition came into view from the highway in the right corner, and as it pulled into the parking lot, I could see it had two people in it. The driver got out, and Zian paused the feed just as the angle became clear enough to capture his face.

"Presenting Mr. Khalim Jones," he said, hitting a couple of keys.

"Where's this at?" I asked.

"Going by the location of the camera I pulled this off, we're looking at the old Ashton warehouse off of Pickfair Street."

Eli was still glued to the video. "Who is the other person with Mr. Jones?"

"Let's find out," Zian said, unpausing the video.

Jones got out of his car and walked around to the passenger side. The person with him was pulled out, and it was evident from the general physical features it was a woman. Something about her gait felt unsteady, and Jones had to drag her inside. As her face turned in the camera's direction, Eli's breath caught. Zian paused it again and gave my client a worried look.

"Are you sure?" I asked, putting a hand on Eli's shoulder.

He nodded somberly.

"You've been talking up what a badass your sister is," I said. "Why is she so weak now?"

"She has been in that vessel too long," Eli said. "As my condition can attest, it is only a matter of time before dead vessels suffer from the ravages of decay. Usually, we can exit the body and find a new one, but..."

"He's doing something that's keeping her in there," Zian said, running with the thought. "What do you think, a classic Seal of Solomon or Seal of David somewhere on her body to lock her in place?"

"Does it matter?" I asked.

"Does if you want to break it," Zian said, working his phone the way he worked his laptop. "Whatever he's using, I'm pretty sure I've got something in my digital copies of Alexandria's library that should do the trick. When you find her, look her over and send it to me."

I started thinking about battle strategies. "How long ago was that video footage?"

Zian glanced up to get the timestamp from the laptop. "Three minutes, twenty-six seconds ago." Finishing up with his phone for a moment, he pulled up the present warehouse footage. "Car's still there, so it's a safe bet he is too."

"And Sarit," Eli said, the fire coming back into his eyes.

I held up my phone. "Wouldn't happen to have a complete layout for that warehouse, would you?"

Zian gazed up from his phone again, a little annoyed. "Bell, this isn't like it is at the Indigo. I can't snap my fingers and get five pieces of data simultaneously."

"Ah, c'mon…you're saying the Prince of Information can't manage one simple set of schematics?"

"Okay, okay," Zian said, turning back to his laptop, with a large grin. "I admit it'll be faster to find those than all the info I've got on breaking protective seals. I'll send it over to your phone as soon as I have it."

"Sounds good," I said, heading for the door, Eli right behind me. Zian didn't glance up as he buzzed us out of the office.

Pickfair Street was a few blocks down, but the ride in the Stingray still gave Eli and I time to talk.

"What should we expect if we do run into the ifrit?" I asked Eli, doing my best to keep to the speed limit despite the urgency.

"All the powers of my kind," Eli said. "Whatever we can do, they can also."

"That still doesn't tell me much. Care to elaborate?"

"In their natural form, the spawn of Iblis can move from place to place at the speed of thought, taking anyone and anything with them in the passage. They can track you by scent, turn invisible, create convincing illusions and, of course, possess people and things."

The hatred Eli had for the ifrit shone through his commentary. I wouldn't want to be a person he hated when he was at full strength. "Does being in a body limit some of those powers?"

"Without a doubt," Eli assured me. "There is also another limitation we managed to lay upon the ifrit's power before his ill-timed escape."

I took a sharp left turn, and the tires screeched. "Which was...?"

"We erased his True Name from the Book of Life. Had we been able to follow through on the execution immediately afterward, a great deal of the harm he had inflicted would have been undone the moment his head and shoulders parted company."

I felt a shudder run through me at the description. True Names are what any person built up over the course of a lifetime, a record of every deed they had ever done. To have it wiped out permanently from the universe's record—which I'd also heard called the Akashic Records and a few other choice names—was a punishment that made the regular death penalty look like an act of mercy.

"If his True Name's gone, then how come he's still out and about?" I asked.

"Much as it takes time for the blood of the body to run out of a bleeding man, so it is that it takes three cycles of the moon for a True Name's erasure to make someone a non-entity."

"So you're telling me all we have to do was wait another couple of months, and he'd disappear anyway?"

Eli made a face at me that reminded me of one of Morgan's "are you honestly this stupid?" looks. "And why would you assume he would stay idle during this time? There are rumors—unconfirmed, but that is why they are rumors—that a True Name can be restored if one offers up the appropriate sacrifices. Such sacrifices usually involve the innocent and the helpless, and I would never countenance leaving them to the tender mercies of such a desperate being."

The warehouse was coming up on the left. A quick scan of the buildings past it showed a defunct hardware store I knew well. It had an old employee parking lot in the back that was out of sight of the street.

"I was wondering why you never referred to this guy by name," I mused as we drove past the warehouse.

"Whatever name he made for himself was forfeited the moment we subdued him," Eli said while the car slowed its speed next to the hardware store. "Now, it is only a matter of making sure his life follows."

While we'd been talking, Zian managed to pass on the warehouse specs to my phone. As soon as I parked the car, I took a close look at it. There was an emergency exit door in the back corner, facing the hardware store building. A little zooming in revealed there was an upper balcony above the warehouse floor with an office that faced the street—my bet for where Mr. Jones was doing his on-site chain-smoking.

Eli looked at the map over my shoulder and pointed to one closed-off section on the ground floor. "Should we need to dispose of any guards, lethally or otherwise, that looks the ideal spot to put them."

"It'll depend on the lock on the door," I pointed out as I put the phone away. "Who knows what kind of shape the overall building's in?"

I leaned down to pull my knife out of my boot. I wasn't sure if it would have the same effect on the ifrit as it did the poltergeists, but it was a lot quieter than the Sig in my pocket.

Eli took in a deep breath and blew a cloud of his "smoke" on the blade. It flared ever so briefly with flame-colored pictographs resembling Arabic. A second later, the edge was shiny as ever. I looked a question at my client.

"Something to deal with any Azif we are unfortunate enough to run into," he explained. "I would much prefer to avoid another taxing fight like the one we had the previous evening."

"With you there," I admitted, undoing my seatbelt. "Let's go."

The sun was setting, which gave us a few shadows to walk through as we slinked around the side of the building. The emergency exit was a few feet away from the back corner of the store. The shadow of a light pole, cast by the departing sun, fell across it like a blanket.

Playing a hunch, I focused enough to trigger my sixth sense. A couple of seconds later, I could make out a pair of Azif standing guard at the door. I pulled my senses back to the real world—even on good days, it wasn't a bright idea to leave the sixth sense on longer than necessary—and turned back to Eli. I pointed to the doors, tapped the nearest shadow and held up two fingers.

My client nodded and grinned. He tapped himself twice on the chest, pointed towards the door, darted two of his fingers towards himself and then made a stabbing motion with his other hand. Classic ambush...I certainly didn't have any better ideas. I nodded, hoping I could get the drop on these things in time.

Eli walked past me into view of the door guards. That's when he started talking to the Azif in hostile tones. Like with the glyphs on my knife, his words sounded Arabic, but something about the diction made me think it predated the language by at least a few centuries. Both Azif gave that indescribable cry that almost made me miss them getting close.

Shadow creatures are always a lot easier to make out in daylight. I jabbed the nearest one with the blade as Eli sidestepped his hand. The words on the blade flared as it slid home, burning him from the inside out like Eli's hands had the previous night. The other Azif stopped dead in his tracks as his buddy became one with the air. Big mistake...which I made him pay for with a quick slice at his throat area. This time, the pictographs were there for an eye blink, but it was long enough to send this shadow monster to the same fiery death.

I gave the blade an appreciative look. "Handy."

Eli shrugged and motioned towards the door. I nodded. I knew better than to talk out loud in a hostile zone. It's like one of my sea daddies drilled into me: "If they don't hear you, son, they aren't gonna know you're coming."

This door was unlocked, but I opened it with caution. For all I knew, there was a tripwire attached to it with a Bouncing Betty on the other end, or a loud alarm. Eli felt up the area between the hinges. He ran his hand up and down it twice before giving me the nod. I inched my way up the door and felt up the outer edge. No wires or laser beams I could see. We both used the opening to slip inside and close it behind us.

The scene on the factory floor was a horror show. Dozens of men, women, and children were seated at sewing machines, laying on them in severely contorted positions. Every one of them had a black set of eyeballs that saw nothing and an open mouth with a silent scream. I did a quick sniff of the air. The coal smell was thick enough that I could have cut it with the knife.

Eli shook his head in mute disbelief. Whatever had happened, this was as much a surprise to him as it was me.

I went over to the nearest body, a matronly woman in her forties who seemed like she'd been a real looker in her younger days. Now she was a fresh victim of a vicious supernatural predator...or maybe more than one. Her natural skin color was bleached by whatever killed her. I could make out the irises and pupils of the eyes up-close, but the whole eyeball was a solid matte black. The positioning of her hands told me she was likely in the middle of doing her regular job when she was killed, further supported by the still-unfinished dress in the sewing machine. The design on the dress was a rough match for one of the rejected designs I found at the previous warehouse.

Eli was checking them over, one by one. His head refused to stop shaking. These were the people he was talking about protecting, and all we'd managed to do was arrive in time to find their newly-dead bodies. It was a cinch all the deceased were illegals, none of whom had rights to a lawyer when alive or to a thorough investigation of their murders now they were dead. If they were to get any justice, it was going to have to be me that did it.

Eli's eyes widened as he got near one of the sewing machines. Taking in a short, harsh breath, he waved me over. I didn't waste any time getting there, but I still tried to be quiet. The Azif may not have been the only things we needed to worry about.

I was halfway there when I saw why Eli was reacting like he was. Sarit was sitting at this particular sewing station. Her eyes were free of the blackness I'd seen in the others, but they were as blank in their stare. My nose wrinkled at the decomposition of the corpse; she was still a head-turner, but she was getting seriously ripe. I fancied I saw a bit of bone poking out from her top left knuckles.

"Sister," Eli hissed. "Sister, it is I."

Sarit did nothing except continue to stare.

"You sure she's in there?" I whispered back.

"Positive...I would know her scent anywhere."

Remembering what Zian said about sealing her in, I started moving her clothing aside to find any marks. I found one on her upper right breast, a bizarre compilation of lines, pseudo-Arabic script and a few other unfamiliar symbols.

Eli's eyes got fearful at the sight of this sign. "Iblis' Bane."

I pulled out my smartphone and activated the camera on it. A couple of flashes later, I had two pictures to pass onto Zian when I—

It came out of nowhere. One minute, Eli was looking at Sarit like she was already dead. The next, a foul coal smell invaded my nostrils as something flashed across the room and swooped up Eli with it. I pocketed my phone and reached for my weapon, but my hand never had the time to get close before it took me for a ride as well.

I thought the after-odor was hard to stomach. Let me tell you, the two seconds I spent in the embrace of that smell's source was like being in a gas chamber. My phone and knife were still in my hands as I stopped. A glance around told me we were in the upstairs office...and Eli and I were no longer alone.

Khalim Jones had a swarthy complexion that looked good on him, if the girl in question was into a "daddy" type. His hair was impeccably styled and groomed, a smattering of ash grey in the midst of the blackness. His smile showed whitened, even teeth designed to charm people. The Armani suit and expensive shoes completed the image. But I was more focused on the red highlights I could spot in his dark eyes and the pair of smoky wings coming out of his back.

The wings receded into his physical body as he turned his gaze to Eli. "I must say, Elijah, you are most persistent in your futile pursuit of me."

Eli looked weaker than ever. Still, he managed to fire an impressive ball of spit in Jones' direction that landed right on his cheek. "Weakened or not, I have managed to find you. How then is my pursuit futile?"

Jones brought a hand to the spit, wiped it off and scoffed at it. Then another burst of the black smoke erupted, and he was right in front of Eli, delivering a punch that knocked him into a wall. I thought I heard bones snap as he hit it.

That shook me out of my stupor. I pulled out my Sig. Maybe he was smoke inside, but his vessel was physical, and it could be hurt. I fired a couple of shots at his knee. At that range, no way I could have missed...and I didn't.

The nine mils drove him to one knee, wincing in pain at my unexpected attack. He had enough time to look at me before I pushed the knife into his body's heart, right under the breastbone. He looked surprised and then annoyed.

I was still wondering why that hadn't hurt when he grabbed me by the throat and said, "Ouch." Then it was another unpleasant ride on the Coal Smoke Express that knocked the wind out of me as my back hit the desk in the corner.

This was getting ugly fast. If I didn't do something to even up the odds, I was going to become the newest corpse on the factory floor. I poured all my strength into my right fist as Jones' iron grip kept strangling me, and I hit him in the right temple.

I may as well have rammed my fist through a wall socket. The shock of whatever this ifrit was made of ran down my arm and all over my body at warp speed. God, did it hurt! It was like subjecting myself to full-body heartburn. Still, it was enough to stun him and make him let go of my throat. I noticed, while I was shaking my head, he was winded. I glanced over at Eli, who was getting back on his feet from his beatdown. He didn't look like he could last much longer in the decaying body he was using.

"I will admit," the ifrit said, drawing my attention back to him. "That blow was impressive, for a human." He paused, and the way he looked at me made me think of a scientist about to dissect lab rats. "Interesting. Very interesting."

Both of Jones' hands found my throat. He opened his mouth to pour out a nasty, vicious cloud at my face which forced its way past my lips and nostrils. My gag reflex kicked in at the assault, my tonsils fighting a hard battle to keep the crap out of my system. I was about to wonder if they were going to lose when a cry behind Jones sent the cloud away.

My eyes cleared enough for me to see Eli bashing the ifrit over the head with an old oak office chair. He kept swinging at Jones like a man possessed...appropriate since that's what his vessel was. Jones was so busy warding off the blows with his left arm that he didn't have time to notice me pulling the knife out of his chest. By the time he did, I was slashing his right arm from the wrist down. He let go from the pain, giving me time to add a kick to the jaw to compliment my client's assault.

I managed to keep a death grip on my Sig the whole time. I brought it up and emptied the clip into Jones' chest. It didn't have the effect I was going for, as the fire in the ifrit's eyes lit up with delight as he absorbed my shots. With a sweep of his left arm, he turned the office chair into instant ash. In the same sweep, Jones' right hand caught Eli's throat, and I could make out the corner of a smile on the bastard's face. Eli's body burst into flames, making him scream in agony as the fire cooked it beyond repair.

"Dammit," I breathed as I jerked myself off the desk. I

ran right at the ifrit with my knife raised in the classic slasher pose. A quick flash of the black smoke whirled in front of my eyes, and I was sent flying through the office window. The glass tinkled as my back broke through it before gravity gave me a one-way ticket to the ground.

I didn't have to wait long to hit the bottom. A couple of seconds later, I landed on something nice and soft, breaking my fall without breaking my body. It took a couple more seconds to realize I'd landed in the Maserati's passenger seat. Days like this made me glad Lady MacDeath hadn't decided it was time to toll the bell.

A quick glance up at the driver's side sun visor showed a key poking out of the edge of it.

I scrambled over to the driver's side of the car, stuck the key in the ignition and was rewarded with the engine firing up the second I turned it. I shoved the sporty antique into reverse gear, spun out to face the street and shifted it into first, so I could tear out of there.

Yeah, I was committing grand theft auto, and Morgan would have loved nailing my ass to the wall for that. But compared to what I was getting away from, it was the least of my worries.

9

THE LADY VANISHES

Once I got on the road, there was never any question of where I was going to take my "borrowed" sports car. Derby was the roughest neighborhood in Cold City, crime being its principal trade and business. That made it a great place to ditch a car, whether it was a junker or a gem. All you had to do was park it in a discrete spot off the main streets, and the local recycling program would send it to the nearest chop shop.

My eye caught a familiar dumpster in an alley off to the left. Not so long ago, I used it to light a signal fire that got me out of another bad fight I was losing. It was as good a spot as any to leave the Maserati.

I turned towards the alley, quick but controlled, parking it behind the dumpster proper. The car's profile was low enough not to be seen from the street, but any enterprising carjacker wouldn't have any trouble taking it to the nearest shop—especially with the keys left in the ignition.

As soon as I got out of the car, I checked myself over.

The brand on my shoulder, which marked me as *hers* and protected me from death, was burning like it was applied using a branding iron. But aside from a few relatively minor aches and bruises, I was actually all right for once. Some of the glass followed me into the car's front seats, cutting me here and there, but aside from a bit of soreness around my throat and a throbbing in my chest from the ifrit's last punch, I was in decent shape for having lost yet another fight.

That made me remember the battle's other casualty. *Poor Eli...*He was so close to his goal, only to get wasted by the perp he crossed dimensions to follow. To hells with what Zian had said. No matter what other secrets he might have been keeping, I never once thought Eli cared less for his sister or any of the ifrit's victims than he ever told me. And he went down fighting with the last of his strength. It deserved nothing but respect...and revenge on the ifrit as soon as I could manage it.

A very faint whisper cut through my whirling thoughts. I looked around the alley; still alone. *So maybe I need to get out of here before—*

I listened to the voice again, a bit more distinct this time. What's more, I could make out what it was saying.

"Bell."

I glanced around; I didn't see anything. The voice came again, a whisper in the wind.

"Bell."

It was too short a time since I last used the sixth sense, but I needed to know. I was able to make out every individual pore of the bricks, every hairline crack on the ground, every mote of dust on the car. Then I made out a faint cloud, such a pale yellow it was almost white, floating around my head. A quick sniff confirmed it smelled of a mix between sage and sandalwood.

"Eli?" I asked, feeling a sense of relief. While I didn't mind dying in the course of my job, I had serious qualms about anyone else paying the same price.

"Yes," the voice whispered again, a bit more distinct with my sixth sense on. "Body...need...a body."

My relief gave way to a bit of annoyance. "What, you can't find one on your own? You did before...twice."

"Ifrit...Azif...searching."

Well, that was reasonable. Sure, Eli could zip over to one of the city morgue and get himself another slightly used corpse to walk around in. But now we were up against Khalim Jones, he knew about me as well as his jinni pursuer. He might get proactive enough to have his Azif finish the job, assuming he didn't want to do it himself. Least I could do was play guard dog to make sure it didn't happen.

I checked my phone. It was 8:05 p.m., a little earlier than I would have felt comfortable dropping by the Cold City Morgue, but I also knew there were likely only two coroners still left onsite. Aside from them, we only had to worry about Ray, who was to that place's security what an inoperative surveillance camera was to a convenience store: all show, no action.

"Listen," I said, putting the phone away again. "We need to leave the car here. Anyway, you can get us to the morgue without—"

My last words got cut off by that cloud wrapping around me and whisking me across town at warp speed. It was a lot more pleasant than the ifrit's abduction; Eli's scent put me in this dreamy state that I never wanted to leave. It was so peaceful that it was jarring to be standing on the ground again.

I took a quick look around. Eli landed me in another alley, this one with contrasting walls. On the right was the beautiful, clean brickwork of the Hidden Falls Center, Cold City's newest hospital; on the left side was an older building, its bricks much more worn down and with some visible cracks in them. Along the foot of this wall were a series of small rectangular windows, rust covering the outside frames from years of neglect. The glass on them was far too thick to break, but I knew from experience popping open the right frame wasn't much harder than picking a door lock.

My sixth sense shut itself off when the ride started, but I could still smell Eli close by as I asked, "And you couldn't transport us inside...why?"

The voice was fainter than with the sixth sense on but still audible. "Sealed...last time...open door."

So the seal on the windows and doors was so airtight Eli couldn't push his way in. That would be why he needed an open door last time, likely during the daylight hours. Well, it wasn't like I hadn't broken in here before.

All was as quiet then as in the later hours, and it took me a minute of careful looking to identify my usual point of B&E entry amongst the windows. Hopefully, only the grave-yard shift was still around this late.

I worked at the window with a piece of wire for another few minutes before it popped open. I stuck my head in to listen for anyone about. The distinct white noise of the portable TV at Ray's desk echoed down the hallway, tuned into whatever pro wrestling match was about to start.

Another minute to make sure the coast was clear, and I whispered, "Alright."

I pulled my head out and put my feet in its place before sliding into the morgue proper. Something soft caught my feet before they hit the hard linoleum floor. I glanced down to see there was nothing there before the invisible hands lowered me to the floor without a sound.

"Thanks," I whispered. Eli didn't say anything back. I guessed he was quiet in case someone was around to hear him. I took my cue from him on the subject.

The corridors were dimly lit by fluorescent lights, a power-saving measure that helped cut the place's utility bill in half, or so I heard. It gave Eli and me plenty of shadows to hide in as we made our way to the cold room. Ray's TV grew fainter and fainter as we drew closer to the cold room's doors.

Even though we were alone, the cold room was brightly lit. I saw a freshly-dissected corpse on the exam table, the distinctive Y-zipper incision still open from the autopsy. There was no way the coroners would leave him like that all night, so I guessed they were due back in the room at any time.

I was walking over to the wall freezers when I heard a low growl mixed with a hiss. "What?" I asked Eli, my eyes scanning for Azif.

"Table...vessel...ifrit," Eli whispered.

Putting the words together, I muttered, "Ah, shit." That had to be the cab driver Ramirez was looking for. I found myself hoping the final report on him would show he'd died from something related to the explosions...but I wasn't betting on it.

Shaking my head, I said, "Alright, let's see if we can find you a new ride, and then we can get out of here."

I froze as I noted how casual the words had come out. *Gee...when had my life taken such a turn that body-shopping in a morgue in the middle of the night was the new normal for me?*

I saw a more distinct shape of Eli's cloud form in the stainless steel of the cabinet doors. "Sealed...need entry."

Even as I opened up the nearest cabinet, I thought over the implications of what Eli was telling me. If something airtight was able to keep him out, would it do the same thing for the ifrit? Hard not to think so; those stories of being sealed in bottles and lamps hinted as much.

The corpse inside was a pretty-looking woman, somewhere in her forties. There were a few laugh lines around her face, but the choice application of cosmetics could have made her look like she was somewhere in her late twenties. Her bare shoulders showed off pale skin that must have had a decent tan when she was still alive. Add in the red, curly hair, and she resembled a rich man's fantasy mistress.

"Perfect," Eli breathed, the last syllable being an octave higher than the first one as a sudden rush of air whooshed by me.

"No, wait!" I hissed. "You can't jump in the first corpse you—"

"So you're sure that's the conclusion we want to write?" I heard a nasal voice from the hallway ask.

Oh no, no, no, no, no, I thought. The timing on the end of the MEs coffee break could hardly be any worse.

"Hey, we do the autopsies," a second voice said. "Morgan's boys and girls get paid to investigate our results."

The woman's corpse opened her eyes and smiled. As casually as though she were getting out of bed, she climbed out of the freezer. The sheet fell away to reveal an impressive nude body. It barely stood at five foot, making me think of a pixie. Under other circumstances, I would have liked to get acquainted with that body...like if it wasn't possessed by a male jinni, and we weren't about five seconds away from being discovered. I grabbed the sheet and tossed it into the freezer before closing the door.

"Do not worry, Bell," Eli said, and his voice was all wrong. I mean, the accent was unmistakably his, but the feminine lust-inspiring voice was new. "I have my ways."

He wrapped slender arms around me—I mean *she*, I suppose...*Hells, but this was going to be weird*—and Eli vanished. A glance around showed me that I did too. I was doing my best to ignore how his—well, *her* new body felt against mine, as lovely as it looked, when the coroners walked in.

The one on the right, a lanky, long-haired young guy with a craggy face and a couple of days of five o'clock shadow, told his pal, "Yeah, yeah, I know you're right, Joe. But..."

"But what?" Joe asked in a nasal voice. He was a portly older man in the age bracket of Eli's newest vessel, with thinning hair and impossibly smooth skin.

Then Joe's almond-shaped eyes narrowed, and he said, "Oh, don't tell me. You think if we could have come up with a cause of death that tied in with the mess downtown, you could have squeezed into Ramirez's pants."

Eli steered us towards the front door. I let her take the lead; invisibility helps keep you out of sight, but it's no guarantee you won't hit something noisy by mistake, mostly because you can't see where your own body is.

"Well...maybe," the young man said, making a face as they got back to the corpse. "What would have been wrong with that?"

Joe was shaking his head. "You mean aside from the fact she's got a boyfriend?"

"So?" the young guy sneered back, spreading his arms. "Word I hear is he's this real pain in the ass who's always breaking up with her. Maybe if she got with a real man..."

Joe gave him the groan I was doing my best to keep from escaping my throat. By then, Eli and I were nearly at the door.

"That's a woman you're talking about, Sam, not a girl," Joe said while the young guy smoothed down the Y-incision. "No offense, but you're nowhere near close to being ready for that in your life."

My arms felt the door on them. Eli stopped walking, waiting for the right moment.

"Well, how else am I supposed to get a date while I'm still young?" Sam snapped. "This job isn't a winning pickup line at the bar."

The echo of Sam's words was enough noise for Eli to get us through the door without being heard. She let go of me, and I was once again distracted by his newest vessel's naked charms.

"So quit," Joe said unsympathetically while picking up a staple gun as the door swung closed. "I could use a little less..."

The door muffled the rest of his words, and we both

went back towards the open window. I was about to jump up when I looked at Eli.

"Is there any way you can...?" I asked, waving a hand up and down her nakedness.

Eli glanced down and then up. "Yes, but it will drain my strength a bit more than I would like."

"Better than being arrested for indecent exposure, not to mention awkward questions on how you got over being dead."

Eli frowned and nodded. A pair of form-fitting black jeans and a purple, ruffled blouse formed around her body. Both were a little translucent, and wouldn't stick upon close inspection, but they'd do the trick from afar. Although the shading of both completely clashed with the red hair.

"This will only last an hour," Eli whispered.

I nodded and jumped up to the window. Even if it wasn't real, it was still better than the full frontal she sported a minute ago. I reached down to get Eli through the window too. Her new height meant I had to stick my arms and shoulders down deep.

Once we were through, I shut the window behind us and glanced around the alley. The coast was still clear.

"So, I'm guessing trying the teleportation trick you did before is out of the question now?"

"It won't work." Eli gave a regretful nod.

"Jones didn't have a problem with it?"

"One more difference between us. I cannot do it, not while I'm in a vessel."

I sighed and slumped my shoulders. "Hope this new body can handle a long walk, then."

10

AFTERMATH

As we walked, I checked my phone. Once we were a block away from the morgue, I clued Zian in on what was going on by text. I would have snapped a pic of Eli's newest vessel for him to run background, but I was worried about the slight chance of it tipping off the wrong people. After reading me a riot act over making him worry, he assured me he'd dig deeper while we were getting ourselves sorted out.

But Zian wasn't the reason I was peering down at my phone. I was keeping an eye on the time before Eli's new clothes disappeared. My apartment was too far away to make it in time on foot. A city bus would help with the time thing, but I didn't have a boarding pass, and that would be the first place I would look if I were hunting Eli and me. So that left one place we could reach if we pushed it.

We got to the Tombs with a total of eleven minutes to spare. The dinner rush had long since left the building, making the neon-wrapped diner look as deserted as its namesake. The only sign of anyone inside was the line of employee cars on the right side.

Tommy was wiping down the bar when we walked in the door. Those charcoal eyebrows of his went up in surprise when he saw Eli's current body. Then they went back down and sighed as understanding dawned on his face.

Shaking his head, he put away his wiping rag and declared, "Just off-hand, I'd say you two have had a rough day."

"Don't get me started, Tommy," I said while I rubbed the bridge of my nose. "Know the saying 'So close, yet so far'?"

"Actually," Eli said, her hand reaching for Tommy's wrist on the bar. "I was wondering if you could fulfill an unusual request."

"If you mean clothes to hide the va-va-voom body you're sporting, I got some old clothes of Tiffany's which might fit."

I wasn't surprised. More often than not, Tommy had a knack for knowing what was up.

"But," he added, holding up a finger. "If you want something to eat, you best explain to me why you're wearing one of my favorite customers."

I rolled my eyes. Somebody would have known a woman who looks this attractive. I hoped Tommy knowing her didn't mean the whole neighborhood did.

While my friend took Eli to the back, I went to my booth. Pulling out my phone, I dialed up Zian.

"Where are you, Bell?" Zian asked as soon as he picked up.

"The Tombs," I said back. "We had to make a pit stop. How's the search going?"

"Making some headway, but it'll take a while. Anything else I can do for you guys while that's going?"

"Yeah...we're going to need a ride back to the spot."

"Are you daft, you geezer? It's not like—"

"The Stingray's still there, Z. We both know its actual owner has a hair-trigger temper when it comes to what's hers."

"Yeah, yeah...but damn, Bell. Times like this, I see why my father has a problem with you."

"Ouch," I said as Tommy and Eli came from out the back. "I'll call you when we're about to leave, okay?"

"Fine. Try not to get in more trouble between now and then."

"No promises," I said with a smile before hanging up.

Eli's new outfit was simple but more color-coordinated. She wore a plain green t-shirt and a standard pair of blue jeans. Realizing she was now wearing shoes in the form of a pair of cheap felony Flyers, I asked, "Did it hurt to walk barefoot on the sidewalk?"

Eli shrugged as she slid into the opposite side of the booth. "Not particularly. I would not have thought of them at all had not Mr. Tommy—"

"Damn, girl, I told you before," Tommy said with a near-chuckle. "It's just 'Tommy'." Then he made a mock-innocent face as he added, "Then again, you were in another body when I told you, so maybe that's scrambling your memory."

Eli's pretty face winced. "I realize you are attempting to add some levity to our situation, Tommy. But it grieves me to think my former vessel will forever be a man who disappeared without a trace."

Tommy's face got thoughtful. "So...not a trace of him left?"

"Just instant ash," I said, feeling the same sting Eli did. "If he had any next of kin..."

"Tell you what...see if your gamer boy pal can come up with anything on the guy. I'll run it down on my end and see if we can't at least tell anybody who loved him he's gone."

I nodded. For all his joking, my mysterious chef friend had a very community-minded approach to life.

"Would I be overstepping my bounds as a guest by asking how you know this vessel?" Eli asked.

Tommy held up a heavily-stained toe tag. Man, I must have been out of it. Eli was wearing that thing the whole walk over, and I never noticed.

"Never knew her real name until I saw it on here," he explained, tapping the tag with his other hand. "But then, Madam L sounds more impressive than Louisa Albertson."

Taking an educated guess, I asked, "She was a working girl?"

"About to be an ex-working girl. She'd saved enough money to get out of the life and was on her way when..."

Tommy's face got sad. Eli made the same grab for his wrist as she had earlier. He looked down at it and gave a sad smile.

"She always used to do that when someone was down," he said. "Guess your body remembers."

"She died from a rupture of the heart," Eli said. "It was very quick...a small burst of pain and it was over. There was no suffering."

Tommy put his free hand over her wrist, toe tag still

dangling in his hand. "I won't say it makes me glad...but it's something."

"So how much do you remember of your vessel's previous life?" I asked, curious.

"It varies," Eli admitted. "If the brain has been damaged, certain memories are distorted or less than clear. Of course, the same thing can be true if the vessel lived a particularly unpleasant life or died in a very horrific way. But Madam L's memories...they are fairly clear."

"You know of her 'getaway fund', then?" Tommy asked.

Eli nodded and let go of his wrist.

"You must know this but...Madam L wouldn't mind in the slightest if some of her money went to Bell here."

"Isn't this grave-robbing?" I asked, getting very uncomfortable with the thought.

"Oh, like you gave away all that cash Eli here handed you in that other body."

"But then I didn't know he...I mean, she was—"

"Tommy is speaking the truth, Bell," Eli said, looking at me in a very Eli way, which reminded of the man she used to be. "I know of a hidden compartment not very far from the warehouse where she has a great deal of money waiting for her."

I guess it's a weird thing to get queasy about. I deal with ancient gods, fight monsters out of myth and send spirits packing back across the border. The thought of taking from the corpse of a mostly-innocent person makes my stomach churn a little.

I tried making one last play to talk her out of it. "You said you'd give me that bonus once the job is completed."

Eli smiled, not fooled by my parsing. "You located my

sister and my mortal enemy. As far as I am concerned, that particular job is done. Therefore, you should be paid in full for your services."

"See?" Tommy chimed in, spreading his arms. "What part of the word 'yes' don't you understand, son?"

I sighed. "Okay, but let's get the car back first. I'd like to keep Zian out of it."

"I'm guessing he's going to be picking you two up?"

"Soon as we're done here."

"Well, you haven't eaten, so neither one of you are done yet. Got a new chicken sandwich recipe I want to try on you two."

"What about paying for—"

Tommy's face got a little sad again. "Tonight's meal's on L's tab. She paid up for a full month. May as well start using it on you two."

Tommy then went towards the back, leaving Eli and me alone in the dining room.

"Something I've got to ask," I said, watching Eli's body language clash with the nearly-retired hooker's body. "Why did you pick the body of a woman?"

Eli shrugged. "It was a body that met my needs. While I could have had you keep opening the cabinets until we found an ideal male match, I knew our time of safety was far too short."

"You mean, you smelled those coroners coming back our way?"

"Is that what those workers of the dead are called? Then, yes, that was it precisely."

Snatches of Cherokee could be heard from the kitchen as

the grill sizzled. I could smell the chicken from our seat. Eli sniffed and smiled.

"So you've got no moral objections to eating chicken?" I asked.

"Far from it," Eli said. "Filthy creatures though they are, chickens are wonderful to eat when prepared properly. What I smell tells me Tommy will not let us down in this matter."

"So let's talk about what we saw in the warehouse," I said, leaning in a little. "You recognized the sign on Sarit's body, even gave it a name."

Eli nodded. "Iblis' Bane, the original binding enchantment used by King Suleiman when he commanded the ifrits to assist in the building of the grand temple of Jerusalem."

I frowned a little. "I'm no magical practitioner, but wouldn't the actual Seal of Solomon—"

"That is merely for protection," Eli countered, holding up a hand. "To command such rebellious spirits requires a different sign. While his father, Daud, passed on much knowledge that aided him, the secret of Iblis' Bane was given to Suleiman through his mother, Bath-Sheba."

I nodded, putting it together in my head. "So this sign also affects jinn and can make them do anything the person who made it wants them to. Since both jinn and ifrit are mostly smoke, it's going to be put on whatever vessel they're attached to. Sometimes that's a bottle, but in this case, it's a body."

"That is what we find ourselves up against at the moment," Eli said, tapping her finger twice on the tabletop for emphasis.

"Do you know how to break it?"

"That, I am afraid, is where my knowledge fails both of us. My sister and I were trained to be warriors, not magicians. I do know defacing the sign by carving over it will do nothing other than making its magic permanent. A counter-pattern must be traced over it to release the prisoner from the dominator's control."

"Zian might be able to help us with that one," I said, grateful I snapped the picture of the sign before our forced eviction from the building. "One last thing...what was the deal with all the corpses around Sarit?"

Eli made a cute face that betrayed her frustration. "That is another matter where my ignorance is quite vast. All I can say categorically about what we saw is that something spiritual was taken from each of those people as they died."

"And the taking was enough to kill them outright?"

Eli got more frustrated by the question. "I do not know... and I swear by the Most High I would dearly like to. Given the condition of their bodies, I am certain it was the ifrit who took their essence."

"Well, two things are for sure," I said, leaning back in my seat. "First, we're going to need more information and a better strategy before we try taking on Jones and his little shadow posse again."

"And the second thing?"

"That chicken sandwich is going to taste very, very good."

The sandwich was every bit as tasty as I thought it'd be. Tommy added some crinkly fries to the side and a genuine

Classic dill pickle. Eli was as enthusiastic about the food, and I saw some color come back into her cheeks as she ate. When Tommy came to take our plates, he gave her a longing look.

"L and I," he said. "We weren't a couple, but...we had a few nights together, which were nice."

Eli gave him an understanding smile. If it was anything to go by, L thought a lot of those nights too.

"I almost want to ask you to stick around until after close," he said, running a gentle hand through her hair. "But...it wouldn't be the same. She's gone to whatever's waiting on the other side."

Eli took his hand and put it on her cheek. "You will see her again, Tommy...be patient."

Tommy stroked it and pulled it back with a smile. "Ol' Bell here and this diner's given me plenty of practice with that one." Then he snapped his fingers. "Damn, nearly forgot. I took a gander at that warehouse on Thames like you asked."

"What'd you find?" I asked.

"Nothing crazy about the warehouse itself," Tommy said, grabbing my plate. "But there was something out on the docks down the street. A cargo container full of dead illegals was uncovered a couple of days ago."

I felt my throat get a little tight. "What was the condition of the bodies?"

"A lot of black eyes on all the corpses," Tommy said. "And by black eyes, I mean the orbs were a solid black. The official word I heard was all those Juan and Juanita Does were the victims of some lethal carbon monoxide poisoning while in transit. But a coyote I know told me a different story."

"What would a coyote know about anything that goes in this city?" Eli asked in confusion.

"Not that kind of coyote," I told her. "It's a nickname for people who transport other people illegally."

"Yeah," Tommy said with a nod. "And this particular one told me he'd dropped that shipment of folks off to the Thames warehouse a week before. He's more than a little pissed somebody stuck 'em back in the container and made it look like he was careless."

I guess there was no point in expecting basic humanity from that kind of a man. Just like with his cousins in legitimate corporations, profits always come over the people who make the former happen. If they'd been killed in a fire at the warehouse, I doubt the coyote would have batted an eye.

"He did pass something else on to me," Tommy went on, the dishes now cleared from the table. "He's willing to pay a small bounty to anyone who could finger the person who made him look bad. He thinks it was Hellfire, but he wants to be sure."

It was tempting, but I asked, "How much does he know about our kind of business?"

"Oh, get the details and let me worry about that. Of course, we are going to split it fifty-fifty, right?"

I groaned and put my face in my hands.

"Is this how a typical conversation between the two of you usually goes?" Eli asked with amusement.

"More or less," I said, dropping my hands. "Okay, Tommy, as soon as I know, I'll let you know."

"Fair enough, Bell," Tommy said with a triumphant grin on his face. "Now...how was the sandwich?"

11

PLAYING WITH FIRE

As he drove his Prius back to Pickfair, Zian couldn't take his eyes off Eli's new body in the backseat.

I nudged him with my elbow from the passenger seat. "Friendly reminder: you need to watch the road."

My friend gave me an annoyed look that wasn't enough to hide the blush on his cheeks. "You have seen me work on my laptop, right? Compared to dancing through multiple data streams, driving is a snap."

Eli looked at him with genuine curiosity. "While I can admit this vessel has its attractive qualities, I remain completely astonished at how every man I have been around thus far finds it utterly captivating."

"I've got, like, a million questions running through my head on how that body-hopping deal works," Zian admitted, his smooth changing of lanes standing as proof of his claim to being a good driver. "But I'm more worried about what may be waiting for us at the warehouse. A 911 call went out before you took off with the Maserati, Bell. I'm hoping you stuck it in a—"

"Nobody's ever going to find it again," I assured him as he turned in the right-hand lane onto Pickfair proper. "Now we need to get my wheels, and we're golden."

"There is a distinct possibility the ifrit is still there as well," Eli mentioned, her face turning grave at the prospect. "Conversely, one or two of his Azif may be lying in wait to see if we are foolish enough to return. Are we certain your vehicle will be untampered with by the time we return?"

My hacker buddy and I traded glances, both of us trying not to laugh.

As Zian had warned, the cops were out in full force at the Ashton warehouse. I counted about four prowl cars, a couple of unmarked vehicles, six or seven techs going over the scene and several strips of police tape blocking off the window I went sailing through.

"Please tell me you had the good sense not to park too close to all this," Zian said, giving the cop convention an uneasy eye.

"Hardware store two doors down," I said, pointing to it. "My ride's in the back parking lot."

Zian nodded but wound up driving past it.

"Z, I said—"

"I know what you said, Bell. But I'm going to make sure the coast is clear before we pull in there."

Couldn't fault him for taking a page from my playbook. True, a Prius was likely to draw way less attention than a Stingray. But even the dimmest flatfoot would be curious as to why any car would be going to a deserted hardware store at this time of night.

Zian eventually pulled into a Walgreens two blocks down. He pulled out his smartphone and started furiously working the screen like he would his laptop back at the off-site. Eli leaned forward in his seat to peer over Zian's shoulder to watch him work. I was curious enough to do the same.

In rapid succession, the phone showed all the CCTV cam feeds in the area. He found the one of the hardware store's rear. There was the faintest shimmer you could make out in the spot where I'd parked the car. Eli didn't catch that.

"Where is the car?" she asked, pointing towards the screen.

"Still there," Zian told her, using his fingers to zoom in the image.

Pointing at the image again, he said, "If you squint really hard, you can make out the outline of where the car is."

Eli nodded but frowned. "I can only presume this inability to be seen by this device is owed to the patronage of the one you call 'Lady McDeath'."

"Yeah," I confirmed, "otherwise, this car would be noticed."

The demonstration over, Zian went back to flipping through the rest of the CCTV feeds. I recognized a few of the feeds he was staring at as ones we'd seen. He nodded and put the phone away.

"Seems like they've done their canvass of the area," he said. "I can check what they know at the off-site later. But first, let's get that car out of there."

"What about the magic eye that is fixed on the spot where we left the vehicle?" Eli asked.

"I've got the footage we saw on a tape loop for the next

hour. Should be more than enough time to get it out of there."

"Sounds like a plan," I said, undoing my seatbelt. "Thanks for the lift, Zian."

"Like you'd know what to do without me," he said with a playful punch of the arm. Then he turned to Eli, and I swear his smile was flirtatious. "And yeah, darling, you can expect plenty more stares as long as you're wearing that body."

Eli completely missed it. "Duly noted," she said, squeezing Zian's shoulder.

I steered her towards the front door as Zian drove off.

"But is not the car in the opposite—"

"It's about having a cover story," I explained. "A friend dropped us off, we got some supplies, and then we met him a few blocks away after he got done with his errand."

Eli arched an eyebrow at me. "Deception, then."

"Oh, yeah," I said. "The last thing we need is the cops getting curious about why we're here at all."

I grabbed some toothpaste and mouthwash while we were inside. I needed them for a while, but now I could afford it. Once we paid for it, we went back out. After a careful gauging of the evening traffic, we made a run across the street to the dockside. Eli started taking discreet sniffs of our immediate area since we climbed out of Zian's car. Now she was sniffing the air like a bloodhound for any delicate scents.

"One distinct advantage of wearing a female vessel," she said as we made our way back towards the hardware store. "The olfactory sense of such a body is remarkably sensitive compared to a male's."

"Won't all the air pollution make finding the scents of the ifrit or Azif harder?" I asked, keeping a nervous eye on the surrounding shadows.

Eli shook her auburn head. "Being around this area earlier helped me get a deep impression of its various ambient smells. We should be relatively prepared to find our foes before they find us."

I found myself wishing she was right, but we made it to the back of the hardware store without a problem. The car park was deserted, and there were no cops anywhere close by. I glanced at Eli, and she shook her head. The Azif and ifrit weren't here either. No need to push our luck any further tonight.

I kept the lights off as I pulled the Stingray back onto the highway. I only turned them on when I confirmed there were no police cruisers behind us.

"Now that our transportation has been secured," Eli said, putting her hand on her chin. "There is still the small matter of me paying you for your time and trouble."

"It can wait," I said. "Right now, I'm more concerned about us getting back to Zian's place without getting ambushed."

She frowned at me. "You desperately need a woman in your life, Bell."

"So everyone keeps telling me," I said, doing my best to bite my tongue on adding how I was doing everything I could to make that happen with Ramirez.

"I mean that," Eli said, raising her eyebrows. "You are as ungrounded as any person I have ever encountered. You think about the immediate moment and never once consider you may need to take certain risks to ensure your continuing survival. A wife would be most helpful to you in keeping such boring but essential matters as finances up to date."

"You can't spend the money if you're dead," I pointed out, looking in the rearview mirror out of habit. It was still all clear.

"But it is equally true you need money to survive in this particular world," Eli added, leaning back in her seat. "Given what I have been able to extract from the memories of my hosts, I have concluded it is costly to be a human in this city."

Thinking of my monthly condominium payment, I grimaced and said, "You're not wrong."

"Therefore, as this vessel has no more need for such currency, why should you not benefit from my generosity and her untimely demise while no one knows where that money is?"

It was hard to argue with that kind of logic. After all, one of the reasons I took this case was because I was seriously short on funds. "Do you remember how to get to the place?"

"Of course...but will you, at the very least, consider what else I have said?"

I promised I would, but I wasn't sure if I necessarily meant it.

———

We wound up in a no-tell motel at the very end of Pickfair. The sign up front was so battered, and so many bulbs were gone I couldn't make out the name. The guy at the front desk, a little man in his late forties with a bald spot on his head, greasy dress shirt and a thin goatee, spotted me first and sneered. "Thirty upfront, sport."

"C'mon, Bryan," Eli said, making her voice turn extra sexy. "I promised him a discount for being a first-timer."

I thought I heard a few of those golden jinn tones underneath her voice, and Bryan got this enraptured look on his face. "Yeah, fine...the boss asks I'll use my end to cover it, L."

"You're a sweetheart," Eli said with a smile that could cause instant orgasms.

Why, yes, I was able to concentrate on walking past the desk instead of having one of those. Why do you ask?

She led me upstairs to a balcony. The usual noises of horizontal entertainment and the cooking smells of sex leaked through the walls and doors.

"This was her regular room," she said when we got near room 316.

I gave the door a look. "Well...should not be hard to break in—"

Eli pulled up the carpet by the right doorframe and retrieved a room key.

"Or that could work too," I added while she unlocked the door.

The inside was like every other motel I've ever been in: a bed, a medium-sized TV sitting on top of a cheap wooden chest of drawers, an empty closet and a bathroom roughly the size of the closet. The eggshell white of the walls was stained yellow, possibly from the occasional smoker, probably from the fact it hadn't been cleaned anytime this decade.

The money L stashed wasn't in any one place. Eli pulled loose bills from underneath the TV, a taped envelope underneath the middle drawer of the chest of drawers, a water-proof plastic baggie inside the toilet tank, another such baggie behind the trap of the shower drain. She pulled the money out and counted it all on the bed. The final count was easily in the neighborhood of $4000.

Hearing some grunts from the other side of the wall, I noted, "This wouldn't be enough to get out of the life."

"It was what she called her 'getaway fund,'" Eli explained, handing me the money. "Most of her actual money was kept secure in a bank on the other side of the city. No one who worked there had any notion of what she did to earn such money. It was assumed she was a...I have no idea what an 'investment banker' is but—"

A female voice on the other side of the wall interrupted her. "Oh, oh, oh, oh God!"

Wincing, I told Eli, "Let's say it's a lot more decent work than what's going on in the next room. How did she know the money would be safe here?"

"She paid a monthly rental fee for the privilege of using this room," Eli said, stuffing the now-useless money containers in one of the plastic baggies. "Every woman in her profession who uses this place does. One of the privileges of having this place was the complete privacy that came with it, so long as certain rules were always observed."

"But she didn't necessarily trust management to be on the up-and-up," I deduced, thankful the shouting and heavy breathing was getting quieter. "So she scattered the money all around the room to give her a better shot at keeping at least some of it."

"Indeed," Eli confirmed. "Well, I think a reasonable

amount of time has passed since we entered this room. If you go ahead of me, I shall join you in your car shortly."

I looked a bit uneasy at this prospect. Eli smiled, reached up to my neck and gave me a quick kiss that left lipstick on my skin; then she reached up a hand to messy my hair.

"It is a testament to your great heart you care so deeply," she said. "But I shall be fine in your absence. It would be best if no one suspects we came here for any purpose other than the usual one. This is the best way to accomplish that."

"Okay," I said, feeling awkward. I wondered how much of L was still left within the vessel Eli habited. It surely seemed some of the personas came along with the memories. "But if you're not back at the car in five minutes, I'm coming back up. And Bryan had better have the good sense not to ask me for money when I do."

Eli shook her head as I walked out.

Didn't turn out to be any need for dramatics. She was out the door three minutes and change later. She tossed the discarded money containers onto the sidewalk a couple of blocks away at a stoplight. After driving aimlessly for a few blocks to spot any tails, we headed back towards Zian's off-site.

———

My hacker friend was glued to his laptop when he buzzed us back into the old warehouse's office. We walked around the desk and saw him going through various CCTV feeds. I noticed each one of them featured Khalim Jones somewhere, either prominently or in the background.

After a few minutes of silence and windows opening and closing, I quipped, "Nice to see you too, Zianyon."

Zian didn't so much as glance at me, even though I used his full name, so I tried again. "I'm fine, thanks for asking."

"Don't quit your day job, Bell," Zian said in a low tone.

Deciding to ignore the fact quitting it would be more trouble than it was worth, I asked, "So what's the story with the *Truman Show*?"

"Now we've got an ID on our ifrit's host," Zian explained, looking over his shoulder at us, "I'm doing everything I can to backtrace his movements. I want to get as close to the day the bombs went off downtown as I can."

"Makes sense, but I'm worried he ducked into a place where he could have done something nasty or important that the cams won't pick up on."

"But it would seem these magic eyes of your world are everywhere in your city," Eli opined with a frown. "Would not being able to do anything completely out of sight be a sheer impossibility?"

I figured a demonstration would make the point better than any words. "Zian, think you can pull up all the cameras in and around that motel at the end of Pickfair without slowing down your search?"

He made a farting sound with his lips, and then he pulled up the surveillance feed. The closest—and only—cam he was able to come up with was a damaged one across the street with a cracked lens.

Eli took it in and asked, "And there are no such eyes within this place?"

"If there were, I would have brought them up," Zian confirmed.

"So you see, Eli," I said, putting a hand on her shoulders. "It doesn't matter how extensive a surveillance system like this is. There are always going to be blind spots."

Zian went back to staring at his screen. "Trying to figure out which blind spots he's been at is going to be the trick. Sorting through a month's worth of video footage is no joke."

"Anything you can tell us about this guy?" I asked.

"Just that, unlike Eli's previous flesh avatar, this one was a living body. Some of the cams I've seen are full-color, and he's got a healthy tan on him."

Eli nodded. "That would make sense. One of his more infamous crimes against the All-High was wantonly taking the bodies of living people for his pleasure. Once he has gotten sufficient enjoyment out of it, he leaves it behind, the body and mind a broken husk."

Thinking about Jones' alluring looks, I concluded that must have been the only reason the fashion designer had caught the ifrit's burning eye. The perks of having power and influence built into the life he stole was a bonus.

"Any pattern to his overall movements?" I asked.

"Nothing you'd think was off for a fashion designer," Zian said, putting the screen around the motel away. "Hellfire offices, employees, the sweatshop op on Thames, the occasional nightclub and, of course, our local fashion show... About everything you'd expect from a guy like this."

"There's got to be something there, Zian," I said, leaning forward to see if anything that flashed on the screen triggered something. I got an achy set of eyes for my trouble.

Eli put her hand on my shoulder. "It would likely be best if I did that instead. I daresay my eyes can keep track of these screens as easily as Zian's own."

I felt the day's events weighing me down. Guess it was more than my eyes that felt tired. Everything in my body was shutting down on me, but there was one more thing I needed to do. "What time is it?"

"Just came up on 9:36 p.m.," Zian said. "Why do you ask?"

I walked over to an ancient, sagging couch to the desk's right. "One of you, wake me up around midnight. I'm going to go back out to the Ashton warehouse to take another look."

Eli stared at me with serious reproach. "That is an astonishingly bad idea to pursue."

"What she said," Zian added while still looking at the screen. "Not only could there still be some cops around—"

"Not unless the city council voted to allow them more overtime," I said, remembering that tidbit from Ramirez as I laid down.

"But there's the possibility Jones or whatever his real name is left a special 'welcome back' gift that's about as welcome as ransomware."

"Also," Eli said, putting her hands on her hips. "What leads you to believe you will find something all the parties who have converged on this place have managed to miss?"

If I didn't know for a fact that Eli's new body was going to rot like the old one, I would have sworn she was auditioning to be my wife. I sighed as I felt myself drifting off. "Nothing...but I still want to be sure."

After that, I was dead to the world.

———

Half-past midnight, I parked the Stingray back at the

Walgreens on Pickfair. It took me nearly ten minutes to get both Zian and Eli to understand I was still serious about going back. It took another ten for me to convince Eli to stay with my favorite online info broker so she could help him search for clues.

I never told her I had another motive: keeping her out of the line of fire. At best, Jones thought Eli was dead. At worst, the ifrit knew she was still out there but had no clue what body she was wearing. The next dustup we had, that kind of surprise could make all the difference.

I made a point of going back behind the hardware store again. That route managed to keep me from being spotted too soon so far; no reason to believe that had changed. As I stuck to the shadows, I turned on my sixth sense to get a feel for the area. I was already sporting a headache from the little late-evening nap I'd taken. The assault of scents, sounds and fine visual details I was now picking up made it worse, but it was better than being jumped.

Leaning against the back wall, I kept my senses open and looked around. The only thing I could make out in the warehouse was the yellow tape stretched over the back door; otherwise, the coast was clear. I shut off my sixth sense and made a beeline for the back door.

I would usually break through the tape and say *the hell with it,* but I figured a little extra caution wouldn't hurt for once. The tape didn't cover the door handle, and it was still unlocked when I turned the knob; maybe the lock rusted out or got broken. I slipped through the gaps in the tape to go inside.

The bottom floor looked about the same as it had when I was there earlier, minus the curiously dead bodies and, of course, Sarit. The ifrit's lingering scent smothered the place like an oily cloud waiting for someone to ignite it. I wondered what would happen to this place once enough time had passed. Would someone use it for more sweatshop ops? Or would it be introduced to the Cold City tradition of the wrecking ball makeover?

I quickly checked around each of the stations to see if there was anything worth knowing. All I got for my trouble was a few bits of cloth half-stitched together. The most complete of the bunch was a full rubber dress, the kind that clings to a woman's body but is small enough to put in your pocket when it's not being worn. I made out some green gemstones on what I presumed was the back of it. I took it with me. Maybe it was another dead end; perhaps I could give it as a gift to Ramirez for a night of fun. Or maybe it'd point me to where Jones was headed next.

It took a minute for me to find the stairs up to the office. I was never so glad to be taking a staircase in my life; it beat being dragged upstairs by an angry fire spirit at warp speed. Nobody bothered to tape off the office door, and it was as unlocked as the back door was.

From the glow of the street light, I saw some traces of the fight here and there: the indentation in the wall where Eli's host landed, what was left of that office chair and, of course, the gaping hole where the window lost the argument with my flying body. I also caught a glimpse of the ashes of Eli's previous body on the floor. Sadness hit me at the sight. That could well have been Eli and not the body, if not for her quick exit.

Pulling out a penlight, I grabbed the nearest desk drawer and started checking it over. It was empty. So were the two under it. Well, what did I expect? Eli tried to warn me there was never that big a chance of there being anything left to take.

I was about to call it quits when I saw a flash of white out of the corner of my eye. It was under the desk's right leg, on the floor below the bottom drawer. Maybe it was a document of some kind?

Getting down on my hands and knees, I slid my fingers underneath the narrow crack to grab it. I managed to extract it and gave it a good look with the flash. It was a document, written in the same script Eli put on my knife. It'd be a cinch if Eli could read it, if not necessarily understand what it was talking about.

The sound of breaking glass tore me from my musing. It came from downstairs. It took me a second longer to realize it was two sounds put together, and when I spotted the orange glow, I felt my heart skip a beat.

Sure enough, the bottom floor had turned into a raging inferno by the time I peeked my head out the office door. It spread like a fungal bloom, swallowing the floor, machines and anything else the flames could touch. No way this was an ordinary Molotov cocktail. Somebody had brewed up some Greek Fire, the closest thing Alternum Mundum had to napalm. If I didn't get out of the building in the next ten seconds, I was going to burn too.

Shutting the door behind me, I ran right at the window I was knocked out of earlier that day. Hells with breaking the tape; in a few seconds, it was going to be ashes with the rest. I jumped out when I realized something important: I didn't have any handy Maseratis to break my fall this time.

"Ah, shit," I whispered as gravity had its way with me. I shut my eyes and braced myself for a rough landing.

I was a little surprised to land with a softer thud than I expected. The distinctive smell of day-old garbage hit my nose stronger than Jones' coal scent. I opened my eyes to find myself on a pile of garbage bags stacked under the window.

I didn't have time to think more about that. The flames spewed out of the window I just escaped through, doing its best impression of a volcanic eruption. I forced myself to get up and ran away from the building as it went up in a spectacular, but controlled, explosion. A ring of fire sprayed out from the building in a starburst, right before the whole thing collapsed in one messy fall.

The fire department was going to be out here ASAP.

I made a beeline for the back of the hardware store and waited a bit. The red trucks and flashing lights followed the distinctive sound of sirens. As expected, a few prowl cars came with their set of lights and sirens to the scene. Everyone's attention would be on the fire and everything around it. If I timed it right, I could slip out without anyone noticing me.

Once I was sure nobody else was coming for the fireworks, I left my hiding place and walked down the street. I went up a few blocks to check for a tail, using the crosswalks and traffic lights like a model citizen. I walked around the neighborhood to make sure I was clear before going back in the Walgreens parking lot for my car.

I pulled out the evidence I grabbed from the scene. Was Jones trying to kill me with that move? Or had the whole thing been about covering his tracks, and I happened to pick the wrong moment for a break-in? Either way, I was lucky to come out of that one without anything too serious in the way of injuries.

I gave the dress another look, stretching it out to focus on the gemstones. The stones made out some pattern on the back, but one gem on the upper left was a couple of inches out of place. It reminded me of the Iblis' Bane brand we'd found on Sarit's breast. Was there a connection?

12

THE BREAKFAST CLUB

Eli, Zian and I dragged ourselves into the Tombs at the crack of dawn. I could hear and smell breakfast cooking in the back, a welcome thing after the day and night we all had. Tommy gave us a big grin from the counter as he put away his wiping rag.

"Well, as I live and breathe," he said. "I was wondering if you ate human food like the rest of us mere mortals, Gamer Boy."

Zian flinched at the mention of his heritage. I gave Tommy a warning look and headed off any unpleasantness by asking, "Anyway, can we get L's tab to buy all three of us breakfast?"

"For another five mornings," Tommy confirmed, waving us towards the booth. "What'll it be?"

"Ham omelet, sausage biscuit, and orange juice," I said, stretching my arms.

"Just blueberry oatmeal for me," Zian said.

Eli gave the question some thought before saying, "I

would very much like some biscuits, chicken and as much coffee as you can spare."

"Well, how about a pair of chicken biscuits and a bottomless cup of coffee?" Tommy asked with a smirk.

"That sounds wonderful."

"Then take a seat, and we'll have it out lickety-split."

My body was glad to stop walking as it dropped into the booth. I sighed and rubbed my face. Thanks to my late-night nap, I wasn't tired, but I was still sore from my second swan dive of the night. Plus, while Eli might be too polite to bring it up, landing on garbage also made me smell terrible.

The breakfast crowd was still an hour from getting in, so we had the place to ourselves for the time being. I couldn't think of a better time or place to go over our findings.

"So," I said to Zian. "You're sure about that pattern on the dress being a rough match for that brand on Sarit's chest?"

"As sure as I am about wiping the CCTV feeds of you after the fire," Zian said, rubbing his boyish face in exhaustion. "There was nothing I could do about your first visit though, as these were already with the police."

I nodded. "I'll worry about it later. The dress?"

"Extrapolation from the sample you gave me shows it to be a 99% match to the pic."

"But would that pattern work as well as the brand we saw?" I asked Eli.

"On clothing or skin, the pattern would still accomplish its intended purpose," Eli said with a sad expression on her face.

"And don't forget those stones went all the way *through*

the fabric," Zian added. "They'd be touching the skin if anyone wore it."

"Alright, what about what was written on the document?" I asked my client. "You sure it—"

"Truthfully, I almost wish I was not," Eli said. "But the words on that paper made the situation extremely clear. The souls of the workers we found were used to help create the magic on the dresses." He frowned. "The script was slightly unclear on one point. It spoke as though only a certain part of the soul was being extracted for such a purpose."

"Like Ancient Egyptian and Native American models suggest, the soul is actually quite a few pieces put together," I said. "So maybe the spellbinding process uses what the Egyptians called the *ka* or the *ba,* or even the True Names of those poor people to make it work."

Both Eli and Zian gave me a look of amazement.

"What?" I asked with a shrug. "I've got a private library full of occult books back at my place. I've been spending the last month looking them over in case our ex-mayor left—"

Tommy came out the back with three breakfast trays. As he sat them down, he said, "Well, don't stop on my account, son. It sounds like the conversation was getting interesting."

Zian opened his mouth to say something when his phone buzzed. He pulled it out and gave it a quick look.

"Hear about that fire over at the Ashton warehouse last night?" I asked while Zian was working.

Tommy nodded as he finished with setting down Eli's plate. "Yeah, a few of the boys in blue and red rolled up in the wee small hours. Made sure I gave 'em plenty of coffee and doughnuts...Works better than booze in getting that crowd to talk. They kept saying how they'd never seen a fire quite like this one before...burned so damn hot the bricks were sizzling when they put out the flames." Tommy gave me the critical eye as I dug into my omelet. "Now you wouldn't happen to have anything to do with all that, would you?"

"Not a thing," I said with a shake of my head. It was the truth, but the expression on Tommy's face told me he knew it wasn't the whole truth. "Okay," I admitted after swallowing a bite. "I might have been in the neighborhood when Greek Fire got thrown through the window."

Tommy took a sharp breath through his teeth. "This hasn't turned into a gig for that witchy woman who holds your life, has it?"

Eli, who was munching on her first chicken biscuit with gusto, raised her hand and shook her head. Tommy held up a hand. "Alright, I trust you, old soul. It's just sounding like one of these non-profit favors he does way too much for my liking."

Zian's eyes were glued to his phone. He looked a lot of shades paler than when he'd picked it up.

Catching up on that too, Tommy said, "Well, I'll let you get back to it. I can help with anything else..."

"You know I'll be around," I finished, raising my fork for emphasis.

As Tommy walked away from our table, shaking his head, Zian glanced up at us. "This thing went from bad to worse."

"I figured as much," I said, using my knife to cut into another piece of the omelet. "I was waiting for you to tell us how."

Eli looked at Zian with interest. Swallowing hard, my

hacker buddy said, "Remember how I had the off-site working on any orders of Hellfire dresses that matched what you found at the warehouse?"

I nodded as I enjoyed the second bite of my omelet. Yes, this was a bad situation. But nothing was going to get in the way of me appreciating my food.

"Well, thanks to the free advertising provided by the fashion show, the dresses are getting distributed to every high-end boutique and store in Cold City. What happened to Sarit is about to get spammed to who knows how many innocent women in this town."

Eli took a pull of her coffee like it was a bottle of Number 10 Jack Daniel's. As she sat it down, I noticed the coffee mug refilling itself to the brim. "Is there nothing you can do with your miracle machines that could stop this from coming about?"

Zian gave it some thought. "I could slow things down... misdirect orders to addresses nobody would be at, cancel some others and make it look like a computer error. But all that'd do is buy us more time. The problem of the dresses and the hellraiser making them is still going to be out there."

"Would killing the ifrit stop all this from happening?" I asked Eli. Sometimes that's all it took to make certain magic fail, but it was never a guarantee.

Eli nodded. "Any binding magic used would have to require the ifrit to invest something of himself to make it work. Killing him would, therefore, kill the magic as well."

I shook my head while I ate my breakfast. Between bites, I said, "I still don't get how someone who lost his True Name could wind up being this powerful, let alone coming up with binding spells."

"Well," Zian piped up after swallowing his oatmeal. "You and Eli said before about how parts of the souls were used to make the binding enchantments happen. What if another part of the souls were used to keep feeding him power?"

I glanced up at my hacker pal. "Like their True Names?"

Eli drank another swig of the coffee, and it once again filled back up. "Such a practice could not work for very long. Between possession of a vessel and the vast amount of power he was channeling, the charge he got from such an unholy extraction would be minimal."

"Which is why he did it in mass quantities," I said, tapping the tabletop. "It would work on the same principle as a camel storing water in his hump. He stocks up on all those True Names, he can put off becoming nothing a little longer."

"And because he's got so much in his system, he's juiced to the point of OP," Zian added. "So he goes nuts on the juice...well, more nuts...and then realizes he's burned through what was keeping him stable."

"Thus, he needs to feed on the workers at the warehouse after wasting the energy he got from the others Tommy mentioned the last time we were here," Eli said, pointing at me.

I nodded. "And took whatever other soul component was in them for the dresses as a side bonus."

It would be while we were on a roll that my phone went off. A quick look showed it was Kennedy. Getting out of the booth, I held up the phone and said, "I'm going to need to take this."

"Should I tell Tommy our conclusions if he comes back before you?" Eli asked.

I frowned and shook my head, walking towards the front door. "Mention it but hold off on the details. I'll tell him what we know when I get back."

Outside was as deserted as the Tombs. There were a few cars on the cold, misty streets, trying to beat the morning rush. But otherwise, I had the whole block to myself. I answered the phone with "Morning, Kennedy. What's on your mind?"

"The nasty little thought you might be keeping me outta the loop," Kennedy replied, her Texan accent growing prominent in her voice. That was never a good sign.

"C'mon, Kennedy. You know how an investigation—"

"*You* c'mon, Vale. When I hear about a nasty fire that's leveled a warehouse connected up the wazoo to a little fashion company you and I've been looking into, what am I supposed to think?"

I sighed, took another breath to get my thoughts clear. "I was hoping you'd trust me enough to tell you all about it when I knew more."

"So you did know about this fire?"

"Yes."

"Did you set it?"

"Why does everyone keep asking me that? No. Of course not."

"You wouldn't be bullshitting me on that last part, would you?"

Maybe, if it were the truth. "No, Kennedy. It's no way to keep a working relationship going."

"True enough, hoss," Kennedy said, her voice lightening

up enough to let me know I was off the hook for now. "So what can you tell me about it?"

"All I know is I had enough time to get out before the whole place went up," I said. "It was pretty touch-and-go."

"Fire marshals I've been talking to say they've never seen a fire like this before."

"One of my contacts mentioned it too. One thing I can tell you about is the accelerant used in that little Molotov was from across the border."

Kennedy knew enough of my code phrases to get my meaning. "Think they might have been trying to snuff you?"

"If they knew I was there, then maybe. Could have been shitty timing on my part. Serves me right for not checking the bad guys' day planner."

Kennedy stifled a laugh. "Level with me, Vale. There anything you can tell me about this? Anything I can use to help out?"

"If there were, I'd tell you," I said, hoping that would be enough to get her to drop it. I should have known better.

"Well, think I'll do a little poking around anyway," she said. "Speaking of which, got a couple of details you might be interested to hear. Guess where Hellfire had their offices up until recently?"

"Downtown where the bombs went off," I said.

"Uh-uh, not just anywhere downtown," Kennedy added. "They happened to be right where I found one of those pyramids we took care of."

That little detail made me wonder how much of a coincidence Jones' possession was. "So what's Detail Number Two?"

"Emma Fawcett, co-founder of Hellfire. Did time in the

fashion trenches as a designer before she threw in with Jones a few years ago."

"Any romantic attachment to Jones in that mix?"

"Going by the fact she likes to go out with some of the models who wear her dresses, kind of doubt it. But here's the thing: she's been MIA since the whole Galatas Incident. But now I'm hearing scattered reports of her showing up at the fashion show."

"Just like that?" I asked, frowning into the phone. "What's she doing there? Has she been seen anywhere else?"

"Trying to run those questions down myself, hoss," Kennedy said with a verbal shrug in her voice. "See why it's an interesting idea to keep each other in the loop?"

I didn't disagree, but I also wanted the journalist to keep from winding up in a mess she couldn't get out of.

"Oh, thought you might want to know," Kennedy added with a little too much enthusiasm. "Our favorite detective lieutenant got his CSI team out to the scene about an hour ago so they can pick things over."

"Great," I said, leaning against the door. If Morgan's habits ran true to form, he'd be seeing me sometime shortly.

"Now I've done you a few solids, Vale," Kennedy said. "Think about doing me one sometime down the line, okay?"

"Okay," I said, not sure if I meant it. "Try to be careful, would you? Over-the-border business always gets a lot nastier than you think it would."

"Hmmm...Isn't this the part where you tell me to drop it and walk away?" Kennedy asked, a bit of a tease in her voice.

"Would you do it if I asked?"

"Hell, no...but you knew that already, didn't you?"

"I ought to."

We said our goodbyes, and I went back inside. Tommy was waiting by the booth as Eli drank her coffee. Seemed like she figured out the cup refilled on its own.

"Your boy here tells me you might have something to say about what happened to the coyote's cargo."

I gave Tommy the rundown on our current theory, stressing that a theory was all it was until we could find out more info. Tommy nodded and said, "Yeah, that coyote might not be as patient as I am. Tell you what, get the full scoop and then I'll deliver it to him. Until then, mum's the word."

I tried taking another bite of my omelet, but it was too cold to be tasty. Tommy sighed and grabbed the plate. "For what L paid me, the least I can do is give you a hot meal."

———

The breakfast crowd was trickling in when we walked back out. I told Zian and Eli about Morgan's interest in the fire after eating my reheated breakfast. Zian was playing with his phone on the way out, hacking into the police database. When we neared the Stingray, he said, "Bad news, Bell. Morgan's named you a person of interest in the arson."

I sighed. "Of course he did. Any way you can—"

"I'll see what I can do."

I gave my buddy an affectionate shoulder pat. "You're a prince, Z."

"The Prince of Information," he replied with a goofy grin and a raised pointer. Then his face grew more serious. "I'd better get back to the off-site. If I'm going to pour sand in the digital gears on those orders, I'm going to need the laptop for the job."

"Need to head home myself," I said, opening the driver's side door. Eli got in the backseat.

"And what of me?" Eli asked as she settled in. "Where shall I go?"

"I'll drop you off back at Zian's off-site," I said, turning the engine over while Zian strapped on his seatbelt. "It'll be safer for you there."

"Safer, perhaps, but hardly more comfortable," Eli scoffed while she clicked her seatbelt in place. "Besides, you have ample protective wards on your home, and your furniture would be much more conducive to my attaining the kind of rest that rekindles my flame."

I bit my lip. She smiled at me the same way she'd unbalanced Bryan as she said, "Besides, it is hardly as though I have not slept in your residence before now."

Zian was holding back a laugh while I felt myself get flustered. She *had* to be drawing from her body's memories to be pulling this play.

"Yeah, but that was before Morgan knew I was part of all this," I said, hoping I was convincing. "Now he's involved—"

Eli pursed her lips with a bit of disappointment. "And why should you have to face such a dreadful man alone? Just because you have done so in the past does not mean you cannot have someone by your side now."

Oh, she was playing dirty. Given what I could remember from the *Thousand and One Nights*, it wasn't wholly unexpected. Jinn were never known to fight fair when it comes to getting what they want. Still, given her talents, she might make things easier with Morgan than they usually were.

I threw up my hands and said, "Alright, fine, you win. We'll go back to my place together." Cocking my thumb towards her, I added, "But I'm getting the couch. Morgan comes in, you don't come out unless it looks like I'm in trouble. Got it?"

Eli gave me a smug little smile that said, "We'll see."

Zian burst out laughing.

"Now, if you're done yucking it up at my expense," I said with a dirty sideways glance at him, "I got someone else for you to look at."

13

LEFT AND GONE AWAY

It didn't matter how long I lay there on the couch; I couldn't sleep. Maybe it was the breakfast at the Tombs. Perhaps it was the shower I took to get the slime off when I got in. Maybe it was because I was so exhausted that sleep wasn't going to happen. All I knew for sure was I was still awake, and I didn't want to be.

I tossed, turned and tried every deep breathing trick I knew to get myself into Dreamland. Nothing worked. After an hour and a half of trying, I gave up.

In my bedroom, I could hear Eli's soft, even breaths as she slept. I wondered if she was exhausted from staying up all night or if it was that my wards gave her enough peace of mind to rest easy. Regardless, I was glad someone was able to get some shuteye.

Her breathing made me realize one of the other reasons I was still up. I was afraid for her continued safety. As long as no one opened the door from the inside, my wards should be enough to keep anyone out. But if Jones had an inside track on me, it was only a matter of time before he found this place. As many soul pieces as he was sucking down, he might have enough juice to huff, puff and blow the door down, either the front or the sliding glass one that led out to the porch. Dammit, why couldn't she have gone with Zian? His place may have been less safe, but it was also less known to the ifrit.

I shook my head. I was thinking about Eli as a woman, even though I knew she was anything but. Helping out damsels in distress always tended to cloud my judgment on the right way to do things. Still, she had a close call during our last dance with the ifrit. Things could go worse the next time unless we changed things up.

Not having anything better to do, I picked up the dress I found earlier off the coffee table. I pulled it from my coat before putting that much-abused piece of clothing in the washer. The thought of it made me realize the spin cycle had stopped on my slimed clothes. I put the stone back down on the table, right between a pen and a sheet of paper, then went over to the laundry room, pulled the load out and put it in the dryer. It'd be an hour before they were done.

That out of the way, I grabbed the dress again. Holding it up in the mid-morning light from the sliding glass doors, I watched the gems sparkle a little. Now, I've been around enough precious stones to know it was no emerald. But it neither looked nor felt like glass. So what was it?

I pulled my knife from my boot with my free hand. Hoping I hadn't made a significant mistake, I dug the point into the side of a gem. The result was nothing like I expected.

In place of the clear, green stone, there was a soft blue

one that had no transparency about it at all. It didn't change size and weight, but the feel of the damn thing changed from smooth to rough in my hand. The whole effect was like watching a hologram flicker and fade out.

I felt my breath catch as I realized what I was holding. *Oh, no, no, no, no, no!* I thought as I dropped the dress back on the table so I could dial Zian on my cell.

He answered on the second ring. "Bell, I was about to call you. What—"

"I've found out what those gemstones are," I told him. "They're lapis lazuli from the pyramids we blew up. Feels like the ifrit put some all-senses illusion on top of them."

"That fits," Zian replied, not sounding a bit surprised by what I uncovered.

"You mean, it fits with what you were about to tell me?"

"Now I know about Ms. Fawcett," Zian explained, "I thought it'd be a bit prudent to go back to the day of the explosions to track her movements. CCTV feeds put her in the downtown Hellfire offices before the big booms."

"And when's the next time we see her?"

"A week after we shut off the portal. She was taking side streets to find a discreet entrance into the fallout zone. Finally found it on Wolfman Street."

"The house at 329, right?" I asked with a sinking feeling in my stomach.

"Wait, tell me you didn't go back—"

"All I'm going to say is I had an excellent reason to do that. Now, how many trips did she make into that hell pit?"

"I've got six on the video files so far, always by herself and always out of sight of the cops. Nothing but her purse going in, but each time out, there's a good-sized gym bag under her arm."

"Here's what I don't get," I said. "Why hide the gems under this kind of illusion? You, me and Kennedy are pretty much the only living souls who know anything about the pyramids. So how likely is it—"

A deep breath made itself heard in the living room. I could still hear Eli's even breathing in the bedroom, so it wasn't her.

"Bell," Zian said on the other end. "You cut out there. What were you going to say?"

"Just saying no one but us would have recognized the stones for what they were."

"The Conclave might have. Hard to believe our Non-Man In Black didn't take them into account when he came over to our world."

The breath came again, louder this time.

"I swear, something is cutting you off," my hacker buddy said with irritation. "Everything alright with your phone?"

"Yeah, Zian," I said, knowing something else in this room was anything but alright. "So what do you think—"

The breath came one more time, turning into a mini-scream. That's when I figured out where the noise was coming from: the uncovered lapis lazuli.

"Bell, what's happening?" Zian asked on the other end in alarm.

The pitch of the scream got higher and higher as blue dust flowed off the gems and into an azure cloud. I stepped back as the cloud took human shape and form. Did I manage to set off a trap?

Eli threw open the door of the bedroom and saw the

same apparition my eyes were glued to. I raised my knife, but Eli grabbed my hand.

"Wait," she pleaded, her face full of hope.

I could make out details of the smoke figure, which had taken a female form. The cloud retained a tether to the stones it came from, seeming to feed it power and energy that made sketching out the cloud's details happen.

"Bell?!" Zian all but shouted into the phone.

When a familiar face formed on the figure's head, I said, "I'm going to need to call you back, Zian."

"Is everything—"

"If it isn't, you'll be the first to know," I said, hanging up.

As the creative process of the stones finished, Sarit slumped over in exhaustion. But her face brightened again as she spotted Eli.

"Brother," she said, her voice a faint whisper. "You still live."

"Only by the continuing grace of the All-High and continued help of Bell," Eli said with relief.

Sarit turned to me. "It is pleasing to...truly...meet you face-to-face, sir. I felt your...presence at the...warehouse. But...I could...say nothing."

"Mind telling me how this conversation is even possible?" I asked, still not seeing how the pieces connected.

"When you broke the seal, you...gave me back a piece of...my power," Sarit explained. "It is...insufficient to be able...to break free of...the ifrit. But it was...enough to project...a piece of my...soul through the gems."

Going on a hunch, I asked, "Is that piece of the soul the same one Jones extracted from the workers to put in the gemstones?"

She raised her eyebrows. "Yes, how did you—"

"As we suspected, dear sister," Eli explained, pushing past me to be near Sarit. "Mr. Vale is quite knowledgeable about how our world truly works. He also entertained a theory that the ifrit's power derived from the taking of the True Names of those poor victims. Can you confirm this for us?"

"It is so," Sarit said with great sadness in her voice. Her form lost some of its definition before swirling back into focus.

"Before we go any further," I said urgently, "how long can you keep the lines of communication open?"

"Not long," Sarit admitted. "But long enough to tell you...the counter-pattern."

"The one that'll break Iblis' Bane?" I asked, not daring to hope.

Sarit nodded.

"But how did you come by this, sister?" Eli asked.

"Our foe is nothing if not boastful," Sarit said, the details blurring yet again. "He showed me how to...undo...my bonds to...toy with me."

More and more of Sarit's cloud projection was turning into smudges. Gritting her teeth, Sarit willed her body to become stable again.

"Hurry," she said with her teeth clenched. "I have not much longer."

Pulling up the picture of Sarit's brand on my phone, I laid it down on the coffee table. Snatching up the pen on the right side, I drew out the pattern on the paper. Sarit nodded and, to my surprise, was substantial enough to take the pen from me. She then drew out the counter-pattern; adding a few extra lines to the existing framework changed the shape entirely. It took everything she had left to draw it. The pen clattered on the table as she fell apart.

"Hurry, brother," she said as the gems sucked her back in. "I have not..."

And then she was gone, the dust receding as though the stones were a vacuum cleaner.

Eli held her hands to her mouth and tears sparkled in her eyes. I grabbed her by the shoulders and comforted her. "At least we know she's fine for the moment. And we've got what we need to set her free. We need to find her and the ifrit, that's all."

Eli dropped her hands and looked at me. "But can you truly promise we will find them in time?"

I knew better than to answer.

———

After that dramatic episode, there was no point in either of us trying to get to back to sleep. We spent the next two hours practicing the counter-pattern Sarit gave us. Eli paid attention to what order the extra strokes were added, and made sure I got them right. We went through half a stack of computer paper in the process.

It was frustrating but necessary. When the time came to break the magic for real, there would be no second chances. Plus, given what we learned last night, it might be more than Sarit we needed to free.

It was getting close to noon when a text came through my phone...Kennedy. Her message was brief and to the point: "Check out my old boss on TV."

I put down the pen and picked up the remote on the couch. Eli watched in fascination as the TV screen came to life. Onscreen was some cooking competition show; the host running it thought his British accent gave him a license to abuse the contestants. I ignored him and flicked over to Headliner News.

The banner on the underside of the screen read, *HELL-FIRE CEO ISSUES OFFICIAL STATEMENT ON WARE-HOUSE FIRE.* Eli's eyes hardened as Khalim Jones stepped up to the podium. He was flanked by security guards who were going for the Secret Service getup: dark glasses, three-piece suits and dead faces. Something about them bothered me, but I couldn't put my finger on it.

I focused on Jones next; he was dressed in a custom-made dark blue suit, and he looked every bit the dapper gentleman he was supposed to be. None of the damage he suffered during our last encounter showed. I shuddered to think how he accomplished that small miracle, and how many poor souls gave up their lives to strengthen his.

"Thank you all for coming," Jones began as he spoke into the microphone. "While the fire at the Ashton warehouse is a blow to our company, I nevertheless remain glad there was no further loss of human life. As with the previous tragedy, we are fully cooperating with the Cold City Police Department and look forward to being able to help them catch the arsonist or arsonists involved."

As he talked, I texted Zian, *Press conference on Headliner right now. Check security personnel for IDs.*

"I would like to take this moment to express my great sadness at the senseless murders of our workers," Jones continued. "To be killed in so horrific a manner for only—"

"Does anything about those people next to Jones look familiar?" I asked Eli.

She shook her head and shrugged. "I am still having trouble adjusting to the idea of a magic eye that sees things from far away as they happen. And you all look the same to me." I frowned, before remembering her kind uses smells to differentiate people.

"So, in conclusion," Jones said, grabbing our attention, "if anyone has information that could lead to the capture of either the murderers of our workers or the arsonists of our building, I urge them to contact the police as soon as it is possible. Should you wish to remain anonymous, you may also contact our corporate offices to pass along such information."

I thought that last part sounded like a field day for the DA's office. Any privacy Jones was guaranteeing would likely evaporate under the threat of obstruction of justice.

I could make out a woman right behind the well-tailored muscle guarding Jones. While getting a good look at her features was impossible, I could see she was roughly five foot five, wore a dark pantsuit and had her eyes glued to Jones at all times. Oh, well...Maybe I'd get a better look at her when this conference wrapped up.

On-screen, Jones did the verbal equivalent of pulling the pin of a grenade. "While this is hardly the forum I would have chosen, I feel compelled to make one more announcement. Despite our recent tragedies, I am pleased to announce we will be opening up our very first boutique within the next few weeks. These will be stocked with designs exclusive to the store, of which we will be providing the opportunity for the public to try them out at this week's fashion show. If you would like to hear further details..."

At that point, I blanked out the rest of his words. A store exclusively for Hellfire's products coupled with a chance to wear them at the most prominent cultural event going on in Cold City...Who needed all those other stores? Jones had leveraged two significant crimes into a marketing coup that would help him finish what the soul extractions started.

Jones walked away from the podium, a flurry of questions right on his heels. His muscle clung around him like a protective barrier, exposing the face of the woman I'd seen behind him. She wasn't what you call beautiful, dull brown hair in a bun, what looked like equally brown eyes, average skin color, and a slightly oversized nose. But she had confidence and poise that made up for her plainness. She was right behind the bodyguards.

Zian fired off a text that provided the final nail on the ugly coffin we witnessed.

Security guys match missing persons from Galatas Incident. The woman behind them is Fawcett.

14

GIRL TROUBLE

A knock on the door stopped my puzzlement short. Holding up a finger to Eli, I called out, "Yes?"

"Open up, Vale," Morgan's unwelcome voice said from the other side. "We need to talk."

"Got a warrant, Lieutenant?"

The irritation in Morgan's voice went up a notch. "You got two choices. You can either open up the door, or I come back with that warrant and bust you for obstruction of justice. How do you want to play it?"

One thing Morgan never did was bluff. So I said, "Yeah, give me a minute."

"Fifty-eight seconds and counting."

I pointed Eli towards the bedroom. She shook her head, her expression getting stubborn. I made a face myself and pointed towards the bedroom again. I wanted to do the bare minimum on explaining anything to Morgan. Having a beautiful woman in the same room would make that more complicated than it needed to be.

Eli stared daggers at me and stormed back into the room with a huff. I noticed her gait was more like a man's as she walked. I wondered how she found the strength to shut the door rather than slamming it like I knew she wanted to.

"Forty-five seconds," Morgan called out, snapping me out of my thought process.

Might as well get this over with, I thought as I shut off the TV. Getting off the couch, I unlocked the door and opened it. Morgan was on the other side, peering down at the watch on his left arm. It was an ancient, slightly scratched up Timex Ironman, held to the arm by a black plastic wristband in place of the original metal one. Morgan hit the timer button on it and nodded.

"Thirty-seven seconds and change," he said. "That's faster than I expected."

"Can we get on with this, Morgan?" I asked, stepping aside to let him in. "I've got things to do today."

"What kind of things?" Morgan asked as he stepped in, his eyes sweeping the place with a cop's eye.

"PI things," I said, shutting the door behind him. "The kind of things that pay my bills every month and sometimes pisses you off."

Morgan grunted. Guess he wasn't too irritated with me right now...which was strange.

Sitting down on the loveseat, he contemplated the door with appreciation. "Nice replacement job on the front door... doesn't come off as cheap."

"Yeah, well," I said, going over to my electric kettle in the kitchen. "Nothing like a serious attempt on your life to make you think about security."

"True," Morgan admitted as I filled the kettle. "The

Hellfire people could have learned something from that line of thought."

Got to give it to Morgan, though he is pompous, self-righteous and hates me with a passion, he's anything but dumb. Sure, he plays at it, but that's a snare. Every time he rattles a perp's cage with his words, his eyes and ears are soaking in every detail that slips through the bars. For me, he's a lot easier to deal with when he's hopping mad. But him being relatively calm made me worried. He was laying out a trap I may not have been prepared for.

"Can't offer any doughnuts," I said as I turned the kettle on. "But maybe you're up for some coffee?"

The scowl etched onto Morgan's face was priceless. One of the few things Morgan hated more than me was cop stereotypes. "We both know you gag at the smell of a latte from Starbucks. Just give me some of that green tea crap you keep on hand."

I threw him a mocking salute. "Aye, aye, lieutenant. So other than insulting my choice of hot beverages, what brings you by today?"

"Ashton warehouse on Pickfair," Morgan said while I got the tea bags. "You heard about what's gone down there?"

"Just saw the news conference on Headliner," I answered, tilting my head towards the blank TV screen. "Don't give a shit about a building in Cold City getting the demolition treatment. But Jones mentioned some dead workers?"

Morgan's face got hard. "Yeah, about a dozen sweatshop workers found dead there the day before. Funny thing...First, we heard about it was from a 911 call that mentioned some-body thrown through the upstairs office window. Then our caller sees a sleek, expensive car fleeing the scene. Anybody with wheels like that should be pretty easy to track, don't you think? And then there's you, buying groceries from a shop nearby a few hours before."

I shrugged. "I was out of mouthwash; that's not a crime, is it?"

"No, but that's enough to make me want to ask you some questions," Morgan said with an unpleasant smile. "Here's a good one: how do all those dead people downstairs connect with the struggle we found signs of all over the upstairs?"

The kettle had hit full boil by this point. I grabbed a couple of mugs. "You got me. Maybe one of them was trying to get away and ran upstairs because the doors were covered. Maybe the perp had a sick sense of humor and wanted to do something special to one of them."

That damn smile was still plastered on Morgan's face; it made me wonder if I shouldn't have taken my chances with him coming back for that warrant.

The kettle shut off. I put the tea bags in the cups and poured.

"So...where were you yesterday between the hours of noon and midnight?" Morgan asked.

"Working a missing person case," I said, glancing between him and the steeping tea. "I've got a client who lost track of a sister after the downtown blasts."

The suspicious look in Morgan's eye told me he wasn't buying it. "And who is this mystery client?"

The bedroom door opened with an audible squeak, and Eli stepped out. In place of the clothes she'd got from Tommy, she was now wearing one of my dress shirts as a nightgown. I did a facepalm as Eli said, "That, sir, would be me."

Morgan's eyes ran over Eli's body appreciably. "And who might you be?"

"Louisa Albertson," my client said as she stepped into the living room with a seductive swing in her hips. "Mr. Vale has been a *tremendous* help in locating my sister's whereabouts."

The smile on Morgan's face turned into a full-fledged leer. "I take it you paid Mr. Vale here with...services?"

Eli's expression went cold. "Mr. Vale works for his money as surely as I do. That is why I paid him the reasonable sum of $4000 to do this job."

"Okay, okay," Morgan said, holding up his hands. "None of my business, I get it. Still, I know a certain detective of mine who would be interested to hear about you."

By then, the tea was ready, and I threw away the bags with more force than was necessary. I contemplated sweetening Morgan's with some arsenic before settling on a dash of the same sugar I put in mine.

I moved back to the living room, my face as sour as the drinks in my hand.

Taking the tea from me, Morgan said, "So...this sister. She was caught up in that business downtown?"

"No, her disappearance occurred after those unfortunate events," Eli said, sitting down on the couch. "Sarit—that is my sister's name, by the way—came to Cold City to help with the cleanup efforts underway."

Morgan took a sip of the tea and asked, "She was contracted through the city, then?"

Eli crossed her legs. "She was part of a private effort. I

would tell you more, but one of the conditions of helping out was the persons behind it insisted upon anonymity."

"Ah, an NDA, huh?"

Eli's eyes got a confused look again, but she covered it with a sad sigh. "Whatever misfortunes have befallen her, I blame myself for not being there to protect her. So...am I now under arrest, Lieutenant?" she asked, staring intensely into his eyes. I heard the gold tones in her voice.

Morgan shook his head a little, and his eyes lost some of their certainty. "No, not at this time. Still, I would appreciate it if you could account for Mr. Vale's movements here during the hours of noon and midnight yesterday."

With carefully chosen words, Eli did that. She mentioned me picking her up—leaving off that it was at the morgue—our going to the Tombs, her getting money from a secure location to pay me and meeting up with Zian to chase down leads.

"Wait," Morgan said, looking up from his notes. "This wouldn't be the same Zianyon who was nearly a victim of the shooting spree that tried punching through your front door, would it?"

"That's him," I confirmed. "All the contact info you got from him last year is still current."

Morgan nodded and finished up his notes. "Well...any friend of yours is usually a suspect. But he seemed like a sweet enough kid. He vouches for you, that should be enough to get you off the hook." I felt myself relax as Morgan got up and sat the cup down on the coffee table. Then the smile came back, and Morgan added, "For now."

The seals we left all over the table caught his attention.
Dammit, why didn't I think of that before?

"Interesting drawings," he said, picking up one of them. "You considering a career in fashion, Vale?"

"The less you know, the better," I said, never uttering more truthful words to my longtime nemesis.

He chuckled as he put the drawing back down. "Let me know how that line works on Ramirez."

I felt my heart sink as I let him out. I was paranoid enough to listen for his footsteps to recede before I said anything else.

"How much does this man know of our world?" Eli asked, concern dawning on her face.

"Nothing, and I'd like to keep it that way," I admitted. "Problem is, Morgan knows I'm always less than honest about this stuff when it comes up. It makes him keep digging like the bear he is."

Eli tilted her head in consideration. "He does resemble a bear, does he not? Territorial, protective, fierce...to say nothing of the clear concern he has for your safety."

"Don't know if you caught that," I said with a crooked grin as I collected Morgan's mug, "but I'm not one of his favorite people. If he'd found me splattered on the pavement outside the warehouse, I doubt he'd bat an eye."

"That would only be because he was deciding how to best avenge your death. He is a man who cares for all human life and mourns every time it is senselessly snuffed out like a candle wick."

Her words made me pause; I never thought of Morgan like that. But the way Eli was describing him, it made a certain kind of sense. I realized it was the only thing making sense in my head at the moment. I got up and felt woozy as I dropped Morgan's cup into the sink.

Eli caught onto that too and asked, "Are you feeling the need to have some rest yourself?"

"Yeah," I admitted. "Couldn't sleep worth a damn all morning, but I feel it now."

"Then to bed," Eli said, steering me towards the bedroom. "It is now my turn to stand watch at the door while you rest."

Before I knew it, she'd steered me to the bed and was laying me down. She pulled off my shirt to reveal the clothes she got from Tommy underneath.

I gave her a look. "I could have sworn you—"

"It is much easier to cast an illusion over a portion of the body than it is to create a full set of clothes," Eli said. "Besides, was it not useful in establishing your alibi?"

I nodded and felt myself fading again. The last thing I remember, before losing consciousness, was Eli leaving the room.

———

My eyes snapped open. Even through the covers on me, I felt a chill in the room. I didn't have to search around long to find the source leaning against the back left corner. I was wondering when I'd hear from Lady McDeath again.

Today, she was wearing an outfit that would fit with a Playboy spread, a matching black lace bra and panties set with garter belt and stockings. It was a nice contrast to her too-white skin, and her platinum blonde hair made her look as pale as the moon. A slash of dark red lipstick contrasted with both colors and her dark eyes pinned me to the bed like a butterfly pinned by a throwing knife.

"Took you long enough," I said in my usual flippant fashion. I noticed how things felt...wrong somehow.

That's when my heart decided to stop beating for a second. It started up again as Lady McDeath pushed herself off the wall to walk over to the bed; her way of saying 'hello' when she was annoyed with me.

Ignoring the squeeze, I asked, "So what did I do wrong this time?"

"It is more than you," she said as she took a step closer to me. "I have a list of grievances that encompasses some of your associates."

I shrugged. "Alright, fire away."

"Candice Kennedy," she began. "You have once again made her privy to matters that originate from Alternum Mundum."

"She's a valuable contact, and I've been doing my best to keep her on the edges," I protested. "Is it my fault she—"

"Yes," she interrupted, putting an extra hiss on the word. "Whatever you were about to say, yes, it *is* your fault she now knows enough to keep searching. Certain parties are very troubled by this development."

I got a smug smile on my face. "Word I hear is it's hardly a unanimous opinion."

"Whatever the Messenger may have told you, Bellamy Vale, it was not the complete truth. But this is...Candice Kennedy needs to be kept away from any further secrets."

I got a little hot. "You hear me arguing otherwise? The problem is I've got nothing that could convince her to back off."

"You better find it...and soon."

"Okay, so that's one associate. Who else is working your last nerve?"

"This man, Morgan…He suspects our existence far too close for comfort."

I growled as I leaned back on the headboard. "Are we really going to go there? The last thing I want is for Morgan to get wise, mostly for legal reasons."

"And yet you insist on antagonizing him, lying to him and laying down false trails he can easily detect."

That one stung a bit. "Oh, I'm sorry. I thought the idea was to keep him away from the truth. You've got a better idea on how to handle it, I'm all ears. The man's a headache."

Lady McDeath gave me a calculating look. "There have been talks of sanctioning him to prevent any—"

"No!" My heart stopped again, this time for quite a few more seconds.

"Do you need another reminder on who takes orders from whom?" Lady McDeath asked while the squeeze was on.

I gasped as she let go, but I gave her a hard stare. "I don't know how it works on your side of the border, but cop killings are never good news here, especially if the victims have rank. If you take Morgan off the count, I'll be the prime suspect. That adds more complications to the mix and makes me being able to do what I need to do for you harder."

She frowned but nodded, her red lips pursing. "Very well…that shall be considered. But there is one final associate who has neither deep ties nor long history with you…The jinni."

Remembering an earlier conversation with Zian, I said,

"From what I've been told, they did something major to piss off Hermes at least a thousand years ago."

"It was more than the Messenger," Lady McDeath confirmed, her frown deepening. "That race took actions so beyond the pale—"

"Pun intended?"

She gave me a withering glare before continuing with, "Suffice to say, those certain parties I referred to before have grave concerns over their presence in this city."

I fought not to let on a smile as an idea bloomed in my head. "Well, from what I've put together, that one *is* sort of my fault. My little game plan to shut down the Underworld gate pulled my client, her sister and their mortal enemy to our city."

Lady McDeath took two more steps towards me, her gait so light it was as though she floated rather than walked. "I feel as though I should be surprised, and yet I am not."

I shrugged, keeping the charade up. "So you see, because it is partly my mess, I owe it to everybody to clean it up."

"No, you do not," she said, the dark fires flicking to life in her eyes. She reached for my throat, her cold fingers making it near impossible to breathe. "The best thing you could do, Bellamy Vale, is drop this case altogether and allow others to handle the situation."

"I don't know how much attention you've been paying..." I wheezed, "...but I am way past being able to let this one go. I'm on the ifrit's radar...and he's on the warpath for both me...*and*...my client."

Her grip tightened on my throat to the point where I felt her fingers link at the back of my neck. The bones should have snapped under the strain—they didn't. "Wait a minute...you haven't been able to keep your usual eagle eye on me, have you?"

"Careful," she growled. Cerberus would have whined at her voice.

"Yeah, careful," I said, running with the thought. "That's why...you're contacting me...right now. You're doing it through...my dreams...because you don't want the jinni to... get wise. Or maybe it's the ifrit...you're trying to duck."

"This was never a task you should have been involved in," she said, getting in my face. "That you persist in it to the point of trying my patience is a terrible idea. So, when you awaken, you will tell your client you are dropping the case completely. If you fail to do this, I promise what I am doing now is the least painful way I can take your life."

The vise around my throat loosened up. As I gasped, I said back, "So I have your permission to break your word?"

Lady McDeath's hostility mixed with confusion on her face. "Say that again?"

"Your word," I repeated. "I gave Eli my word that I would find her sister and take down the ifrit. And since I'm your representative on this side of the border, it meant I also gave *your* word."

She pulled her head back as her eyes narrowed. She glared at me as a hawk looks at a mouse. "This is a trick."

"What, you're saying that your word isn't your bond?" I asked, sensing I hit the right sore spot. "Bet some of those 'certain parties' you keep bringing up might want to know about that. They might have to do something drastic to fix the situation you're going to like even less than what I'm going to do."

The confusion faded away to understanding...and more

anger. I swore I could see dark clouds roll up behind her lithe silhouette.

"Yeah, I get it, you don't like jinn," I continued. "But as I said, it's way too late to turn back now. I've got to see this through to the end...for *all* our sakes."

I was bluffing a little on the "all" part of that last sentence, but Lady McDeath seemed to think I was onto something.

"Very well, finish it," she said, gliding away from the bed. "But understand that incurring my wrath will one day have severe consequences."

She vanished, and I felt a wave of pain hit my head...

———

It stayed with me as I woke up in a cold sweat. I gasped for air while I wiped it away with the sheets. Conversations with my patroness were never pleasant, but some were worse than others. All that went through my aching head as the phone rang...

Ramirez.

I said hello with a sinking feeling in my stomach. The only answer back was a stream of Spanish invective that went on for a minute and didn't pause for a single breath.

"Nice to hear from you too," I said back.

"What was that woman doing in your apartment?" she asked back, her voice in no-bullshit-accepted mode.

"She's a client, Mel," I said. "Just a client and that's it. She and I didn't—"

"I know you didn't."

It stopped me colder than Lady McDeath's stare. "Huh?"

"Oh, I know what Morgan wanted me to think happened," she explained. "I ran her name through the system, and it lit up like a Christmas tree."

The pounding in my head got worse at her words. "I didn't ask for her resume before accepting her case."

"Per her rap sheet, we have her down for solicitation, a few counts of petty theft, even a vagrancy charge back in the day. But the scuttlebutt was she'd become a high-end hooker with a very exclusive clientele, top dollar. She'd be way out of your price range."

Sensing an exit, I added, "But that'd also explain why she was able to pay better than my usual rates to search for her sister."

That was all the opening Ramirez needed to pounce. "Yeah, about that...her juvie file has her down as an only child. Then there's the part where she's been dead in the morgue for the last three days. Care to explain, Mr. Vale?"

"Is this my girlfriend or the homicide detective asking?" I snapped back.

"Both...so talk."

"Alright, how about this?" I asked, doing my best to improvise my way through the conversation. "We both know the State doesn't always recognize true family if there's no bloodline involved."

"Okay, I can buy that, but what about the part of getting over being dead?"

"Misidentification of the corpse," I said. "Happens all the time. Why not recheck the body to see if they got it wrong?"

"It's not my first day on the job, Bell," Ramirez said. "That's what I did before calling you. Imagine my surprise when Sam tells me he can't find the corpse and is very certain where he left it in the freezer wall."

"Maybe something happened while he wasn't working?" I suggested. "It's not like she could have got back to her feet and left on her own."

"Exactly what he said," Ramirez continued. "That's why he'll be running it down for me when he goes on shift this evening."

Rubbing my head, I said, "Look, Mel...if nothing else, the money she pays me with is genuine. So is the missing sister. I'm close to a breakthrough in all this, and I'd appreciate if you give me the space to wrap this up."

Ramirez's voice was far from comforting. "If you're bullshitting me, Vale, we're done. Do you understand? You want a relationship with me, you keep it by being more honest than this."

I was still figuring out what to say when she hung up on me. I moaned and got out of bed. The door opened to show Eli on the other side.

I gave her a wary look. "I hope you appreciate the trouble I'm going through here. The women in my life are no joke."

"I do," Eli said. "Otherwise, I never would have come to your aid when the lieutenant was interrogating you."

There was a spike in pain in my head. "Let me get some aspirin. After that, there's someone I want you to meet."

Yeah, I wanted to keep Kennedy out of all this. But I had a hunch she was the one contact I had who might be able to show me the way out of this.

15

TROUBLED STONES

Kennedy gave the lapis lazuli hunk a hard stare while we all leaned against the side of her news van. I was on her left, looking at her as hard as she was looking at the stone. Eli gave her a more casual look from the right. If you went by her lean, you'd think she was waiting for the bus to roll up.

"Correct me if I'm wrong here, hoss," Kennedy said, "but wasn't the whole point of blowing up them pyramids was so these stones couldn't cause any more trouble?"

"There is no way you could have known," Eli said with a gentle shake of her head. "Either of you."

I peered down the street to get a look at the Taco Bell on the corner. Kennedy got my attention with an annoyed swat on the forearm. "Would you relax already, Bell? My boy Ralph ain't coming out of that restaurant until five minutes after the lunch break is over. I'd say it still gives us about ten minutes."

"Yeah, well, force of habit," I admitted, turning back to

her. "This is the sort of thing I don't like talking about in public." I nodded towards the small stream of passing pedestrians walking around us.

"And why exactly would they care again?" Kennedy reminded me. "Most of them are going to their jobs, going to lunch themselves or going home. I'd think a certified bigshot PI like you'd know how this whole 'hiding in plain sight' thing works."

She had a point, sort of. Eli was wearing one of my shirts, which she tied above the waist, and a black skirt that had to be something Ramirez left behind. Kennedy went for a more casual look, rocking low boots, tight jeans, and a pale rose turtleneck sweater. Both women had their hair untied. There was a breeze disturbing the air, which forced them to rearrange strands and curls at intervals. All in all, I guess we looked like three friends having a chat in a parking lot.

"It certainly has its advantages," Eli admitted. "So long as certain...precautions are always maintained."

"You see what she's saying there? So relax already."

"I don't know if I can," I admitted. "Frankly, Ralphie-boy coming back too early doesn't make the top twenty list of problems we've got in front of us."

Kennedy tapped the pointer of her free hand on the side of the van. "No way Zian can head off any of the stuff going to those new shops like he did the others?"

Eli sighed in frustration. "We have requested he try this. Those deliveries were made under false pretenses the same day the other orders were sent out."

Kennedy turned to her and frowned. "Ain't sure I'm following you, girlfriend."

Eli pulled her head back. "We are not currently in a relationship. Why do you call me 'girlfriend'?"

I winced. Eli's cultural illiteracy remained a great way to stand out to any of Jones' people or hench-shadows. "She's saying the orders to the new shops falsified their invoices to be stuff other than what was in them. As long as it wasn't drugs or people, I doubt anybody would care."

"Speaking of shipping people," Kennedy said, pushing for the side of the van. "I think I might have a line on our mysterious Ms. Fawcett."

She reached into her pocket to pull out a notepad. Using the hand holding the pad, she thumbed the pages until she got to the middle section.

"Here we go," she said. "A contact of mine in the precinct—"

"They don't know Ramirez, do they?" I interrupted.

Kennedy gave me an irritated glare. "He's a file clerk the regular cops don't notice anymore. Now, if you're done interrupting, I'd like to tell you what I found, okay?"

I glanced over her shoulder to see Eli holding in a laugh. At my annoyed look, she shrugged. I sighed, looked at Kennedy and nodded.

"Anyhow," Kennedy said. "My contact mentioned how they managed to bust and hold onto some coyote a few days back."

"A people-trafficker?" Eli asked, seeing the connection.

Kennedy glanced at her over her shoulder. "Surprised you know that one."

"We ran across one while we were sniffing around," I explained, leaving out the Tommy-related details. "Did this guy specialize in menial labor transport?"

Kennedy turned to me in surprise. "Yeah...yeah, he did.

That's what made what the CCPD caught him with a little strange. They arrested him with a load of girls."

"Children?" Eli asked in alarm.

"Not that young, honey. But they were the kind of young and dumb I've seen plenty of rich men keep for trophies."

Eli's eyes narrowed in understanding. "In other words, they were the kind of women that would populate a seraglio."

"Damn, girl!" Kennedy said in amazement. "I haven't heard that term outside of Robert E. Howard's *Conan* stories. Where did you say you came from again?"

"I'm still missing the part on how this connects back to Fawcett," I said, wanting to keep Kennedy's attention on the case and away from Eli's origins. I told her most of what we knew, but I seriously fudged on all the ins and outs of Eli's true nature.

"Well, our coyote boy clammed up until his lawyer got there to bail him out," Kennedy said, looking back down at the notepad. "The girls got turned over to ICE, on their way back to whatever hellhole they got scooped up from. The standout detail was the lawyer, Rex Rodgers. Judging from the perp's financials, that mouthpiece was way out of his price range."

"The slave trade has always been a very profitable business," Eli said with deep sadness. "Riches enough to retain those who would protect them are far from unheard of."

Kennedy nodded but kept her eyes glued on the notepad. "Sure, but this guy was a minnow. Last year, he tried starting up a gang of baby bangers that broke up when shooting up a block party landed most of them with a quarter-to-forever."

Eli looked at me with her usual confusion over the strange terms.

"They were thugs who were sloppy about who they killed," I explained. "And worse at getting away with it."

Kennedy pointed at me with the stone as she nodded. "So how does a guy like our wannabe human trafficker rate a lawyer he couldn't have afforded if he'd worked a drug corner for the next hundred years?"

"He didn't," I said, putting it together. "Someone else paid for Rodgers, and that someone must have been Fawcett."

"Our clerk boy didn't know that bit, I oughta add. But yeah, it's who I found at the end of the money trail when I did a little extra poking around. But it's not the best part." Her thumb flicked back one more page. "My snooping found one other tidbit that didn't make sense. It turns out our Ms. Fawcett is now the proud owner of a strip club."

I looked at Eli to explain, but she raised her hand. "No need to explain that one, Bell. My time watching...reality TV, I think Zian called it...informed me on this matter."

"It's called *Ali Pasha*," Kennedy explained. "It's set to open up at the end of the month. Funny thing, though...I slipped into the place and, as far as I can tell, it could open for business tonight."

"How much do you want to bet the girls that got caught were supposed to be the club's dancers?" I said. "And now they're gone..."

"Yeah, since there's no cast, there's no play." Kennedy scrunched up her face in frustration. "But why do this at all? Fawcett is part of the hottest fashion company in Cold City right now. There should be enough business coming to Hellfire to keep them busy until the next ice age. There wouldn't be the kind of time they'd need to run a strip club on top of all that."

"But does this company not employ women who are... less than shy about nakedness?" Eli asked with her hand on her chin.

Kennedy gave her a smile that felt like it was reserved for educating the intelligent but naïve. "Despite what you might have heard, sweetie, models usually make lousy strippers. Sure, they look hot in high-end fashion clothes, but a lot of them lack in..." She dropped her hands under her bust. Given what I'd seen of the semi-nude models backstage the other night, I could see her point.

Eli leaned her head back against the van and closed her eyes. Any decent photographer who'd snapped her in that pose would have had a job about five seconds after he showed it off. "Still, my sense of the matter is these things are connected...The dresses, the exploited we continue to find, the establishments that treat women as chattel, the stones."

I banged my fist against the van door. "I don't see how, though. I mean, in the beginning, we thought our perp wanted to get away. Now...it's looking a lot bigger than I thought."

Kennedy casually tossed the stone up and down. "Still, going by what you two are saying, it's bad...and likely gonna get worse." Taking another hard stare at the lapis lazuli, she added, "Just one thing I don't get...why all the trouble to disguise this thing if you, me and Zian are the only ones who even—"

I pushed myself off the news van as I realized something. "It wasn't about disguise. It was about function."

Eli and Kennedy gave me a curious look as I asked, "Eli, that thing you did with my knife the other night...Could that be the reason we were able to uncover the stone?"

Eli's eyes widened as understanding dawned in them. "Al-Khem...of course."

"Hey, is that related to alchemy?" Kennedy asked, pointing at Eli with her notepad hand.

"Yes, it is the base root of what you call alchemy, the great tradition of transmutation. But in Al-Khem, the material itself remains unaltered. But the energy within it..."

"Energy is neither created nor destroyed, only changed."

Eli pointed at Kennedy herself in excitement. "Yes, that is it exactly! How did you know?"

"Second Law of Thermodynamics," Kennedy said with a bit of embarrassment. "I was a little bit of a science geek for a while."

"The important thing is it wasn't an illusion," I said, running with the thought as I got in front of Kennedy. "Jones altered the stones' energy to make them work for him."

Eli's eyes got sad again. "With the purloined materials he got from those poor, unfortunate souls we failed to save as paint."

"And now he wants to sell these to the public," Kennedy said, aghast. "He's planning on sucking the life force out of thousands."

I nodded and was about to say something when my smartphone went off. The familiar ringtone of *Do You Wanna Date My Avatar* told me it was Zian. I answered it.

"I have good news and bad news," Zian announced.

"And I don't have time for games," I replied.

Kennedy and Eli were both staring at me, and I mouthed Zian's name to let them know who it was.

"Good news it is," my hacker-friend said, and the fact he sounded anything but joyful told me how bad the other news had to be, "I have a location on Jones. He pulled up at some new strip club downtown."

It was easy to guess which one. "Ali Pasha?"

"Correctamundo," Zian said, "How did y—"

"Never mind, what's the bad news?"

Eli tensed at my words. I raised a palm to halt any questions she may have.

"I ran the club's name into several databases to see what I could find," Zian explained, "and my computer lit up like the Red District. Which means..."

"...someone else's been looking into it," I finished for him. "Tell me it's not..."

"...our friends at the CCPD?" Zian finished. "I wish I could, but one Detective Sergeant Melanie Ramirez filed the latest info request."

A lump of lead settled in my stomach. "Does it say why?"

"Something to do with a missing persons' case she's working." Zian paused. "Surprised me, I thought she was homicide."

"Yeah, but the MP unit is short-staffed, and they've been working round the clock since the Galatas Incident. They asked other units for help. Who is she after?"

There was a long pause on the line, and I realized I hadn't heard the bad news yet. I leaned a hand against the side of the news van as I waited for the shoe to drop.

"Emma Fawcett."

16

WEAK FLESH

I tried calling Ramirez several times as we drove to Ali Pasha, but I kept getting her voicemail. Eli was in the passenger seat while Kennedy sat in the back. We left her van in the parking lot and the keys in the ignition for her cameraman to find whenever lunch break was over.

I hung up the phone with a curse and hit Zian's speed dial.

He picked up on the first ring. "Yeah?"

"I can't reach Ramirez; can you track her phone?" I asked.

"Trying," he said. "Give me a few minutes."

"You've got about five until we reach the club," I said, taking a sharp turn onto Eighth Avenue, a long, linear stretch of black asphalt that crossed through Cold City north to south. The V8 engine of the Corvette roared through the midday flow of soccer mom wagons and door-to-door salesmen hatchbacks.

Eli grabbed the side handle as I zigzagged through cars

and trucks, all the way down south. I could see the ocean-front on the horizon when I was forced to slow down and turn into a smaller street. Two more left turns, and we would reach our destination.

"I'm afraid I have more bad news," Zian said, as I completed turn number one.

It didn't take a genius to figure it out. "She's at the club?"

"I'm sorry," Zian said. "I'm on my way. Don't do anything stupid before I get there."

He hung up as I took the last turn. I felt like kicking myself. I was so wrapped up in my case that I hadn't called Ramirez in days. I had no idea what she was working on. *If I'd known, if I'd taken the time to call her up and see what she was up to...*

"I'm sure she'll be fine." Kennedy laid a reassuring hand on my shoulder. "She's though; she can handle herself."

I parked the Stingray in front of a 7-Eleven at the end of the road, and we made it to the club on foot.

As we neared it, my phone pinged with a text from Zian. It was something he'd pulled from his Library of Alexandria database. Knowing my knowledge of Sanskrit was right up there with my understanding of rocket science, he texted me a phonetic version of an incantation. Per his text, it'd counter the energy of the lapis lazuli stones.

There was a short alley before the club. I peered into it and found what I'd hoped for: the club's service entrance.

"That's our way in," I said to the two women as I glanced down at my phone. I had a chant to learn, and time was running out.

"I'm pretty sure it's locked," Kennedy said with a frown.

"I'm pretty sure it's never stopped me before," I replied

with a smile the right amount of smug. The petite blonde rolled her eyes as I pocketed the phone and took out my lock-picking toolset. The door lost the fight.

On the other side was a dressing room for the dancers. It reminded me of the ones at the fashion show with its lights around the mirror frames. The only thing missing was a forest of cosmetics on each counter and notes of conflicting feminine perfume in the air.

Eli sniffed the air twice. She turned to me, looked over at the closed door on the other end of the room and then back at me before nodding. Kennedy shot me a questioning look. I pointed to the door and made the throat-slicing gesture to explain who was waiting for us.

I took out my Sig Sauer as I flattened myself against the side of the doorway. Just as Kennedy did the same on the opposite side, she gave me an expression that said, "Really?" She extended her hand and opened and closed it twice to indicate she wanted the gun. Meanwhile, Eli took up a position behind her on the wall.

I kept my sigh quiet as I passed her my firearm. I pulled the knife from my boot and pointed the tip at the door. *Who knows?* I thought. *It might be more effective than any pistol would be.* As soon as Kennedy locked both hands on the gun, she nodded at me. I kicked the flimsy door like it was made of toothpicks.

The door took us straight to the main stage. A sea of round, one-support tables separated us from half-a-dozen burly men in suits. They were armed with a mismatched assortment of guns you'd usually find in a street gang's hide-out. Though their gazes were vacant, something in the way they held themselves assured me they retained enough focus to aim and shoot.

They faced the front door before I let them know we were here. They whirled around as one, their fingers moving to the triggers of their weapons.

Khalim Jones stood over someone draped over one of the tables by the stage. As he turned, I could make out the form of Sarit, now wearing a long, dark, tissue-paper-thin dress. The pyramid stones, transfigured into red gems, winked off the overhead lights in the Iblis' Bane pattern. It was like she was wearing a piece of the night with red stars.

Even if you could ignore the black smoke wisps coming out of his mouth, the smile Jones greeted us with was the stuff of nightmares.

"Clever, Elijah," he said, drawing up to his full height. "To think I judged it beneath your dignity to wear the flesh of a mere woman."

Eli pushed past Kennedy and me to look Jones in the eye. "I would say the same of using mere humans as your shock troops, ifrit. But I know better."

There wasn't a sign of Ramirez, and I wasn't sure if this was good or bad news. The lump of lead was still firmly anchored to my stomach as I shifted the knife to an under-handed grip and took a step forward.

"Give up Sarit, and I might think about not ruining your week."

Jones laughed as three long shadows pulled themselves off the wall. "Why do that when I can certainly ruin yours?"

Kennedy fired at the nearest Azif on her left. The bullet hit nothing but the opposite wall. As the shadow man grabbed her, I ripped through its side with my blade. The cut sent it screaming into oblivion with a flurry of ash.

Shots rang out from behind the overhead lights, punching holes in the stage around us. We dived for the tables as Jones dragged Sarit for yet another exit door on the opposite end of the room. Kennedy yanked one of the tables down towards the stage to give us some cover. I saw the Azif slink off the stage and into the same shadows we hid amongst.

From the left side of our hidey-hole, I patted Kennedy's shoulder and pointed at the lights. "Focus on that! I've got the Azif!"

Kennedy took a second to nod before returning fire. I made out the strange shadows coming our way. They were on either side of the table so they could pin us in a squeeze play.

Below the gunfire, I could hear Jones yell at his brainwashed humans in the jinn's tongue. They charged at us, plowing through chairs and tables like a power drill through balsa wood.

I yelled out and jabbed the Azif on the left while Eli took a deep breath. She threw up her right hand as she made a grasping motion. When she closed her hand, her eyes flashed. The last Azif grabbed her hand long enough for me to cut his off.

Eli then switched hands as she gestured towards Jones, this time with a flat palm. The ifrit couldn't touch the door. I could see the faint shimmer of another hardened air barrier brought to us by jinn magic. The Sig clicked empty as I fell to the floor myself. I thanked my marine training for drilling into me the habit of always carrying several spares in my pockets.

"'Cause you never know what's around the corner, son," our LT used to say.

"Clip," I said, holding up the item in question to Kennedy. She dropped the magazine out, took my spare and reloaded without looking away from the lights. The lack of gunfire told me Jones' goons were having the same issue.

Speaking of problems, Jones was busy punching the invisible wall with his bare fists. Black flashes rolled through the barrier when each blow landed, but the wall held firm. As Eli kept her hand pointed at that spot, the flesh on her fingers began their much-delayed decomposition. She wouldn't be able to hold it forever.

"Cover fire!" I said, patting Kennedy's shoulder before I ran out from behind the table. She obliged me by aiming at the lights. One by one, they winked out while I ran over and around the tables to get to Jones. Losing the lights didn't make it harder; I only had to follow the sounds of the ifrit's fists.

I flipped the knife back to an upright position and slashed Jones across his back. A spinning backfist from him connected to my cheekbone. I blacked out for a second before I skidded across the floor, landing right next to Sarit. From what little I could make out of her features, she looked worse than the last time I saw her in the flesh.

The thought ran across my mind as a large hand grabbed me by the neck. I went flying up to the ceiling, hitting it with an agonizing crash. As I came back down, I heard Kennedy scream, "Bell!" before laying down some more shots in Jones' direction. Each shot sounded a little closer to my location than the last.

A table broke my fall, letting me bounce off it before I hit the thinly-carpeted floor. Jones didn't notice the bullets thudding into him before grabbing the charging Kennedy by the throat. To her credit, she kept shooting. She fired her last four rounds in an arc from Jones' chest to his forehead. He gave a little grunt before tossing her back towards the darkened stage.

Much as I wanted to help Kennedy, I used her distraction to my advantage. I crawled back over to Sarit, who was lying on her back. I put the knife blade next to her partially exposed chest and started cutting into the pattern on her borrowed flesh. I kept my hand steady as possible while letting my muscle memory draw out the counter-sigil. By the time Jones threw my reporter wingman into the shadows, I had finished the final cut.

Sarit gave out a big cry that immediately brought Jones' attention back to both of us. He ripped the top off the nearest table, making a jagged wooden stake out of its support. He raised it over his head to impale me through the chest. As he was about to bring it down, he tripped over the top he wrenched off and hit the floor.

My knife went across his throat the second he got close enough. He wrapped my knife arm around both of his and flipped me across him. I made out the makeshift spear he dropped sticking in the floor before I came back down again. The wood scraped my shoulder but missed my head and vital organs, but my back still felt like another sledgehammer hit it when I struck the floor.

While I struggled to get my breath back, Jones crawled

on top of me. He slammed his fist into my face with Mach one punches, demanding in a harsh whisper, "Why...will...you...not...die?"

Even with all the battering I'd been put through, I kept a death grip on my knife. When he managed to miss my head, I drove the knife under his breastbone and right into his heart. Remembering the last time I tried this, I twisted the blade. He gasped from the move, giving me enough time to wrap his left leg with my right one. I bucked my hips, rolled him over and twisted the knife one more time before I yanked it out as I stumbled back to my feet.

A glowing red light spilled out from the hole I carved in his chest. The light drew a lot closer as he slapped the floor with both arms before rising to his feet, Nosferatu-style. His hand hit my windpipe a second later and squeezed.

"Maybe you cannot die," he snarled, tightening his grip. "But I can make you wish for death's release."

He slackened the grip as he lifted me up. I slashed at him again, but he held me out of the reach of the blade. I lashed out as he squeezed, and the knife hit something solid. It set off another bright flash, which blinded me and made him let go. It also made me let go of my weapon.

I fell to my knees and shook my head as I looked up. Sarit held up a purified lapis lazuli stone while reciting an incantation. It took a second for me to realize it was the same phrase Zian gave me before the start of this lopsided battle.

She said it over and over again as she tried pushing the glowing stone into the red spot on Jones' body. All those weeks of decay took too hard a toll on her muscles, however; the ifrit had no trouble keeping the stone away from him. I got to my feet as she was knocked back.

"Grab it!" Sarit yelled as she let go of the stone.

I caught it and took up Sarit's struggle. I could hear her recite the incantation behind me, watched the crimson glow being sucked into the stone at her words. He had a harder time fighting me off than he had my client's sister.

"*Enough!*" Jones bellowed, blowing out a gust of wind that knocked me backward yet again. I managed to stay vertical while Jones lunged at the door. Nothing stopped him this time, so he was outside in seconds.

Eli has to be out of juice, I thought. Then I stopped thinking and started running.

I needn't have hurried like I thought. A dozen steps down the alley, Jones was gasping for breath like he'd run the New York Marathon twice.

But nothing was wrong with his hearing. The second he saw me over his shoulder, he said another incantation that made wings appear on his back. They looked a lot more solid than they had at the warehouse.

My hypothesis was confirmed as he used them to fly. Before he got more than a couple of inches off the ground, however, I leaped onto his back and hung on tight. The extra weight slowed him down, but he still lifted both of us straight up to the sky, flap by flap.

I wrapped my arms around him and started reciting the mantra. Yeah, I'd only seen the phonetic version twice, but hearing Sarit say it in the club was enough for me to memorize it. I could hear him grunt with each repetition of the phrase, the wings straining to keep us both aloft. My hand did its best to force the stone into his chest, fighting against both of his hands pushing back. I got so caught up in the struggle that I didn't realize we were only going up, not across.

I figured that one out when Jones looked at me with one last cheeky smile before a black cloud blew out of his mouth. The wings faded, and the dead weight of Jones' body dragged me back to the ground. The sudden tug of gravity made me lose my grip on the stone. We'd reached a height of about forty stories.

And this time, there wasn't a single soft place to land in sight.

For all the good it would do me, I let go of Jones and furiously racked my brains on how I was going to get out of this one. The ground was racing to meet me, going impossibly fast. I closed my eyes and hit something invisible and soft that slowed my descent. My eyes flew open again, and I had enough time to guess I was roughly fifteen stories up when my unseen air cushion gave out, and I dropped again. A second air mattress caught me inches away from the ground before letting me touch it.

I caught my breath before glancing around. We were in a smelly back alley behind what had to be an Indian restaurant. The smell of curry in the air was so thick that I was sure to carry it home with me.

Sarit and Eli were there, leaning heavily against a wall. Both of them were visibly drained, decayed and gasping for breath as Jones had. Sarit held my knife while Eli had my Sig in one hand and a person's wrist in the other. I struggled to my feet as I ran over to them, fearing the worst about the body. When I saw the face, I relaxed.

"The ifrit?" Sarit asked me with an anxious expression.

I slumped my shoulders and shook my head. Looking at Eli, I asked, "Kennedy?"

"Taken," she said, and I felt my inside grow cold.

Eli looked at me seriously. "How far are we from your car?"

I frowned as I tried to think. "Near as I can tell, we're about three blocks from it."

Eli gestured towards the other end of the alley, which felt like it let out on another street. "Let's go."

With some effort, Sarit ran up to her sibling's side to grab the other arm of the person she was dragging. I rang Zian's phone, reflecting on how this battle cost all of us dearly. Still, the jinn twins were dragging an unexpected consolation prize...

Emma Fawcett.

17

BETWIXT AND BETWEEN

Zian was waiting for us in the parking lot of the 7-Eleven, his bright blue eyes scanning the area for trouble. The poor kid's face went into shock as he saw Eli and Sarit. Or maybe he was reacting to our fourth passenger.

"Athena, protect us," my hacker pal said while we got her into the back of his car. "What in the depths of Tartarus happened out there?"

I lowered my way-past-weary head before putting a hand on his shoulder. "Sarit, this is Zianyon. Zian, this is Sarit, the woman we've been looking for."

"Hades damn it, don't dodge the question!" he said, passing a nervous hand through his mess of bleached-blond locks.

Eli finished pushing the comatose body of Fawcett inside the Prius before closing the door. "It would be best if we discussed this in a more protected and private setting."

I nodded in agreement, and the motion made the world go blurry around the edges. Zian grabbed my arm to steady me. "Yeah, sure...but you gotta tell me what happened to Kennedy."

Even withered from imprisonment and abuse, Sarit's face had a spark of beauty. It made her sighing look like a work of art in motion. "That, too, is something we should discuss elsewhere."

Zian's eyes grew scared, but he stopped asking questions.

"Tell me you've got info on Ramirez' location. I didn't see her at the club."

Clearing his throat, he pulled out his smartphone and swallowed hard.

"That...that lines up with what I found on the CCTV." His British accent took a quiet, defeated tone; his fingers moved slower than they usually did.

To Sarit's puzzled expression, Eli explained, "Magic eyes which watch most of this city and its people."

A minute later, he turned the smartphone to show footage of a limo pulling up at the same alley exit we escaped through. One of Hellfire's security goons had Kennedy draped over his shoulder caveman-style, apparently knocked unconscious. As he threw Kennedy into the open door in the back, Ramirez came around the corner, service weapon drawn and ready to be used.

After saying something which sounded official, she opened fire on the goon. He shrugged off the nine mils about as easy as his boss did. Three steps later, he grabbed her head with one of his catcher mitt hands. A slam into the wall stopped Ramirez's struggles completely. I blew out an outraged breath at the sight. He threw her into the back of the limo before climbing in himself, and the limo took off.

"Tell me you got a license plate, a location, something," I said.

Zian closed his eyes and shook his head. "They knew where the CCTV wasn't. I lost track of them about two blocks from that spot. Also tried tracking Kennedy's phone but..."

"Alright, we need to regroup and interrogate Fawcett. She's our only lead. Eli, you're with me." I nodded to Zian. "You take Sarit and follow us back to my place. We'll be safe there."

Zian nodded, and we got on our way.

———

The sun had set by the time we reached my building. The Prius followed me into the underground carpark and stopped next to the Corvette. The spot Zian took belonged to one of my neighbors, a senior woman who no longer owned a car. Today wasn't the first time Zian borrowed this spot to park, but he'd never dragged an unconscious woman from his backseat to the lift before.

Once everyone was situated—me on the loveseat, the jinn siblings on the couch, poor Fawcett between them and Zian next to the door—we gave my young friend the highlight reel of the fight we survived.

I spared a glance at the elusive Ms. Fawcett. "Guess that makes her our only lead. Can somebody tell me why she isn't attacking us like she and the others did in the club?"

"A psychic filter I put upon her mind at the club," Eli explained. "He cannot see through her eyes, hear through her ears, nor move her limbs as he once did."

I noted the lack of stones on her clothes. "Doesn't look like she's wearing recent Hellfire designs."

Sarit moved Fawcett enough to face her back. "Sadly, Mr. Vale, you are very mistaken."

With one motion, my client's sister ripped open the back of the dress to reveal Iblis' Bane carved on the skin. Untouched lapis lazuli stones stood out on specific points of her back, embedded into the flesh like something out of a Clive Barker film.

Zian walked up to Fawcett and aligned his right palm with hers. He closed his eyes for a minute before opening them up and putting his palm away. "She's not alive, but she's definitely not dead."

"Caught betwixt and between," Sarit confirmed. "During my captivity, I saw this pattern through the fabric of a thin shirt she wore. Iblis' Bane is a terrible thing to inflict on any human soul. Yet our quarry has done so innumerable times over the centuries."

She turned her gaze onto Zian, looking at him quizzically. "I'm surprised you were able to discern so much." She sniffed and frowned. "The smell of the old ones..."

Zian shifted uncomfortably but was saved from answering by Eli's intervention. "Not now, sister. We have more pressing matters at hand."

Sarit nodded and returned her attention fully to Fawcett. She held out a hand, and I lent her my knife as she eyed the mutilated back with some thought. "The counter-sigil will set her free as it has myself. But she is only a mortal... her body was never meant to withstand what it has. The instant I finish the design, we shall only have a few moments to converse with her."

"What about you?" I asked, finding the strength to rise from my seat. "Did me drawing the counter-sigil put you on track to have to leave that body?"

Sarit gave me a sad smile. "Nothing can truly stop that now, Mr. Vale. But you have given me leave to do so when the time to depart approaches." Putting down the knife on her lap, she raised her cold, dead hand to my shoulder. There were tears she refused to shed in her eyes. "For this, I thank you from the bottom of my heart and soul."

I took her hand and squeezed, icy touch and all. "It's fine. I know what it's like to be trapped."

"As touching as this is, sister," Eli interjected with a note of criticism. "None of us are served by the delay. Let us begin."

Sarit sighed as she dropped her hand. Picking my knife back up, she began cutting into Fawcett's back. I went around to the front so I could question her the moment she came out of it.

She gave out a gasp like Sarit did in the club. Then her breathing became jagged, shallow and rapid. She looked around in confusion, trying to figure out how she got here.

"Oh, no," she moaned. "No, no, no, no..."

"Ms. Fawcett," I said, putting my hands on her shoulders. "I'm Bellamy Vale."

The gesture made her look at me. Her eyes lit up with recognition. "I know...know you. You're the...monster hunter. You went into the blast site again and again...before I did."

"Yeah, that's me," I said. "And you're the co-founder of Hellfire. You've been enslaved by—"

"It wasn't slavery," she said in a rush.

She drew a breath, calmed down and repeated, "It wasn't slavery...it was salvation. I was...trapped in the ruins for a week. By the time...he found me, I was...I wanted to live. I wanted to keep going. I didn't care...care what I paid."

"That's when he put the stones in?"

She shivered a little harder, rattling in my grasp. "Oh God...oh, God, it hurts. It hurts so bad. I...I..."

I could feel her fading in my arms. Whatever I wanted to ask her, now was the time. "The guy who saved you...he's got a couple of friends of mine. Both of them are women. I need to know why."

She chuckled, bordering on hysteria. "Women...you know, he told me...why he brought me back. Only...a lesbian. So he tasked me with...finding quality women like...like what he was wanting."

"He put you in charge of bringing those girls to Ali Pasha," I said, hoping she'd stick on the main track I needed her to walk.

Her eyes grew glassy, her body slumping back into Sarit's arms. "Was...always Plan A. Get girls...girls who wouldn't be...missed and had...all—all the right qualities. No missing persons reports...no one who counted...just...just..."

She ran out of breath and Sarit stroked the dying woman's hair. Fawcett's breathing changed again, getting steadier. "Amanda...is that you?"

Sarit stared at me with a confused expression. I gestured for her to roll with it.

"Yes," Sarit said, a little unsteadily. "Yes, it is I."

Fawcett didn't seem to notice the voice was wrong. Her right hand pushed past me as she reached up to Sarit's cheek. "I'm so sorry...I should have married you when..."

"I forgive you, Emma," Sarit said. "But please, tell me... why did Jones need all those girls?"

Fawcett's hand dropped to Sarit's neck and gave her a protective squeeze. "He's not Jones...anymore, Amanda. He's...something else...something terrible."

"I know, beloved one, I know. But why did he need the girls?"

Fawcett's breathing slowed down as she whispered, "Never understood...what he was saying...True Name...dissipation...binding...food."

The last of her life force departed with her final words. I shut her eyes and thought about this Amanda she talked about. If there was any justice, that's who she was going to join right then.

"What about you guys," Zian asked. "How much longer are those bodies going to last?"

Eli held up her ruined hand, now almost complete skeletal from our last clash with the ifrit. "I daresay, friend, the ravages you see on our borrowed flesh speak more eloquently than any words either of us could offer."

My phone rang, and I bit back a curse when I saw the caller ID. I stood and moved to my bedroom to take it.

"Vale," I said, in the receiver.

"What do you know?" a slightly out of breath and pissed off Detective Lieutenant Morgan asked at the other end of the line.

I had no idea how much he knew. Ramirez hadn't been missing for more than two hours...Was he looking for her?

I baited him for Intel. "About what?"

"I don't have time for your games, Vale." Morgan bellowed. "Not when my sergeant is missing."

Well, that cleared things up. If he knew Ramirez was gone, it was a safe bet he'd seen the same CCTV footage I had. "I don't—"

"Oh, cut the crap," he all but growled into the phone. "She was last seen being dragged into a car alongside your reporter friend. Don't insult me by pretending you didn't know about it."

"I don't know where they are," I said and hoped my tone was enough to assure him I was telling the truth.

"But you knew they were missing. I could arrest you for that alone." He scuffed. "Hell, I'm sure if I keep digging, I'll find the evidence you were on the scene."

I pinched the bridge of my nose. Having a conversation with this guy was like trying to talk to a brick wall. "Morgan, it's not—"

"I have four bodies here, Vale. How much do you wanna bet them bullets will be a match for that P226 of yours?"

Damn, he had me. Time was running out for Ramirez and Kennedy, and I couldn't fight both the jinn and the authorities. One way or another, I had to get Morgan off my back.

"There's a one-way street before the Tombs. Be there in fifteen minutes," I said. "Alone."

Morgan grunted his acquiescence, and I hung up. It was a small miracle he was willing to talk to me at all. Any other day and he'd have stormed into my flat, arrest warrant in one hand, handcuffs in the other. Ramirez was one of his team, I guess that changed things.

Three curious pairs of eyes settled on me the instant I returned to the living room.

"Detective Morgan?" Zian asked as he saw my face.

I nodded. "He's searching for Melanie."

Sarit, who was arranging Fawcett's corpse, turned a questioning gaze to her brother.

"Mortal authorities," Eli indicated. "Can he help us?"

I shook my head. "No. We can't involve the police in this. It would be dangerous for them, and it would make... certain persons cross with me if I did."

Sarit stood up and walked closer to me. Zian knelt before the body and started reciting a prayer in ancient Greek. I recognized the name Hades a couple of times.

"How are you going to get him off your back?" Zian asked after he finished his prayers. He kept kneeling as he started digging in his pockets for something. "A lot can be said about the man, but he genuinely cares for Ramirez. If he thinks she's in danger, he won't back down."

"Haven't figured that out yet," I said, shrugging my jacket back on. My battered body protested the action, but I silenced it. Out of the corner of my eye, I saw Zian pull out a pair of *drachmae* coins.

"Hold the fort, try to find something, anything to tell us where Jones is," I told him. "I'll be back as soon as I can."

Zian nodded as he got up from his crouch. The coins covered Fawcett's eyes, payment for the ferryman Charon so she could cross into the Underworld.

As I said, I'm used to battling through pain. My time with Lady McDeath means I do that more often than I'd like to think about. One of the weird things I've found is that driving a car in this state was easier than walking. I had no trouble whatsoever steering the Stingray past the Tombs and down into the alleyway where I would meet Morgan.

The spot was deserted when I got there. I killed the engine and stayed in the car as I waited for the detective lieutenant to arrive. I leaned back against the headrest and caught my stare in the rearview mirror.

"You're an idiot," I told the guy looking back at me. "An idiot with a bleeding heart and not the beginning of a plan."

Morgan came around the street corner on foot a minute later, and I got out of the car.

He didn't seem to care there was a faint drizzle of rain outside. The bottom of his trousers was wet, as were the top of his shoulders, indicating he'd been spending quite a bit of time outside in the rain. He must have searched the alley behind Ali Pasha himself before the forensics arrived.

The minute he was close enough, he zeroed in on me like a bull charging a red-shirted *torero*. I didn't have time to put up a fight, so I let him. Faster than you can say *olé*, he pinned me to the nearest brick wall. Man, but people liked doing that do me a lot lately.

"Right now, only two things are keeping me from beating the crap out of you," he seethed, inches away from my face. "*Who* and *where*."

I was surprised to find out Morgan was smoking. I thought he'd given up the habit, but today he smelled like an ashtray. "I don't kn—"

"Don't you dare finish that sentence," he all but growled.

Morgan moved his right arm up, pushing his forearm down onto my trachea. "I *know* you were on the case long before us, so cut the crap."

"Fine," I wheezed out. "Got the who...still working out...the...where."

Morgan lessened the pressure on my throat, "Keep talking."

I took in a deep breath, before saying, "I can't."

The pressure returned in full strength.

"I mean it, Morgan...I...can't." It was hard to get the words out. Harder to focus through the loud thumps of my heartbeat resounding in my ears. "Wouldn't...be safe...for you."

"Oh, give me a break, Vale. I've been a cop for twenty-five years," Morgan added more pressure to my throat. "I can handle myself."

The world blurred around the edges, but the rage and contempt on the detective's face were still easy to spot. He meant his earlier words—my knowledge was the only thing keeping me alive. I looked around for a way out, but couldn't find any.

The two of us stood alone in a small alley that never saw any activity during peak hour. Night had fallen, and the faint drizzle of rain had turned into a downpour. It was a safe bet no one was magically going to pop up behind us to rescue me.

I had to give Morgan the truth, or at least enough of it, to buy me some time to save the girls.

"You can't. Not...not against these...guys." I managed to get the words out through sheer will. "You...were right...about me. There's stuff...I keep from you...and from Ramirez." It killed me to have to admit it, but I was out of options. If that admission wanted to haunt my ass sometime soon, I'd worry about it then.

The pressure lessened on my windpipe, but the detective's eyes kept blazing.

"We don't live in the same world, Morgan," I continued, voice raspy. "Trust me when I say you're not equipped to go up against threats from my end of the street."

I prayed to all the gods I knew Morgan would have the good sense to recognize the truth when he heard it. I glanced up, caught his gaze and held on. "I'm sorry, Morgan. I am."

"What the hell are you on about?" he asked.

"The oncoming fight, it's gonna be a big one. I'd love nothing more than to have additional backup, but in all honesty, you'd be more of a liability."

"The fuck?" Morgan seethed, and I lost his gaze amidst the anger.

I fought to get it back. Forced him to hear me, to really listen to me. "I'm honest here, man. I swear, I am. Ramirez got caught up in something bigger than you can imagine. Big players that scare the living crap out of me.

"Now, there's a lot you don't know about, Morgan. And I'm sorry, but I don't have the time to catch you up. I know who took her; I need a little bit more time to find out where they're keeping her."

Morgan let go of me; the motion as quick as when he'd grabbed me. "Ramirez is one of us." He pointed at himself. "The police won't stand on the benches while some down-on-his-luck PI" —He pointed at me— "does the job."

"And she's my girlfriend, Morgan." I played the last card I had, spilled more of the truth and laid my heart bare for him to see. "I *love* her. I will get her back."

The words hit their mark; I could see it in his eyes.

"I'm begging you, Morgan. Trust me, please. I know the

man who has her, and we're close to finding his location. I can get her back. But I need to go there alone. If you and your men storm the place, it's going to turn into a bloodbath. Twenty-four hours; it's all I'm asking for."

Morgan took a step back and groaned. I moved away from the wall and pulled at my shirt to rearrange it. It was a lost cause, and I was as damp as the man facing me. He'd made his decision, and I could see he was regretting it.

"Do you realize how much you're asking for?" he asked, his voice no more than a whisper.

"All I'm asking for is for you to trust me." I turned my collar up. "Don't do it for me; do it for *her*."

With one last shake of his head, Morgan stepped to the side, resignation replacing the fury on his face. I gave him a nod and walked back to my car.

His voice was hard as steel as he called out after me. "You better deliver on that promise, Vale. Or I swear to God, there won't be a rock large enough on this planet for you to hide under."

I gave him one last glance as I got in the car. He stood where I left him, a dimly lit silhouette standing tall in the pouring rain. He had both hands curled into fists at his side.

"I won't hide," I said, turning the key in the ignition. "If I fail, you can have me."

18

SENSORY OVERLOAD

"Any way you can pick up the ifrit's scent again?" I asked Eli once I got back to my flat.

I opened the nearest window a crack. I would have suggested she go out on the porch, but the protective measures only extended as far as the inside of the apartment.

Eli frowned as she rose from her seat. "I have no great hopes that this is so, Bell. Still, as we have recently been in close contact with our foe..." She walked past me to get to the window.

Meanwhile, Sarit climbed off the couch herself. Someone had placed one of my afghans over Fawcett's body.

Zian was working on my laptop on the kitchen table, but he had yet to turn up something useful.

"What about what Fawcett said?" I asked of the jinn twins.

"I am unable to say whether my knowledge of what Emma's last words referred to is either a blessing or curse," Sarit said.

"The first two words of those were clear enough to me," I said, glancing over to see Eli sniff the fresh air like a blood-hound. "Jones, or whatever his real name was, has been harvesting True Names to get his power. Dissipation goes back to what's going to happen to him if he doesn't do that."

"As for the rest," Sarit said, "I heard it straight from the mouth of my boastful captor. He intends to marry women to feed off their True Names."

I tapped my chin as I worked out the dynamics in my head. "So, by marrying them, he'd be taking on *their* names as opposed to his own, since he doesn't have one. And it wouldn't be like what he did with those poor illegal workers. He had to devour those to stay alive. But this kind of True Name would keep charging him up like a car battery."

Sarit gave me a small frown. "Assuming such a device gives what it feeds continuous energy, then yes. When I was first captured, his ravings over the failure of the slave-trader to deliver his 'goods' went for many long hours. He attempted to bind me in such a manner."

"Which is why you're in the dress," I said, motioning vaguely at her now torn and soiled black dress.

Her dark eyes blazed while her face hardened.

"So, between the failure to deliver the girls and make you his new ball-and-chain—"

Sarit jerked her head back in disgust.

"Yeah, I know, a very unflattering term for a wife," I admitted. "Anyway, that's why he got involved in the fashion show. It was a perfect cover to find yet more women for him to pick and choose from."

"And vessels for his Azif," Sarit added with an arched eyebrow. "You saw one such specimen in that magical picture show Zianyon showed us. The men who bought or were given his specially-tailored shirts soon found themselves hollowed out to make room for those abominable shadow creatures."

Eli continued to sniff the air furiously.

"So the fashion show and all the dresses aren't *quite* as good as the illegal strippers would have been," I said. "But if you can make one woman disappear out of—"

"It would have been more than merely one," Sarit interrupted. "Multiple wives are an accepted part of jinn culture. Also, the more True Names he has to draw upon—"

"The more power he gets," I breathed.

"Nothing!" Eli declared, slapping the wall with her ravaged hand. "Not a trace of his scent to be found, no matter how hard I breathe."

Sarit looked over my shoulder at Eli. "I had hoped, Elijah, my failure to find our quarry belonged solely to me."

Zian shut off his computer to join us.

"You were sniffing for him the whole way back?" my hacker buddy asked in amazement.

Sarit shrugged. "We just managed to fight him off. I was his captive for several days. For all we knew, he may well have been tracking our steps from the establishment we escaped to this sanctuary we currently stand in."

Zian nodded, but the nod slowed as his eyes widened. "Wait a minute, wait a minute...You're able to track people by smell too, right? Why not try tracking Kennedy's scent instead?"

"However much I applaud your ingenuity," Eli said, turning back around. "The fact remains that the scents of most mortals are as unremarkable to us as the smell of fresh grass or flowering trees is to you. While I have spent a great deal of time in Ms. Kennedy's presence, I fear—"

"Well, what about Bell?" Zian interjected, jabbing his finger in my direction. "He's been around Kennedy a lot longer. Maybe if he could give you the memory of her scent, you could use that."

Eli and Sarit exchanged glances with each other. They looked hopeful, but a little concerned too.

"Such a thing might be possible," Sarit said in a careful tone. "But how would we—"

"I've got something that might work," I said. "Usually, I use this ability on corpses to pick up sense impressions from before they died. I've got no idea if it'll work for living jinn, but…"

Eli smiled and grabbed my shoulder with her more intact hand. "We lose nothing by trying. Let us attempt this experiment."

I sat back down on the loveseat while Eli and Sarit stood on either side. I could feel Zian behind me.

I reached inside my jacket pocket and took out a small amulet made out of painite, one of the rarest gemstones on the planet. It was about three inches long, two inches wide, and shaped like a bident. It was given to me by Lady McDeath and allowed me to communicate with the recently dead. It allowed me to get into their memories and relive their last moments alongside them.

That was never a pleasant experience, but I often had to piece together what happened when I was on a case. That being said, I never tried to turn it inwards and reach for one of my memories. I wasn't sure if it was possible. And it was almost certainly ten kinds of nuts to bring someone along for the ride.

I cupped my hands and placed the bident in them. Lady McDeath's mark on my shoulders burned as the amulet touched my flesh. I don't know if it was jinn consciousness or pure coincidence, but both of their hands touched mine at the same time. I closed my hands around theirs and felt my way into their minds. The shock of the memories ripped right through me like a buzz saw, making me jerk.

The world I knew faded, and a dark summit replaced it. The air around us was warm and acrid. It smelled of sulfur, and I could taste the smell of soot on my tongue. I took it in, bewildered. The soil of scorched black rocks went all the way to the cliff, and beyond lay a bottomless pit of black darkness. I couldn't figure out where the light came from. There was no sun and no stars in the sky, no visible source of light I could find. And yet, I could see.

The light was in the air, I realized. Tiny incandescent particles, carried by the winds. They were burning and dying at the same time. Like fireworks, there one instant and gone the next. I didn't know where they came from though; there was no—

A cry of anger tore me out of my thoughts, and I turned back to face the sound. I saw shapes moving in the distance, climbing the summit and aiming for the edge.

They were jinn in their pure form; I understood as they drew closer. They were made of smoke so dense they were tangible. They had legs and arms that made their silhouette look human, though the proportions were wrong. At their center, beneath the smoke, shone a light alternating between hues of red and yellow, like the beating of a heart.

The tallest of the group was in chains, dragged by two burly guards. His form was less human than the others. His skull was elongated, his limbs crooked and longer. He was of another race, I understood. I didn't know how I knew it, but I could name it. He was an ifrit. I knew sure as I knew we stood on the Mountain of Judgment, the most sacred place in all the realm.

As the jinn assembled around the prisoner in a semicircle, one of them moved to stand in front of the condemned. He looked older, and it was apparent the long day's climb of the mountain took a lot out of him. I did not know his name, but felt like calling him "Father". He bore the two symbols of his office in his hands: the blazing scimitar Eadala in his right hand and a scroll in his left.

"You are a curse upon creation." Father's words resounded around us, booming over the desolate summit. "As you stand here, bound and defeated, we ask if you have anything to say before we douse your cinders and be rid of you once and for all?"

Laughter like rocks grinding together preceded the reply. "Do you know how many times I have been brought to this mountaintop, old one?" the ifrit asked, standing as tall and menacing as his chains would allow. "Why do you believe this time shall be any different?"

"No more," Father said, as he unfurled the scroll. It was a page taken from the Book of Life, the one where his True Name was written at the dawn of time.

The ifrit recoiled in surprise as the words sparked, burned and joined the ashes in the wind.

"No more," everyone echoed around him. "No more."

The ifrit screamed, rage turning to fury as he tried his

bonds again. They held true, but the guards stepped closer. Father lifted his sword as a light tore through the sky and—

—we were standing on a rooftop in the middle of a bustling city. All around us, as far as the eye could see, stretched a sea of metal and glass.

We were in the heart of humanity's kingdom; "Cold City", it was called. A city buzzing with activity, humans running left and right in their metallic vehicles. The sounds of the traffic of life, echoing around the walls, an ever-present distraction. And the smells—oh, my Lord, the *smells*. There were so many, all of them overlapping each other in a constant battle to come out on top. It was hard to focus and harder to track in that oozing mass. Despite it all, I made it this far. The borrowed skin wasn't enough to hide the stench of my enemy.

Black smoke belched from the ifrit's mouth as he proclaimed, "Did you not think I could smell your presence a mile before your arrival?"

"What you have smelled is your own death," I declared, crouching into a fighting stance. I knew this vessel was far from ideal. I knew my odds would be better with my brother by my side. But the monster needed to pay for what he'd done.

I charged at him only to find—

—myself falling to the ground far below. I felt a calmness settle upon me as this vessel met its fate. True, I could have stopped my descent with a simple burst of air. But why would I have fared any better in a future struggle with the ifrit than I did? I needed something better...something that could take the brunt of—

—the blow struck my face. These damned Azif...They

must have been waiting for such an opportunity. Every jinni in the company struggled with these abominations while the ifrit struggled through his chains to join the fight. Father was standing in front of him, ready to finish the execution, only—

—Father missed his strike. Eadala destroyed the Nameless One's chains with its ill-aimed stroke. The monster laughed, his eyes matching the blazing red core of his chest. With a swat of his hand, he—

—pushed me inside the warehouse where rows of white sewing machines gleamed in the dimly lit area. I fought against his control, tried to resist him, but I could not. At the move of his hand, I sat and saw. I—

—screamed. My head was burning, inside and out. It was too much. Too many memories, ebbing in and out of my consciousness. Eli and Sarit's were mixing with my own, replacing them, and I was losing sight of Bellamy Vale.

The pain took me to my knees as I reached up with both hands to cradle my head. My skull was too small; it couldn't contain all of these memories. The world kept dancing around me, the past and the present entwined in an erratic waltz. I shut my eyes and buried the tip of my fingers deeper into my skin. Our consciousnesses were blending like a *piña colada*. The close contact made all three of our minds struggle with each other. They'd fight until one of us came out on top. But if one of us did, the other two would be condemned. What had I done—

I felt a pair of hands on my shoulders, squeezing me. They were reassuring, and they made some of the pain go away. I dared reopen my eyes.

The maddening dance was over, and the world had settled onto something new. Rain fell from the dark-grey sky onto paved streets. A young boy with light brown hair stood under a fine-looking black umbrella. He was eight or nine years old, and he wore a navy-blue uniform which screamed 'private school'. He walked away from the dark limousine on his own and took measured steps towards the old Victorian-looking building ahead. He paused an instant to look at the other children arriving. They were the same age he was and wore the same uniform. They let go of their parents' hands, kissed them goodbye and walked inside.

The boy turned back to the car and waved at the man behind the wheel, though he knew the driver wouldn't wave back at him. He tried not to let the pain resulting from that particular piece of knowledge show on his face.

The scene blurred as the day passed, and it was time for the boy to go home. The estate was large, and though it was old, it was well-maintained. The friendly smiles of the staff welcomed the boy at the door. A plump senior woman took his coat to hang it off to dry on a peg placed high on the wall, while another younger lady—who could only be the first woman's daughter or much younger sister, for they looked so much alike—leaned down to present him with a plate of freshly baked cookies.

The child took one mechanically as he moved forward without a word. The moment they were out of sight, they and their smiles faded from his awareness. For though the boy was young, he was no fool, and he understood all too well the staff were paid to smile at him.

He kept walking, small steps treading soft carpet. He walked past the vast sitting room and the library, and with little more than a shudder, he walked past the study with its perpetually closed door. It was a forbidden place where he could never enter. He learned that lesson a long time ago.

He took the stairs up, walked down a corridor and up the second set of steps until he reached the only room that mattered to him. He knocked once and entered, without waiting for an invitation to come in. He knew full well the person resting inside was too weak to provide one anyway.

His mother lay in her bed, motionless as always. Long auburn hair provided deep contrast between the cotton-white pillow and her ashen face. Her eyes fluttered open, and it took her a moment to focus on the boy waiting patiently by the entrance. Porcelain-white fingers rose to beacon him closer before resting once more atop the soft mattress. "How was your day, my son?" she rasped.

The boy sat by her bedside and told her all about it. He kept talking long after she'd fallen asleep.

Days passed. They blurred into weeks, which morphed into months, and the boy grew older. He retreated into himself, disconnecting from reality, until the day he connected to something else. Something greater, another world where he was no longer alone. A world where people admired him, a world where he had friends...hundreds of them. It was such an intricate construct, woven in a way that connected people like a spider's web.

But to the boy, it was so much more than that. It was almost as though the web was alive. It spoke to him, surrendered secrets and vast knowledge. And the boy's blood thirsted for more. Something long-denied was fed as Zian found his home, the one place where he could be himself.

Thus, it was one late afternoon he entered the room that was forbidden to him all his life. He was only sixteen, and he'd never been so afraid in his life, but he knew he had no choice. He didn't smile as he entered the room. He couldn't be bothered to fake it, and unlike the staff, no one paid him to do so. Instead, he chose to wear a mask of total blankness. Like the computers he loved so much, he was now made of ones and zeros, a collection of logical reactions and facts, emotions banned like the viruses they were. He walked into his father's study with a straight back and his head held high.

If his father noticed his feeble attempt at an insult, he didn't let it show. Hermes was, after all, the king of binary code. He spoke in a neutral tone, his voice not rising once. So confident was he that his son would see the error of his ways. So certain was he that he could bring him back into the fray.

For this was not the future he'd planned for him. Zianyon was of a greater lineage; he was meant for more. The choice was drawing ever closer. Only two years separated him from adulthood and the moment where he'd have to decide where his future would take him.

If he so chose, Olympus would welcome him. In the white citadel, he would take the place that was rightfully his, or he could stay on Earth and stand by his father's side, rising in society until he was all but a prince amongst humans. The choice was his, but his father made sure Zianyon understood these were the only two options available.

Zian let a sneer pass his lips. It wasn't hard to see which side his father favored. All these lessons about antiquity, about the gods, about their lineage, who was connected to who, who owned who. All these lessons weren't for nothing. His father wanted him on the other side. Because he, Hermes, was stuck here on Earth, condemned by his compact to remain on this side of the border he'd helped create. Oh, how badly he needed someone to take his place on the other side, someone he could manipulate like a puppet. Someone who would strike deals on his behalf and who would ensure the information flowed.

Zian wanted no part of it, and he told his father as much. He saw a third option for himself, and this was the way he chose. Volumes rose as their discussion took a nastier turn. Words that should have been kept quiet were exchanged.

Zian stooped low enough to use the nastiest weapon in his arsenal, the forbidden subject never supposed to be spoken of, not since she'd passed.

With tears in his eyes, he screamed, "This is not what *she* would have wanted for me!"

Silence met his words. And he saw more than felt the impact they had on his father. It was the moment's pause in his action, the flicker of pain that crossed his eyes.

Zian gasped at his foolishness, and he almost apologized. A second passed, and another. And the moment was gone.

"I gave you everything," Hermes said, his voice colder than the wintery wind outside. "And this is what you chose to do with it." His hand rose, encompassing Zian's thin frame from bottom to top noting the saggy pants that needed a wash, the oversized t-shirt with a neon-colored logo, the tattoo on his torso that couldn't be seen but was known to everyone in the house, the ring inside his nose, and the messy mop of hair dyed in an off-putting variety of colors.

"You are a disgrace to this family," his father said.

And those also were words that could never be taken back.

"Father of the year," a familiar voice said, and I turned to find my hacker friend standing next to me. "I'm sorry I had to intervene, but it looked like you were in pain."

I nodded, remembering the painful mix of memories I'd been tossed into. "It got too much, their memories...I got lost in it."

"I know, that's why I gave you some of mine." Zian stepped closer and reached both hands to my shoulders. "You're running out of time, Bell. You need to focus on Kennedy."

I shook my head, "I can't; it's too much."

"Sure you can," Zian said, with a goofy smile, "Just think —for once."

It was easier to yank back from Zian's memories than the jinn's. I could still feel the overwhelming force of Eli and Sarit's experiences weighing down on the edge of my mind, but Zian's presence acted as a bulwark, long enough for me to concentrate, to focus on a memory of my own.

I felt myself slipping back towards the news van, where Eli met Kennedy for the first time. I let myself recapture the moment, take in the sights, the sounds and the warm feel of the sun coming in from between the buildings. I focused on the journalist facing me. She wore low boots and tight jeans that betrayed her origins. Her pale rose turtleneck was the perfect shade to match her wavy, long blond hair and golden earrings.

As she stood next to the van, with a chunk of lapis lazuli in her hand, she looked like a hunter focused on its prey. The gleam in her blue eyes said, "I'm on a case, and I'm not letting go, just you watch me."

That was no mere promise; I knew she wouldn't let go. If there was one thing Candice Kennedy had in spades, it was resolve. That, and determination. She clawed her way out of her little Texan town on her own. She made it up the journalist ladder, here in Cold City, thanks to her intelligence and dedication, and she was not going to stop before she reached the top. She was as annoying as she was brilliant, determined and cunning, kind and compassionate, and always, always eager for more.

I poured that into my thoughts. My knowledge of her, what I knew in my head and heart, and I anchored myself to the memory.

Next, to me, I could feel Eli and Sarit stand to attention. Kennedy brought the little stone closer to her face, her blue eyes narrowing in concentration.

A breeze disturbed the air and blew a strand of hair in her face. She tucked it back behind her ear with her free hand. A faint smell of jasmine joined the wind. I recognized the scent of Kennedy's perfume; remembering she wore the same the first time we met. I latched onto this particular memory and heard Eli and Sarit inhale.

The memory faded as the jinn twins let go of my hands. I panted and felt myself slump forward.

Zian pinned me to the back of the chair with his hands and asked, "You back with us, Bell?"

"Yeah...Better, now..." I looked behind me at Zian, thinking of the sad memory I'd touched on in his head. "You?"

He squeezed my shoulders. "Later, when this is over."

I nodded, mostly because I couldn't put into words how sorry I felt for him.

I managed to orient myself enough to see both Eli and Sarit had gone back to the window. A few seconds of furiously sniffing the air later, Eli declared, "Yes...I have her scent."

Sarit gave her a sudden hug. "As do I, beloved brother. She is not far."

That news made me rise to my feet. "Think you can track it?"

"To the ends of this earth," Eli proclaimed as she smiled at me. "Let us prepare for the struggle ahead of us and be done with it."

I glanced at Zian, a request on my lips.

"Don't even think about it," Zian said, cutting me off with a pointed finger. "Kennedy's my friend too. So I'm coming along, whether you like it or not."

I closed my mouth, smiled and asked, "Sarit, do you still have my knife?"

19

BATTLE PLANS

With the Stingray's windows down, Eli and Sarit leaned out over either side of the car. Eli sat right behind me while Sarit was in the passenger seat in front of Zian. My suspicion that these two had some telepathic link got stronger while I watched them work. If the scents were stronger on the left, Eli would tap my shoulder. If on the right, Sarit did the honors. I wasn't paying much attention to the streets, keeping an eye out for overly curious cops who'd wonder what this pair of fading beauties was doing. Zian had the same idea; his smartphone was tuned into the police band while he listened in on an earbud.

The rain stopped falling, but the streets were still wet. They looked oily black, as they glistened under the rays of a nearly-full moon. There was something familiar about the direction we were taking, but I couldn't put my finger on it until I spotted a familiar diner on the right. I yanked the Stingray into the parking lot, choosing a free spot far from the main road. I heard some complaints from the jinn siblings that I couldn't make out until I shut off the engine.

"We still have some distance to go," Eli insisted in a perturbed voice.

"Yeah and I'm pretty sure I know where we're going," I said, looking over her shoulder. "Or haven't you noticed we're getting closer and closer to Hellfire's offices?"

Eli looked around the diner in surprise. "I...must admit we are going in that general direction, yes."

"Makes sense," Zian added, glancing up from his phone. "Nobody but us knows Hellfire is a compromised outfit. It'd make too much sense for that to be their bolt hole."

"What were the characteristics of this...office?" Sarit asked, not quite getting it.

"Cramped little place," I explained, turning to face Sarit. "Not much better than a cubby hole sitting on the third floor of the Clarke Building."

Sarit's eyes hardened as she shook her head. "Our foe would never make his final stand in such a location."

"And yet, sister, does your nose not draw you further and further in this direction?" Eli asked, pointing up the block.

Sarit's eyes softened and put a gentle hand on Eli's shoulder. "Just as I know your own does, Elijah. Nevertheless, I have spent far too much time with our quarry to believe he would change his habits at this late date. One of them is the need for wide-open spaces."

I opened the door and got out. "Well...it *is* called the Clarke Building, not the Clarke Storage Locker. Maybe there's some other space in there he's got access to."

"We can know nothing until we have gotten closer," Eli

asserted, climbing out behind me. "I assume we shall make the rest of this trip by foot?"

"Yeah, but let's stick to side streets and back alleys. Even with the cover of the night, we have to be careful."

As he was getting out, Zian worked the screen of his phone to pull up a map. "I do believe I have us covered on that point, Bell. If you'll follow my lead..."

Sarit shut the passenger door behind him as I said, "You got a point, Zian. Any sign of cops?"

Zian started walking towards the alley to the diner's left. "A couple of patrols in the area, neither of which are anywhere close to us."

The area my hacker buddy led us through was a typical city labyrinth. I wouldn't have risked making my way through there without Zian as my guide. I fancied I spotted the dumpster where I took down Eli during my last visit to Hellfire, but the area had a lot of them, and one looked like the others.

Both Eli and Sarit lost the spring in their step after three blocks. Without mentioning it, Zian slowed his pace so they could keep up. I fell back a little to talk to Sarit, who was getting shorter and shorter of breath.

"Is the scent getting stronger?" I asked, not wanting to confront the elephant in the room.

"Yes and, as you fear, both our vessels are getting weaker," Sarit said, her tone telling me she didn't have time for my bullshit. Every woman in my life always had that problem with me sooner or later.

"I...don't want either of you getting hurt," I said.

"And by 'hurt,' you mean 'killed' or 'destroyed', correct?"

I turned to Eli for help. She gave me a shrug. "I did warn

you my sister has never possessed much patience. That sadly extends into the social graces."

"And how have the social graces benefited you in this hunt, my overly cautious brother?" Sarit asked with enough amusement to tell me she was teasing her.

"Well...I was able to secure the services of Mr. Vale here and, by extension, his friends. So I would disagree with you if you characterized my aptitude for speaking with people as completely useless."

I chuckled at the banter. Only siblings could toss this kind of talk off. "Seriously, you two, are you sure you're up for this? I've got no problem doing this one solo."

Eli grabbed my hand and squeezed. "We started this hunt together, my friend, and that is how we shall finish it."

"And I owe the ifrit a great deal of pain that I intend to repay him in kind," Sarit added, her eyes flaring with inner flames as she clenched her fists.

"And you know why I'm here," Zian said over his shoulder. "We're here."

I sighed and shook my head. "Let's hope the four of us is enough."

A look at the Clarke Building made me seriously question our adequacy. In place of the night watchman, flesh-wearing Azif now circled the building at regular intervals, using the foot traffic for cover. Their heads swept the area, looking for anything out of place. Hard to believe the inside wouldn't also be crawling with the ifrit's internal security.

I took point on this one, sticking my head around the corner to see what was going on. I pulled back and glanced at Eli. "The scent?"

"Goes right into the building itself," she confirmed. "It would seem your hypothesis is once again correct."

"How's security look from here?" Zian asked, working on hacking his way into the local CCTV through his phone.

"Nothing your average SWAT team couldn't handle, but way too much for us," I admitted. "How close are you to getting eyes inside and out?"

"Almost...got it!"

We all gathered around his phone as he pulled up the various cameras he tapped into. He spent the next few minutes checking them over, getting a headcount and a patrol pattern. Then a digital version of a navy klaxon started going off on his phone.

"Shit!" I hissed, taking up my position on the corner. Just as I feared, one of the Azif stopped and looked in our direction while the crowd walked around him. I glanced back at Zian and made chopping motions with my right hand across my neck. He nodded back at me, keeping his eyes glued to his screen. He got it to shut off a few nerve-wracking seconds later, but the damage was done. The guard was coming right at our position.

Thankfully, Zian was on top of the situation. He pointed back down the alley we came, and we made as quick and silent an exit as we could. He got us around a corner on the left that took us out of the guard's line of sight.

I inched my head around the corner. The guard seemed taller in person than his brothers had on camera. His inky-black wraparound sunglasses contrasted with his milky complexion, sort of the way his black three-piece suit contrasted with his NFL physique. He wore a severe blonde buzzcut that stood at as much attention as the Glock.45 he swept the area with. The pistol looked like a derringer in his hand.

He withdrew from the area, satisfied nothing worth his attention was there. I exhaled and gazed at Zian. He was typing furiously on his phone.

"You want to tell me what the hells that was all about?" I asked.

Zian blushed in embarrassment. "Ever since...well, the mayor, I've set up monitoring of any ley line intersections being tapped in the city limits."

"And I am hypothesizing the unwelcome and unexpected alarm we heard meant such...tapping occurred, correct?" Eli asked.

Zian nodded. "I doubt the ifrit didn't know about those two lines crossing here before moving Hellfire's office. So it's him tapping into the extra juice now."

"Which means he is preparing the bridal binding ceremony as we speak." I glanced at his phone. "Can you see where they are?"

Zian shook his head. He was frustrated and minutes away from throwing his phone into the nearest wall. "Can't get into the system anymore. Must be the ley-lines; it looks like everything's fried."

Looking at Sarit, I asked, "Can the Azif pick up scents like you two?"

She shook her head. "No better than your average mortal...and that is because they are wearing flesh. They go strictly by sight in their natural form."

"How much of the security did you see, Zian?"

"Got it pegged as between eighteen and twenty," Zian

said, pocketing his now-useless phone. "And that's not counting any other Azif which might—"

"Any remaining Azif should be in those bodies," Sarit interjected. "More than once, I heard the ifrit rant about how he needed enough shirts to clothe their vessels."

"But couldn't he have done that with some of the women too?" I asked.

"Easily...All the same changes to strength and physique would have taken place."

Zian snorted as he frowned. "So why didn't he?"

I got a nasty smile on my face. "Because he's a male chauvinist pig who thinks his gender helps make him the undisputed master of the universe." Eli's eyes darted to me in surprise. I shrugged. "What? I heard what he said to you at the club."

"We need a plan of attack, and fast."

"You will hardly need both Sarit and me to help you find Ms. Kennedy," Eli said. "Therefore, I volunteer to stay behind to create a diversion."

Sarit blanched at Eli's casual statement. "Need I remind you, brother, our vessels are nearing the end of their usefulness, and we are far from the height of our powers?"

"Which is why I've got a little backup I can provide," Zian said with a grin. "Courtesy of my digital Alexandria library card."

He pulled up a screen full of a line of squiggles on a sandstone background. I would have pegged the writing as Arabic if I didn't know what actual Arabic looked like. Eli gasped at the sight, putting her decayed hand on her still-kissable lips.

"This is the Vessel-Piercer," she whispered. "It can

destroy a spirit from within a mortal body it currently possesses with one shot. This is one of the greatest secrets of the jinn warrior caste...How did you—"

"Somebody put it in the Library of Alexandria," Zian said. "Then somebody else saved it when the original library burned. And then yet somebody else put it in the digital archive. That's as much as anybody's ever going to know."

Sarit said, "Father never taught us this because he thought we were less than ready. Even if you now are, Elijah, there remains the problem that it only works on one target at a time."

"So we use it as a stage magician would," I said. "Keep them so distracted with something else while we pick them off one by one."

Sarit looked unconvinced as her expression got stern. "Tell him, Elijah, or I will."

Eli sighed. "You do not understand the amount of power this spell requires. It is one thing to summon it into our world, but here...in a fresh vessel, I'm not sure how many times I could use it."

I had a pretty good idea of how to circumvent that particular issue. "Do as the ifrit does," I said, tapping my foot to the floor for emphasis. "There's all the juice you need."

Eli's expression didn't change. "Even so..." she sighed. "That spell wouldn't transform the energy, only displace it for a little while. It would destroy our foes, yes...but all things set in motion must go somewhere."

She stared at me as though I was supposed to get it. I didn't and motioned for her to elaborate.

"There's only so many times I can use this spell before the built-up energy is too much for me to control. And then a raw force will gather into a vortex that'll destroy any living creature within one hundred feet."

That time I got it. I gave it some thought, stroking my chin. We were given a cool gun, but only a handful of bullets. So we had to make each shot count. Then I remembered something I said a few minutes ago. "Can you two still manage grand illusions?"

20

WHAT YOU WISH FOR

I pointed the tip of my knife in the direction of the passing guard. So far, Sarit was right about their inability to detect us.

Just the same, Sarit held my Sig in her hands with surprising familiarity. She'd explained that it was buried memories from her borrowed body, though she had no recollections on where and how the woman had learned to shoot. Watching her handle the gun told me she'd have no problem using it if things got ugly.

I did my best to keep my breath steady, and my knife gripped between loose and tight. Any minute now...

A series of sirens louder than Zian's phone rang out on the streets, followed by the screeching of tires. No way the whole block didn't hear them. I could make out the hum of engines under the blare. The vehicles came to a stop at the front of the building; doors opened and shut. Then came the bullhorn voice we'd been waiting for: "Khalim Jones, come out with your hands up!"

The guard broke off his patrol pattern to run towards the front of the building. A quick scan of the block showed me nobody bothered keeping an eye on the back door. We had no way to know how long it would last. Waving at Sarit with my free hand, I got off the wall and ran across the street. I felt Sarit move right behind me, covering the area in case of any unexpected interference.

Once we got there, Sarit set up watch as I picked the lock on the door again. Two minutes later, we were inside, Sarit on point. I was about to ask which direction Kennedy's scent was when an oblivious woman walked in front of us. I pegged her as being in her late forties with her lined face and grey hair. She wore a conservative dress that fit with her rather-plain features and unremarkable physique. She was leafing through documents in a manila folder, going through the pages like a fax machine. The sheets hit the floor in perfect counterpoint with the commotion at the front door.

She gazed up at us and smiled as though it were perfectly reasonable for us to roam the corridors at this time of night. "Oh, hello there. Are you here to see Mr. Jones?"

Sarit and I exchanged puzzled glances before I said, "As a matter of fact, yes, we are. Are you his secretary?"

The woman laughed as she handed me a card from inside the folder. "Good heavens, no. I'm a public accountant on the second floor...Molly Springfield. Come visit me next tax season, and I can give you a reasonable rate on helping file your return."

She said all this while the sound of gunfire echoed through from outside. The way she acted, you'd think she came to work through blazing gun battles every day.

"You mentioned Mr. Jones?" Sarit asked, covering Molly with her gun.

"Oh, so I did," Molly said with another laugh. "Silly me...He wanted to let me tell you he isn't in his office at the moment."

My heart sank. "Will he be back in the morning?"

"My apologies, that wasn't clear. He *is* here, not in his office." Molly laughed again—hells but the woman was jolly. "He's in the basement with his new secretaries...pretty little things."

"How do we get there?" Sarit asked, voice cold, gun still aimed at the woman.

"Oh, take the stairs down," Molly replied, pointing at the door to our right. "You can't miss it."

She stopped finding us interesting enough to talk to and went back to her folder. Jones messed her up good. *How many years of therapy would it take to bring her back?* I wondered.

While she walked off, I heard a weird gasping noise from the fight outside. Then another one...and another one. The Vessel-Piercer didn't mess around.

I grabbed the door, and we headed downstairs. This time I took the lead, keeping my knife in front of us as we went down the narrow flights.

"Guess the ifrit's still got serious powers of persuasion," I noted as we hit a landing.

"Which means he has found another host," Sarit added. "He would never have been able to cloud that poor woman's mind otherwise."

"Think Eli's SWAT team illusion drew all the guards away?"

"One can hope...as I hope your escape plan for my brother works as intended."

While we hit the bottom of another flight, I pulled out a lapis lazuli stone. "Me, I'm glad your dress had spare stones."

"You are certain Zianyon can indeed do what needs doing?" Sarit asked, matching me step for step down the last flight of stairs.

"Sure," I said with more confidence than I felt. "There's more to him than he lets on."

The look she gave me told me she saw through my bull-shit yet again. But we had more important things to worry about.

We opened the door to the basement to see a fiery sight. Right in the center of the room, a table-sized vortex the color of pre-eruption magma swirled and stirred on the floor. The heat coming from it made me back out to the stairwell. Sarit pushed past me and started sweeping the room with the Sig.

Kennedy and Ramirez stood on opposite side of the vortex, left and right respectively. Both stood stock-still in their new Hellfire-made porcelain-white dresses, the red gems on them sparkling in the hellish light. They resembled life-sized Barbie dolls, which wasn't far from the truth of what the ifrit turned them into. The worst part was their vacant gazes. It was as though nobody was home, no emotion whatsoever, and it chilled me to the bone.

"I knew you would come back," a voice beyond Ramirez said. The deepness of its growl told me who it was. But there was something...familiar with it. As the ifrit stepped out of the shadows in his borrowed flesh, I understood why. He wore the security guard who was unlucky enough to catch Eli and me the last time we were here.

Poor guy. This hasn't been his week.

Sarit swung her gun at our body-hopping opponent with uncontrolled rage. "Not another step, accursed one."

"Or what?" the ifrit said with a laugh. "We both know pathetic firearms can do nothing to kill—"

The shots from the Sig echoed like cannon booms in the tight space. The ifrit gasped in surprise as he clutched at his chest and went down to one knee from the shots. I did what I could to ignore the ringing in my ears, to circle to the right.

"As my father taught me," Sarit said with grim satisfaction. "To partake of a foodstuff is to partake of all its qualities, both good and ill. Thus, partaking of this energy nest's forces has made you more vulnerable to harm."

His eyes stayed glued to the gun that hurt him. I was so close to Ramirez I could have reached out and touched her. She kept looking forward without noticing me, and it tore at my heart to see her like this.

"Impossible," the fire demon spat through his stolen lips. "The source forces of this world are the same, regardless of how many lines cross it."

Sarit started circling to the left, keeping her target in sight as she edged closer to Kennedy. "If it were true, how is it I am now able to wound you with a weapon you previously laughed off as a nuisance?"

"The energy of the gateway left me immune to such problems," he protested, walking closer to Ramirez...and me, even if he didn't realize it. "Since my arrival, I have managed to jump from body to body with no ill effects."

"But we drained your strength at the nightclub," Sarit said, shifting from one side of Kennedy to the next while keeping a steady aim. "The gateway has long since closed, and you were foolish enough to think this nest of power had what you needed to stay safe."

Ramirez was in front of me now, the ifrit within arm's reach of her. Getting her out of the line of fire looked pretty tricky, even by my standards.

I could hear the sneer in the ifrit's voice. "And yet I have opened a gate to our world through this nest. As soon as I finish the binding—"

I saw Sarit's face tighten before she pulled the trigger. I grabbed Ramirez as the shot rang out, dragging us both to the floor and rolling across the room. Two more thundering rounds split the air, but I didn't stop until my shoulder hit the wall.

I only *thought* my ears were ringing before, but now nothing but a high-pitched whine filled my eardrums as I struggled to get back on my feet. Ramirez hadn't reacted to our tumble, and she lay still where I'd left her.

I could see the ifrit's lips moving in profile before his back was to me. He was facing in Kennedy's direction when red energy surrounded his whole body.

I wasn't sure what was going on, but I ran towards him anyway. I could hear myself yell, "*No!*" at the top of my lungs.

My shout made him turn his head long enough for Sarit to empty the rest of the Sig's clip into him. One shot even came out of his lower back and missed my hip by inches. The sounds of the shots themselves dimly registered in my abused ears. Two steps before I could grab him, the ifrit turned back around. The red energy left his body to fire out of his hands in one big blast. Instinct told me he was leaving the vessel to rejoin his world. Without thinking, I tackled him by the hips from behind...and I knocked both of us into the red pit.

21

RED SKY AT MORNING

I glanced up, but all I could see of Sarit's body was a hand still wrapped around my Sig. The rest of the basement was gone, replaced by a red sky and black clouds. Nothing resembling solid ground was to be found. I felt the guard's body go limp and realized the ifrit flew the coop yet again, but that was the least of my problems.

The good news was that I managed to spot a bottom to my fall in the form of some brownish ruins standing on the slightly more-crimson-than-the-sky ground. The bad news was that I was still a long way away from the ground. Hoping the dirt would be soft enough, I put the ifrit's abandoned vessel between me and my upcoming landing.

I hit the deck with a bone-jarring impact. The air whooshed out of my lungs, and I lay motionless for long seconds. Though you'd think the fact I'd landed would ring loudly throughout my body, part of me still felt like I was falling. I wasn't sure where I landed, but I could venture a guess.

Only one way to find out if I was right though...I rolled off my human airbag with a groan, to see if my limbs still worked. That action sent me rolling down a hill and getting more dust in my nose and mouth than I would have liked before I came to a halt at the bottom.

Oh, and did I mention I somehow lost my grip on the knife while all this was happening?

I shook the dust off me as I got to my feet. Given more dust swirled around me in a constant windstorm, it was an exercise in futility. The ruins ahead of me were a temple, complete with a golden dome, grand spires and acreage the equivalent of three city blocks. I checked my other hand to confirm that, yes, I did still have the lapis lazuli in my hand. I wasn't sure how much good that was going to do me right here.

A louder version of the ifrit's laugh echoed across the landscape. The echoes hadn't faded before a coal cloud grabbed me. I felt myself slam into hard stone structures four or five times before I flew through the air on a prolonged flight. I had enough time to realize this when the clouds cleared enough for me to see the massive doors I was about to slam into.

"At the temple of mine ancestors will you pay for your interference, mortal flea!" the ifrit's voice promised two seconds before impact.

Somehow, he managed to strike the doors before I did, knocking them open as he let go. That sent me sailing through the air on my own power before I hit the stone floor yet again.

It didn't hurt as much as I thought it would, and I realized gravity was different in this place. I got to my feet with a groan as the doors slammed shut. I jumped up and down a couple of times to confirm my theory, counting the seconds before I landed. The difference with our world wasn't much, but it was still noticeable.

A lack of lightning sources painted the room where I stood in black, and I had no idea what was around me. Without my doing anything, a brazier on the wall to my left flared to life. I had all of two seconds to feel grateful for the light before I heard a sharp whistle. Something pierced my leg, numbing it as the air crackled and hissed around me. I reached for the wall to keep from falling.

Another brazier on the far end lit up, showing a giant made of black clouds, big muscles, sporting a bald head and a grin roughly the size of the Grand Canyon. After that trip down Bad Memory Lane with the jinn twins, I'd know the ifrit's true form anywhere. He held an unstrung golden bow in his left hand, partially blocking off the crimson center of his chest.

"Let us see how fast you can run with an injured leg," he sneered as he drew back his free hand like he was pulling back a bowstring. The thumb of his gripping hand rubbed the space above his fingers. When a white lightning bolt appeared in his other hand, he released it right at me.

Thankfully, it didn't move any faster than a regular arrow, and I did a forward roll that got me out of the way in time. The bolt slammed into the wall with an impotent roar, even as my leg gave out on me as I tried to get back on my feet.

My slump got me out of the way of the ifrit's follow-up shot, my arm and neck hair standing up with the electricity that zipped over me. I was a sitting duck, here in the open.

I waited until he aimed with his third shot before I made my move, and rolled across the floor before the arrowhead could hit home. I steered my roll to the left in anticipation of the next shot and wound up bumping into something big and robust that stopped me dead in my tracks.

"Not good," I muttered as I saw the lightning arrow flying right at me. I pushed off with my uninjured leg to get to the other side of my obstruction. This time, I felt a burst of electricity strike me as the bolt hit the floor. It blew me back across the room like a catapult, making me slam into the wall. Something metallic hit the wall too before clattering onto the floor next to me.

"Every shot increases the bow's power," the ifrit said, pulling back his hand once again. A thumb rub later, the bolt was back in his firing hand, illuminating the room with a blue-white light reminiscent of fluorescent bulbs. He gave me a big grin as he taunted, "So how long do you think you can—"

Then his eyes spotted the thing that made the trip with me. The smile turned into a look of horror. "No..."

I followed my attacker's eyes and frowned. Why would a scimitar hilt with no blade scare him so badly?

I didn't have time to think any further before he fired at me. I grabbed the hilt with my free hand and pushed myself off the wall. I crawled forward and waited for the next shot to light up the room. When it did, I caught a glimpse at the structure that stopped my progress: an altar. I did another quick roll to dodge my involuntary light source; the impact blew me right back into the altar. I bit the inside of my cheek at impact and cursed as the taste of copper landed on my tongue. Hells, but the day kept getting better and better.

I put the altar between me and the ifrit as the next bolt lit up the room. When it hit, the force of the shot pushed both me and the altar back a few inches. Bits of stone shattered upon impact, but I figured that was the least of my worries. *I better figure out why this hilt makes the ifrit so afraid, and quick.*

The light from the bow hadn't shown me anything that explained it. On a hunch, I rubbed the hilt all over. If it worked for the bow, then maybe...

A fiery blade erupted from the center of the handle, broad enough to chop off a head. The sword felt as hot as the weather outside the temple.

As the ifrit shrieked his frustration, I realized I'd seen this weapon before...in the hands of Eli and Sarit's father. The memory reminded me of its name: Eadala—the Arabic word for justice.

I was so caught up in activating the blade I didn't notice my head poking a little above the altar. I almost saw the ifrit's shot too late, but I reflexively swung the scimitar at it. The flaming sword batted the bolt aside, making it smack against a wall on the left. The ifrit fired again, and I knocked the shot to the right. Using my other hand to steady myself on the altar, I inched my way towards my foe while I deflected another shot.

His aim grew worse as I made my way around the altar, close enough for me to fear for my safety, but he was nowhere near as precise a shot as he had been. Since my leg was crippled, I knew I was going to have to time this next part right.

With a firm grip on the blade, I rolled forward. I screamed as I pushed back to my feet. My leg was on fire—

not literally, but it might as well have been. Everything below my knee was yelling at me to give up the fight, lie down and curl into a tight ball.

I brought the blade up as the ifrit shot another bolt at me. I struck it, and the shot ended its course in the wall to my left. It exploded and sent fragments of stone flying. They broke the skin of my arm in two places, and I heard the ifrit hiss as well. I wouldn't have thought mere stone could hurt him, but it did. Maybe some of that light from the bolt latched onto the rock it touched?

I didn't have time to think about it any further. Whatever happened, it enraged the ifrit. His smoky form was denser and darker; anger in its purest form.

I lunged at him, scimitar in hand. I poured my last strength into the motions, taking quick steps forward.

I wasn't fast enough, and the ifrit moved back before the blade could strike him. I swung the sword and took another step, but the ifrit was quick to parry my attack with his bow.

Despite the strength I put in the coup, the ifrit stopped it cold. Before I had time to realize what was going on, the ifrit trapped my blade within the hook of the bow simply by flicking his arm. He lowered his arm and left me with two choices: let go of my only weapon, or hold on and follow the motion.

A kick in the gut was my reward for choosing option B. I fell to the floor upon impact, gasping desperately for air. I had just enough time to roll to the side to avoid the beast's foot connecting with my back.

The ifrit screeched. "Why won't you die, mortal?"

I saw him create another bolt and remembered what he'd said earlier. Each shot was more powerful than the previous one. How many shots had he fired? At this close a range, even if he missed me, the blow could be fatal. I pushed myself to my knees, forcing most of my weight onto my good leg. This was going to hurt, but I had no choice.

The ifrit took aim, and I bent my knee and pushed with all the strength I had left. I jumped as high as I could, and my feet left the floor for a handful of seconds, but it was just enough. Thanks to the low gravity, I flew higher than I usually would, and the bolt flew beneath my legs. It kept going, flying through empty space until it hit the temple's entrance doors. I touched the floor as they exploded into a million shards.

"Sorry," I said, getting back to my feet on sheer will. "I don't die easy."

The ifrit shrieked in rage. His form thickened some more, and the deep red center in his chest stood like a bulls-eye. It was what I was waiting for.

For one brief instant, I saw my target clearly, and I threw Eadala with all the strength I had left.

It flew right at the ifrit's chest. I swayed, vision blurring, as I watched the blade soar straight for my target.

It landed squarely in the center.

The ifrit screamed as the force of the toss pinned him to the wall, the bow flying from his hand. By the combined light of his chest and the sword, I saw him trying to claw at the hilt, not quite able to grab it.

Limping, I moved forward as fast as I could. It was little more than a drunken stagger, but it would do. I reached into my jacket pocket and found what I was looking for.

The lapis lazuli felt warm in my hands, much warmer than it should have from being held. The ifrit's fingertips managed to touch the hilt of the scimitar as I got close enough.

Holding up the stone, I recited the containment incantation Sarit and I tried at Ali Pasha. Once again, the energy from his chest was sucked into the stone, making it burn in my hands. I used the pain as a spur to quit thinking about my numbed leg and concentrate on the incantation. Every time I repeated it, the ifrit grew more and more frenzied. He thrashed around like one of his lightning bolts had struck him.

But then the flow stopped, reversing in the other direction. Stupid...I should have known he could use the stone as a battery if he concentrated hard enough. I kept up the chant, but it felt like a losing battle. The grin was back on the ifrit's face, which pissed me off. In a fit of rage, I shoved the stone right into his chest and played my last card.

I reached deep. Deeper than I ever had within me. I summoned more than my strength into the motion. I poured my pain into it, the worry I felt when I discovered my friends were taken. The anguish Kennedy and Ramirez's vacant gazes elicited in me.

I let the feelings rise in me like the tidal wave they were. A beast's furious growl rose alongside them, coming up from some deep, dark place I seldom acknowledged existed. As the primal scream tore from my throat, I forced the energy down my arm and released it.

The smile disappeared, turning into shock as the vacuum fist sucked the ifrit's energy out of his body and back into the stone. The pitch of my scream changed at the flash of pain that coursed through me. It felt as though each one of my nerves was screaming too. The stone grew hotter and hotter in my fist, but I held on. I forced down my scream and took up the incantation again, reciting it as loudly as I could.

The red in the ifrit's chest grew brighter, to the point where I had to close my eyes. I kept up the chant until my flesh sizzled enough from the heat to make me let go.

A horrific cry tore out of the jinni's throat as his body fell apart. It surrendered to the winds, and the last of the crimson light sucked into the stone.

The tiny gem fell to the floor with a clinking noise. I reached out a hand to hold onto the sword still pinned to the wall. It came away, as though it were stuck into cheese. I took one last swing with it, and the stone vaporized on contact, leaving behind another howling scream, nastier than the last one.

Spent, I slumped down the wall 'til my bum hit the floor. The scimitar's hilt hit the floor beside me as my loose fingers let go of it.

In a daze, I watched as, one by one, the wall braziers lit up. The room it uncovered stretched out to the length of a couple of football fields. The golden dome above my head reflected the light, making it warm and inviting. The only trace of the ifrit having been there was the bow, lying on the dusty floor like a discarded toy.

22

SCATTERED ASHES

I dozed until I had enough strength to get back to my knees. I had to use the scimitar as a makeshift cane to rise to my feet. I knew it wasn't the proper way to use a jinni family sword, but it was all I had within arm's reach. I hobbled my way across the room to the shattered double doors; it only felt like it took forever.

On the other side stood a welcome wagon of what I guessed were jinn. A variety of cloud colors made up their bodies, some wisps pulled off by the wind. They appeared solid enough to touch but loose enough to become one with the wind if they let themselves go. The man in the lead pointed at the sword I leaned on.

He said something in a tongue I didn't comprehend. It sounded airy, like the sound of the wind coursing through leaves on a dark stormy night. I was sure his words were a question, but I had no clue as to their meaning. I raised a curious eyebrow at him.

"Apologies," he said, in a reedy voice. "How can a mortal like you wield Eadala?"

"You got me," I admitted. "I'm glad I could. Otherwise, your ifrit problem would be anything but solved."

That caused a whole bunch of crosstalk amongst the gassy residents of this world. Of course, I couldn't understand a word of it, but hey, it was a private conversation I wasn't being paid to record, so who cares?

I wondered how long they were here and why none of them had entered the temple to help me. I was about to ask them that, when a golden light shined over our heads, making everyone look up. It took a dip in the luminosity department as it got closer to us, and by the time it landed in front of the crowd, I saw a golden cloud in the general shape of a woman. If she'd been flesh, she'd have been lusted after by every straight man and lesbian in sight. A gust of air pulled away a few wisps of her cloud form; they flew like hair billowing in the wind.

My heart skipped a beat as she held up a lapis lazuli stone in her hand. That had to be Eli in it, which made the cloud none other than Sarit. She said something in the jinn language to another woman, who gave her an affirmative reply. The stone was passed to the latter, who recited a chant. The rock melted away into dust at the words, gradually becoming yet another golden cloud much like Sarit, only taller. It solidified in front of me as a man-shaped figure.

I sighed with relief. "So the plan worked?"

"Indeed it did, Bell," Eli said. His voice was different, but it retained those all-too-familiar golden tones. "As you hypothesized, the stone's power kept me safe from the Vessel-Piercer's final fallout."

It was a long shot, but I figured using the spell would be the end of Eli's human vessel. I was relieved to see my hacker friend managed to trap his essence into the stone long enough to save him.

Speaking of, "Is Zian okay?" I asked, worried.

"Quite safe and helping sort through the aftermath," Sarit said over Eli's shoulder. "Where is the ifrit?"

I put more weight on my uninjured leg before holding up the sword. "In a lot of itty bitty pieces of lapis lazuli, courtesy of your father's sword."

The woman grumbled something as she turned her head to look at me.

"This is incredibly rude, Jasmine," Eli said with a rebuke in his voice. "On balance, which problem would you prefer to have at this moment: a temple that needs cleaning, or a fallen one with enough power to dominate two worlds?" Eli drew up to his full height as his voice got louder. "For I say to you all, were it not for this man who stands before us, we should have a greater menace to our safety and that of his people than we could have ever imagined."

I wasn't sure how to take this. I mean, sure, I liked being told I've done a decent job as much as the next guy. But putting a spotlight on my alleged good deeds always made me uncomfortable.

I covered by holding out Eadala to Eli by the hilt. "Think this belongs to you."

Eli took the sword from me but said, "No, my friend... this belongs to her."

Even without clear facial features, Sarit's body language told me how shocked she was to be given their father's sword. She wasn't the only one. More chatter rippled through the crowd.

The beige jinni next to Jasmin came forward and protested, "But you are your father's son, Elijah. That makes you the next—"

"And with the accident of my gender, you would so casually dismiss my twin sister?" Eli retorted, leaning forward to let everyone know his displeasure. "She has as much right to Father's throne as I ever did."

"But you are better suited to be king," Sarit countered, rubbing the hilt to make the blade go away. "My only true skill is battle...and this unfortunate episode has proven how even I can be defeated."

"No less than I was, dear sister," Eli said, putting his hands on her shoulders. "I never wanted the responsibilities of the throne because I know I am unworthy of it."

Sarit moved closer to him, their forms touching and mingling in places. The equivalent of a hug, I assumed. "The fact you are saying this tells me how worthy you truly are, brother."

"Why don't we put it to a coin toss?" I quipped.

The beige jinni growled a little and talked to the siblings in their native tongue.

"Show some respect for our guest by speaking words he can understand," Sarit snapped, cutting him off in midstream.

"Very well," the beige jinni said in defiance. "I believe the time has come for this outsider to leave for his own world."

"I've got to agree with him," I said, raising a hand. "Not that it hasn't been fun, but..."

Eli laughed as he and his sister dropped their embrace. "It has been anything *but* fun for you, Bellamy Vale, but we shall pass over that detail." Then his tone shifted gears. "Just know, from this day forward, the jinn owe you a great debt that can be repaid at any time."

Sarit nodded and reached into her porous chest. She pulled out yet another lapis lazuli stone and handed it to me. "When the time comes for you to summon our aid, merely use your knife to tap the stone twice on each of its sides, from right to left."

"Oh!" Eli said, reaching his hand out to the hill. "Speaking of which..."

A silver blur zipped from the hillside and straight into his hand. He then presented me my knife the way I had presented him with Eadala.

Smiling, I raised the knife blade up to him. "The enchantments still on it?"

"Judge for yourself," Sarit said right before blowing on the blade. The jinn script lit up on the steel in glowing red letters before fading once again.

I was still staring when Sarit hugged me. She enveloped me on all sides, in a soft yet firm embrace. "Thank you for my life," she whispered in my ear. "And for that of my brother."

"With Your Majesty's permission," Eli said as she broke off the hug. "I would like the honor of returning Bell to—"

"Oh, just return our friend to his world so we can discuss how you will be ascending the throne instead of me."

Eli wrapped his arms around me. "We shall see, sister... until later."

We floated up into the red sky, reminding me of a hot-air

balloon ride I took when I was a kid. My leg agreed with the whole flying thing, and it felt nice not to have to do anything. I waited until we were out of earshot of the crowd below us before speaking again. "Would I be canceling the debt if I asked you a few questions?"

"Oh, quite the contrary, Bell," Eli said with another amused chuckle. "I imagine you are ignorant of a few details that will give you the complete picture of what has taken place."

"Yeah, you could say that. Let's start with how you and Sarit are doing...No ill effects from being in those vessels?"

"Now we are in our world, those effects no longer apply to us, no. But I would be lying if I said I had an inkling of how much of a challenge being in your world was for my kind."

"And by 'my kind,' you're not talking about jinn in general. You're talking specifically of your type of jinn."

We passed through a black cloud as Eli glanced down at me. "While you are quite correct as always, my friend, I confess to being a bit mystified on how you reached such a conclusion."

"Just before our friendly neighborhood ifrit shoved me through the temple doors, he talked about how it was the temple of, and I quote, 'my ancestors'. That told me ifrits are another branch of the jinn family tree. Plus, I noticed how you and Sarit not only are the leaders all your people follow, but how not as much dust came off your bodies compared to them."

Eli sighed in admiration. "Your keen eye misses very little, Bell. Yes, my sister and I are Marrit, the rarest of our race. For time out of mind, we have served as this world's chieftains, kings, queens, caliphs, emirs and whatever other title has been in vogue amongst my people for those who must lead."

"And you have a tradition of always leading from the front, which is why you think Sarit is the better pick to be your dad's successor."

"That is so," Eli confirmed with a nod. The gate shined above our heads. "Now it is only a matter of convincing *her* she is the leader our people truly need."

As the gate got closer, I thought of one last question. "So...since the ifrit doesn't have a True Name now, will it undo any of the damage he did while in my world?"

Eli sighed again, this time with genuine regret. "I am afraid that would have only been true had he never taken the True Names of others for his purposes. As it stands, any memories others have of him in his true guise will fade. But the lives he has touched make it impossible for his taint to be expunged from the fabric of your world."

I slumped at the depressing prognosis. "I hoped that—"

"I know, Bell," Eli said. "But the time for us to part has arrived. Please extend my best wishes to Zian and Kennedy."

Eli tossed me through the gate. Once I was through, it shut behind me with a slurp. Gravity was back to its regular level, and I hissed in pain. The concrete floor aggravated all the abuse my body was put through.

Rolling to the side of my uninjured leg, I noticed my gun still in the clutches of Sarit's dismembered hand. Other than that, the room was empty. Ramirez and Kennedy were gone. Unsure if this was good or bad, I crawled over to Sarit's hand and pried the cold, dead fingers open. I managed to stuff the gun in my pocket when the door opened. Kennedy came running into the room barefoot. She still wore the white dress, and it hung to her lean body perfectly.

"Holy hell, hoss," she breathed as she knelt beside me. "What happened to you?"

"It's a long story," I said, "Help me up."

I groaned as she helped me to my feet. With only one leg functioning, I had to lean on her to make it out of the room. "Short version: the ifrit's taken care of, and Eli and Sarit are back at home. They say hi, by the way."

Kennedy guided me up the stairs, holding me on my bad side while I used the railing to steady myself. A rapid-fire stream of Spanish greeted my ears as we got close to ground level. The open door showed Ramirez talking to a young police officer in the lobby. She stood with her back to me, still barefoot, but she'd found a black vest to wrap around her tight shoulders. I didn't need to see her face to know her temper was flaring.

"What did I miss?" I asked Kennedy as we paused on the landing.

"Ramirez and I both woke up down there 'bout ten minutes ago—" She gestured to herself. "—in these rags. Seriously, tell me this isn't what it looks like?"

"Sorry, but yeah, it is." I couldn't help the corners of my lips from lifting up. "Congratulations."

With her free arm, she punched me in the shoulder. She kept it soft, a gentle nudge to carry her point.

"Anyway," she resumed. "There was this giant, fiery hole in the ground next to a severed hand with a gun. And we had no clue where we were or how we'd got here. Not my proudest moment, I'll admit. Thankfully Zian showed up, with an explanation and everything. Gotta say, that boy's good at thinking on his feet."

Zian. I half expected to find my friend hovering close by when I emerged from the portal, but he was nowhere in sight, and this worried me. "Where is he?"

"I'm not sure," Kennedy said. "He helped Ramirez out of the basement and asked me to stay behind to monitor the portal until he came back."

"Let's find out," I said, gesturing for Kennedy to help me get moving again. The sound of our footsteps made Ramirez turn her head. She marched over to us the second she caught sight of me.

"What did you do this time, Bell?" she asked, pointing an accusatory finger at me.

Kennedy picked that moment to let go of my arm. "I'll, uh, go find Zian, yeah?"

Ramirez gave her an annoyed look but jerked her towards the nearest officer. "In there."

When Kennedy was gone, Ramirez got close to me and whispered, "No bullshit, Bell. What the hell happened? One minute I'm getting shoved into a limo after getting knocked semi-conscious, the next, I'm waking up here in some basement while dressed up like a department store manikin."

Then she gestured outside. The cops had shown up, setting up a perimeter and cordoning off the area where the abandoned bodies the Azif inhabited lay. Eli's former vessel was also there. "On top of that, I've got a pile of bodies outside no one can explain and your buddy Zianyon talking about some designer drug called GHB 2.0."

"Yeah, a new designer drug," I said, improvising my lies in the hopes Zian kept it vague enough to get away with it.

"Jones was using Hellfire to smuggle it using the threads...or maybe it was the gems. Never did figure out which one, honestly."

"So you're saying these threads or gems then got used in dresses people wore?"

"Looks that way," I said. "The way I figure it, somebody screwed up and left a batch of it in the material they were smuggling it in. Then that stuff got put into the dresses and dress shirts and, well...you're looking at the results."

Ramirez's eyes narrowed. "Okay, this might explain the guards outside. But your client didn't have any of that, and she's just as dead."

I tensed; time to see if my storytelling skills were up to the task. "Yeah, she got...dosed by some other means. The stuff gave her some Lazarus effect that kept her walking up until now. She wanted to make sure her sister was safe."

"And is this sister around to corroborate any part of this story?"

I sighed in weariness. "No...She got blown to hell with some low-yield explosives. The only thing left of her is a hand you'll find in the basement."

Ramirez nodded, and I could see she was committing every detail of my story to memory. It would all end up in her report, word for word. But there was a light in her eye that told me she was far from convinced.

With a shake of her head, she said, "You're a talented liar, Bell. I gotta hand it to you, you really are." She sounded sad and resigned. It tore at my heart a little. "It lines up. It does...Every time, it does."

She took a step closer to me, her chin angling up to look me square in the eye. "What aren't you telling me, Bell?"

Gods, how I wanted to tell her flat-out. But today was the latest in a long line of proof of why I never could. I held her gaze, but the words refused to come out.

I tried for a hug. She pushed me back with her right hand and said, "I think we need a break."

"Mel, this isn't fair, I—"

She reached her hand up, palm facing me. "Stop it," she said. "Stop lying to me. What happened to me wasn't some drug. There was something more. What about that hole on the floor, huh? What was it? And those men...their wounds— I've never seen anything like this."

I opened my mouth to speak, but she beat me to it.

"Don't!" Her voice rose in volume, and it stopped me cold. She met my eyes again, a mixture of sadness and anger swirling in them. "If it's to tell me more lies, it's best you remain quiet."

I nodded, for it was all I could do. I wished the regret I felt displayed on my face with enough accuracy for her to get a feel for it.

"Thank you for the lovely bedtime story; it will fit in nicely into my report." She turned to walk away, took a few steps and then stopped to turn back to me.

I took a moment to appreciate how beautiful she was. The pearly-white dress hung close to her hips, accentuating each delightful curve. The red gems on the front, sewn over her breast area, drew in the eye to the right place. Even the oversized black vest, with its collar rolled up around her thin neck, complimented her figure.

The sun was rising outside, and morning rays shone through the large windows behind her. They enveloped her tiny frame, a halo around her dark hair that came in at the perfect angle. What tore at my heart the most was Ramirez's face. There was a coldness there I wasn't familiar with and a hard-set determination. Somehow, I knew the flirtatious smiles I was accustomed to were gone.

"It's my job to find out the truth," she said. "And I'm good at my job." With those last, cold words hanging in the air, she walked out the door, the interview over and our latest stab at a relationship with it. Compared to my breaking heart, the rest of my body felt like it'd been given a massage.

I made it to the room where Zian and Kennedy were sitting with a cup of coffee each. Paramedics took over while some junior detective waited to take my statement.

Eventually, they let me go home. Zian insisted on driving me back to my apartment in the Stingray. It gave me time to chat with Kennedy on the way via smartphone. I gave her the rundown of everything that happened.

"Damn, Bell, I'm sorry," Kennedy said on the other end. "Call me a hopeless romantic, but I always hate to hear about breakups."

"Ah, forget it, Kennedy," I said, wanting to talk about anything else. "You got all the details you need to break the story?"

"Sure do, hoss. I'll recheck your statement to make sure everything lines up, but looks like I got another blockbuster story on my hands."

I chuckled.

"Think we'll see 'em again?" she asked. "The jinn siblings?"

I hoped the answer was no. But with the life I had, I knew odds were high I'd have to call in that favor sometime. Hopefully, not too soon.

"Nice having friends in the right places, isn't it?" she said with a smile in her voice that made me wonder if she meant the jinn or herself.

"True enough," I agreed as the complex came into sight. "Well, we're nearly home. Talk with you later, Kennedy."

"Just don't make it too long next time, alright?" Kennedy requested, the Texas twang making the last word come out like a sharp point.

I promised her I would and ended the call.

"She's right, you know," Zian said as he pulled into the parking spot.

"About what?" I asked, undoing my seatbelt.

"About having friends in the right places," Zian said, putting the car in park. "How well did going off on your own work out this time?"

I covered up my discomfort with a chuckle. "First, he gives me dating advice. Now he thinks he can tell me how to do my job. Seriously, which world are you from, and what have you done with my hacker friend?"

I expected a smile from Zian but received a frown and an expression part sad and part apologetic instead. He wet his lips, thinking it through, before answering. "When I helped Eli and Sarit tap your sense memories...I got a glimpse of some things. Your past, it...explained a lot, actually."

It could have been a million things, but the sad look in his eyes made it clear which secret of mine he'd uncovered. I felt a lump grow in my throat, forced it down and glanced away.

"I'm sorry," Zian said. In the eerie silence of the carpark, his voice sounded small, honest.

"Thanks," I said, and remembered my past hadn't been the only one on display.

I turned in my seat, placed a hand on my friend's shoulder. "That connection went both ways, buddy. If you ever want to talk about things..."

Zian squeezed my hand. "I always do, Bell. The trick is doing so in a manner Father doesn't get wise to. That's a fairly tough nut to crack, as you can guess."

I laughed at the joke, and Zian smiled wide. We both pretended we didn't notice the other was faking it and decided to leave it at that.

I pulled my hand back and opened the door. "Think dear old dad will be pissed about you getting involved again?"

"Oh, livid," Zian said, opening his door. "But keeping the ifrit out of Cold City might be enough to keep him from banishing me to Antarctica...I think."

"Good." I smiled. "If he gives you hell, stand your ground. You did the right thing; he won't be able to argue with that."

We both got out. I was less sore than I was before but still stiff. My young friend came around to walk me to the door. While we made our way up in the lift, I asked, "You'll coordinate with Kennedy to make sure all the pieces of the cover story fit?"

"We'll be talking about it in half an hour," Zian said, handing me my keys. "We both know the Conclave will appreciate not having to worry about the cover-up."

The lift stopped, dinged and opened its cold metallic doors. We crossed the corridor in silence, and I felt sad and lonely as I opened my front door. The flat felt empty without

Eli's presence—in either gender. Now it was back to just me and my work.

Zian must have sensed it because he asked, "I do need to go somewhere before linking with Candice. But if you want, I can—"

"I'll be fine," I said, shrugging off his supportive arm to stagger inside. "Need some rest. Go take care of the details, buddy."

He stood poised by the entrance, an expression impossible to decipher on his face. "If you say so," Zian conceded. "But if you want to have that talk sometime..."

I arched an eyebrow at him as I collapsed on the loveseat. "And what about your dad?"

I saw a flash of steel in my friend's eyes. "Father will just have to deal."

It hit me then, how much Zian had grown this past couple of months. He still looked like the perpetual teen he was, bleached-blond hair a total mess, *Age of the Geeks* t-shirt two sizes too large for his bony shoulders. But there was something new behind his eyes, a hardness that wasn't there before. I recognized it for what it was: the strength of will and maturity. I gave him a smile and an encouraging nod.

We said our goodbyes, and Zian shut the door behind him. I thought about locking it, but my whole body did not want to move. I closed my eyes for a second, feeling the droop in my eyelids. Hells with this...If I was going to fall asleep, let it be in bed. That thought was enough to open my eyes.

Lady McDeath sat on my couch, dressed in widow's weeds. A veil covered her face and head, and solid black gloves encased her hands. She held a bouquet of white roses.

"Gotta ask this first," I said, stifling a yawn. "Did I fall asleep?"

She got up from the couch and kicked my shin. The pain told me everything I needed to know about that question.

"Okay," I said, pulling my leg up to rub it. "Now that's out of the way, why are you here?"

She set down the roses on the coffee table and pulled back the veil. "To offer my congratulations on dealing with the situation."

This put me on edge. "Really? Last time we talked, you made it sound like the worst idea I ever had...which is saying something."

Her dark eyes blazed with a surprisingly restrained fire. "I was...concerned. That old brigand once took something of mine. It has been worth the long wait to see him pay for his stealing ways."

As soon as she said that, I got it. "That's why Hermes stopped having dealings with the jinn. It wasn't that they violated the Concords. The ifrit did."

She pouted like a schoolgirl who had her cookie stolen. "Perhaps there is something to what you say, perhaps not. But no one takes what is mine and gets away with it forever."

"Especially if the guy he possessed has taken the same deal I did with you."

Her usual annoyance flashed through her eyes as she dropped her veil back in place.

"And while we're on the subject, how many guys have had this job before me?" I asked. "And what happened to them?"

"This story does not befit your ears, Bellamy Vale. Be

grateful your actions have managed to spare you any retribution from your early carelessness."

"I'll settle for being grateful you kept me from dying as usual," I said, getting back to my feet. "Still, think you could make it to where it doesn't hurt so bad?"

Lady McDeath took up her roses. "Pain keeps you grounded. It will be helpful for another matter we have for you to handle."

Should have known there'd be a catch. "What now?"

A knock on the door interrupted the conversation. "This time, you've got five seconds before I kick in this door, Vale."

I turned to glare at Lady McDeath, but she'd vanished. I wasn't sure if I should feel grateful or angry. I managed to get to the door before Morgan tried his luck.

"What the hell, Lieutenant?" I asked in exasperation.

Morgan pushed past me, nearly knocking me over in the process. "I know you're bullshitting me and the rest of the department about what happened. Something happened to my sergeant, and I want to know what. So I'm going to turn this place upside down until I find something that tells me the truth."

He then reached in his pocket and pulled out a slip of paper. "And here's the warrant, before you ask. So are you going to stay out of my way, or are you going to give me an excuse to toss you in jail for tonight?"

I closed the door and shuffled towards the bedroom. "Whatever, man. Turn the dump upside down if it makes you feel better. Just let me sleep while you're doing it, would you? I need some rest."

I didn't bother looking at him before going into the bedroom and collapsing on my bed. A little later, I heard my front door open and close. Guess Morgan got the message: there were no answers to find here.

That out of the way, I felt myself drifting off to sleep. Maybe I'd be up to whatever Lady McDeath had in mind by the time I woke up.

NOTE FROM THE AUTHOR

Thanks for joining Bellamy Vale's team!

If you loved this book and have a moment to spare, I would really appreciate a short review where you bought it. Your help in spreading the word is gratefully appreciated.

Did you know there are more books in this series?

- Hostile Takeover #1
- Evil Embers #2
- Avenging Spirit #3 (coming 2020)
- Seasons Bleedings (Christmas Special)

All the books are available in ebook and print.

FURTHER READING

The Neve & Egan Cases Series.

Described by readers as 'a refreshingly unique mystery series'.

- Russian Dolls #1
- Ruby Heart #2
- Danse Macabre #3
- Blind Chess #4

All the books are available in ebook and print. There's also an ebook Box Set, with the complete series, at a bargain price.

ABOUT THE AUTHOR

Cristelle Comby was born and raised in the French-speaking area of Switzerland, on the shores of Lake Geneva, where she still resides.

She attributes to her origins her ever-peaceful nature and her undying love for chocolate. She has a passion for art, which also includes an interest in drawing and acting.

She is the author of the NEVE & EGAN CASES mystery series, which features an unlikely duo of private detectives in London: Ashford Egan, a blind History professor, and Alexandra Neve, one of his students.

Currently, she is hard at work on her Urban Fantasy series VALE INVESTIGATION which chronicles the exploits of Death's only envoy on Earth, PI Bellamy Vale, in the fictitious town of Cold City, USA.

The first novel in the series, *Hostile Takeover*, won the 2019 Independent Press Award in the Urban Fantasy category.

KEEP IN TOUCH

You can sign up for Cristelle Comby's newsletter, with give-aways and the latest releases. This will also allow you to download two exclusives stories you cannot get anywhere else: *Redemption Road* (VALE INVESTIGATION prequel novella) and *Personal Favour* (NEVE & EGAN CASES prequel novella).

www.cristelle-comby.com/freebooks

Printed in Great Britain
by Amazon

35548960R00182